BANISHED SONS
OF POSEIDON

By the Author

The Seventh Pleiade

Banished Sons of Poseidon

Visit us at www.boldstrokesbooks.com

BANISHED SONS
OF POSEIDON

by

Andrew J. Peters

A Division of Bold Strokes Books

2015

Credits
Editor: Jerry L. Wheeler
Production Design: Stacia Seaman
Cover Design by Jeanine Henning

Acknowledgments

When the kind folks at Bold Strokes Books gave me the opportunity to pitch a sequel to *The Seventh Pleiade*, I have to admit that I dragged my feet.

The first book was a six-year writing odyssey—another humble confession—that left me feeling shipwrecked from the squalling sea of monomyth and Greek pre-history that I had endeavored to traverse. Though imperfect, that hero's story felt finished to me, and I was quite content to leave Aerander living in asylum, with a suggestion hovering that returning to Atlantis just might be possible, however distantly in the future.

With *The Seventh Pleiade* complete and in press, my hiatus from writing about Atlantis was part celebratory, part self-pitying, and in the end short-lived. The notion of creating a follow-up story from a different character's point of view started to appeal to me. Stripped away from Aerander's adventure in the first book, his relationship with his cousin Dam had always felt to me like the heart the story. And that story was incomplete. I realized that it was important to me for Dam to have a chance to be better understood, and for him to have an adventure in his own right.

Happily, writing Dam's story was a much shorter journey. Perhaps I learned a bit about the craft of storytelling since my last novel. Maybe writing Dam came more naturally to me. Will this book be my last story about gay boys living in Atlantis? Once again, it feels that way, but I'm cautious about saying never.

I want to acknowledge and thank the Bold Strokes team: Len Barot, Sandy Lowe, Cindy Cresap, Sheri Lewis Wohl, Stacia Seaman, and especially my editor, Jerry L. Wheeler.

Perennially deserving of my gratitude, my appreciation, and my apologies is my husband Genaro Cruz who allows me to disappear into imaginary worlds far more often than I should. I love you.

For Genaro

PART ONE

CHAPTER ONE

The boys liked to bathe in the hot water lake not far beyond the Old Ones' underground city. The lake was embanked in black rock, and in the cast of torchlight, its waters glowed as blue and bright as a summer sky.

Dam pitted his metal torch in a cleft in the bank. It cast an aura of light a few yards onto the water and up the black shore. Beyond that stunted perimeter, everything was smothered in darkness. Dam had heard that the barren country around the lake had once been trenched with lava streams, but that was in ages past. All that was left was scarred troughs through rolling fields of bedrock, and none of that could be seen at the time when Dam was out.

The Old Ones had shuttered the watchtower where they kept their brilliant Oomphalos that washed a thrumming, red crystalline tide over the underworld. The charioteer of the sun didn't make his rounds to Agartha, the continent below the earth, so the Old Ones uncovered and eclipsed their magical relic at intervals to give the aboveground refugees some routine of day and night.

The underground peoples said no gods were in their realm. They certainly didn't have any Titans to hold up the sky or to heave the sun or the moon over the land. Some of the refugees said the underworld had been abandoned by the gods, though Dam knew well that it was a place of powerful magic, more ancient than anywhere in the above-world. Whether that came from the gods of his country who had once traveled there or from underworld spirits whose natures he had yet to comprehend, Dam couldn't say.

The boys weren't supposed to venture outside of the city unless they were in threes or fours. Two nights ago, a stranger had been sighted stalking around the deep canyon beyond the city drawbridge. Dam wouldn't have trekked out that way on his own, but the backcountry of dead lava fields seemed like safe territory. He came and went as he wanted to. Aboveground in Atlantis, where he had been a novice priest, he had snuck out of the walled priest's precinct all the time just to walk the city streets at night and claim some freedom.

If his cousin Aerander found out that he had gone to the bathing lake by himself, he would get a scolding. Those lectures never rooted themselves in Dam's head as much as they grasped for purchase. Dam was sixteen years old. He had been minding his own way long before everyone had come underground. Aerander was sixteen too, so he had no right telling Dam this or that anyway. Dam thought they had sorted this out a while ago, but since Aerander had taken on leading the refugees, he fell back on his bossy ways sometimes.

Dam stripped off his sandals and his tunic, laid them on the bank, and delicately made his way into the water. The lake was plenty warm. The whole region around the city stayed comfortably mild like high season back in Atlantis due to heat that rose from lava pits deep beneath the city shelf. The initial sensation of entering the lake was always strange, going from dry to wet. Since Dam had been living in the underworld, his skin had become more sensitive while his eyes had grown lazy from lack of use.

Dam imagined his muscles soaking up the minerals of the lake, making him strong like iron. That was what happened when the Old Ones' warriors bathed there, so they said. He plunged his head beneath the water, disappearing into the mumble of the pool. Afterward, his skin would feel as smooth as a stone washed by the sea.

There was only one detriment to bathing in the mineral lake. Since Dam had given up the habits of the priesthood and stopped shaving his head, the hard water made his thick black hair coarse and unruly when it dried. Whenever he caught his reflection in the silver-plated walls of the refugees' bathing yard, he was startled and amused by what he had become. He looked like the child of savages raised in the depths of a jungle. The Old Ones didn't have the grooming oils that people used aboveground.

That didn't bother Dam much. It suited him fine to look a bit wild, especially considering the strange new country where he was living.

He swam out farther from the bank, beyond the harbor of torchlight. Dam didn't know how extensive the lake was or if it ever got deep. As far as he had ever swum, he could touch down on the rocky floor. The water only reached his clavicle. He dove for the bottom, did a handstand, and kicked out with his feet. That made a noisy splash. Dam crested the water and gathered some sense. If he was going to sneak out on his own, he had to remember to be quiet about it.

His ears pricked up from a distant sound. He looked across the shrouded lava field. Four, then five, then six fuzzy globes of light approached the bank of the lake, with bantering, howling voices.

Dam crawled quietly through the water toward his torch and his clothes. They were boys and likely no one he would relish crossing paths with. They had probably come to practice wrestling in the lake and would harass whomever they came across.

Woefully, Dam had swum out too far to make it to the bank before the noisy group pitted their torches in the ground. Dam drifted back to the shadowed side of the lake. He didn't want to look like a coward scurrying out of the water from the sight of them. It was best to go unnoticed and wait for them to leave. But his torch, sandals, and tunic back on the shore announced a bather in the lake.

From his distance, Dam watched a tall member of the crew step to the edge of the bank. He looked like he was peering out in Dam's direction. The boy uttered something to the others, and then they all shucked their clothes and went bounding into the water.

So much for a peaceful getaway.

Dam kept an eye and an ear on the boys' movements while he idled in the water. Sure enough, they started wrestling and hollering like lunatics and throwing each other down with big splashes. He heard the voices of Leo and Koz, two boys with whom Dam had a not-so-friendly history. Dam recognized Perdikkas, Boros, and Mesokantes. Those three had never paid him much mind, arrogant as they were. They were all *Poseidonidae*, descendants of the god's ten royal houses. Before they had come below to escape the flood, they had held claim to a share of Atlantis' ten kingdoms. It hadn't occurred to them yet that there was no more Atlantis to inherit.

The tall boy was Calyiches, prince of House Mneseus. Since the evacuation, he had cropped up as the favorite of the highborn survivors. On the night that the sea had burst through the island-city's breakwaters, they had all been gathered at the Citadel for the kingdom's sacred festival, the Panegyris. Being on the city's highest ground had been a stroke of luck and bought precious time for Aerander to lead them through the hidden gateway to Agartha. Some eight dozen highborn boys had been rescued while nearly everyone else in the city had perished.

Calyiches emerged from the noisy grapple. He wandered near, homing in on the spot where Dam was idling in the water. "Who's there?"

Dam wasn't going to hide in the shadows. He drifted toward the torch-lit side of the lake, revealing a greater portion of himself in the wallowing shallows. Calyiches' high, broad shoulders towered above the water. He was only covered up to his hair-dusted navel.

The older boy held Dam with his gaze. Calyiches had been the top wrestling and boxing competitor at the Panegyris and had been headed to a career as a military general. He had also been Aerander's sweetheart for a time, though Aerander didn't like talking about that, especially now that Aerander had Lys.

"You're not supposed to be out here alone."

Dam wasn't sure how to answer that, so he didn't. Calyiches' grin was a mesmerizing terror. Calyiches splashed some water on his arms. He nudged his eyes in the direction of his friends. "You want to join us?"

Beyond them, the wrestling commotion squelched. Dam heard muffled side-talk.

"No," Dam answered.

"Suit yourself."

Dam shrugged and started toward the shore. Calyiches tried to block his way. Dam shifted to pass him. Calyiches overtook Dam again, stretching out his arms as though he was gauging a tackle. They kept at that stupid game until they were an arm's reach from each other.

Dam halted. Calyiches laughed. Was Calyiches playing around for fun, or did he have a crueler punishment in mind? The other boys had fixed on the standoff, and they were laughing as well.

"Where are you going in such a hurry?"

"Minding my own business," Dam said.

"Why do you have to leave so soon?"

Calyiches had a way of flipping from threatening to flirtatious. That had been awfully confusing to Dam in the past and disastrous for his cousin. Now Dam saw Calyiches for what he was: a pompous prick. Dam told him, flatly, "Because I want to."

Calyiches glanced at his friends. Then he looked back to Dam with a spark of humor. "I know you."

Dam stared back at him.

"You're Aerander's cousin. You renounced House Atlas to work for the High Priest." Calyiches glanced lewdly at Dam's body. "Do you miss selling favors to temple patrons?"

The muscles in Dam's neck strung up tight. He had never been that kind of priest. That was the ugly rumor Leo and Koz had started before the evacuation. That was the stupid opinion highborn boys had about all the novice priests even though they knew nothing about them.

"Is that what you're doing out here?" Calyiches peered around as though there could be others on the dark side of the lake. "I don't mind. I think you're pretty." He reached for Dam's neck.

Dam shirked away from his grasp. He could show Calyiches he ought to shut his lying mouth, but that required time and opportunity. Calyiches could easily wrestle him down and hold his head beneath the water just for sport, and he had his friends to join in on the abuse if they cared to. Dam trudged past him and the others, climbing up to the bank where he pulled his tunic over his wet head and body. All along the way, the idiots had laughed at him. Seeing that they weren't going to get a rise out of him, they had gone back to their games in the lake.

Dam stepped into his sandals. He would have left straightaway, but he caught a whiff of something odd. Peppery, flinty. Dam placed it: niterbats. The flying little devils lived in caverns above the lava fields. You tended not to smell them until it was too late and they had swarmed right into you, leaving you covered head to toe in soot. They also shied away from the sound of people.

Dam shifted around, listening keenly, but he didn't hear their flapping wings. The boys must have brought that smell with them. Traces of it had to be on the clothes they had left on the bank. If you trapped niterbats, ground them up, and prepared the powdery remains right, you could use them to blow holes through rock with a flame. Dam wondered if Calyiches and his friends had been messing around with that. If they weren't careful, they could blast out one of their eyes or a finger.

Dam smirked. Then again, maybe that wouldn't be so bad.

He grabbed his torch, stepped around the litter of the boys' clothes, and started down the craggy trail back to the city. The lights and the boisterous voices from the lake faded behind him. That ought to have made Dam relax, but the encounter left him feeling like he needed to keep looking over his shoulder.

Darkness swallowed both sides of the trail. Shortly along the way, Dam heard a phantom sound. Someone or something rustling beyond his sight? He stopped and peered in the direction of the noise. He couldn't make anything out, and he wasn't about to go scouting with just his torch. It couldn't have been one of the boys. He still heard their racket at the lake.

A stranger had been staking out the city. Was that person in the backcountry now, come back to spy? Dam quickened his pace down the trail. He couldn't explain it, but he felt certain that someone was watching him all the way home.

CHAPTER TWO

The city of the Old Ones was built and walled on a high plateau of basalt, with only two ways into town: the drawbridge on the canyon-side and the tunnel from the dead lava fields. Otherwise you would have to ford a trench that guttered around the plateau. The trench was twenty yards across, twice as deep, and smoldering with lava at the bottom.

The watchmen at the tunnel gate showed Dam the way as he approached. Their race could make light from their bodies. It spread across their skin like the warm glow of a lantern behind a thin leaf of paper. They also grew their own armor—leathery scales that covered their chests like a hero's cuirass. They only needed helmets and chain mail skirting to be prepared for battle.

Dam had met the two watchmen when he had gone out that night. They knew he liked to wander around on his own, and they gave him no hassle about it. Dam thought about telling them that he had heard something or someone out in the fields, but it could have been his imagination so he said nothing. The watchmen greeted him in Atlantean, and Dam answered back in the few words of their language that he had learned. The watchmen stood aside with their iron crooks to let him pass.

When Aerander, Lys, and Dam had come below to find refuge for their countrymen, they had to retrieve the Oomphalos from the serpent slave-drivers of the underworld, the New Ones, and return it to Old Ones' warrior-queen Ysalane. Ysalane had promised to shelter their people. The survivors had been living in asylum for seven fortnights as best as anyone could figure. Some of them were still frightened of the underground people. Some made up ridiculous stories about them, like they were unclean or backward, or secretly planning to keep them as prisoners.

Atlantis had been the Navel of the World, beckoning traders from all its exotic colonies and importing domestic slaves from conquered nations. Dam had met enough different sorts of people to understand that a man's character, whether virtuous or evil, was tempered by peculiarities much more complex than physical appearance or race. It stood to reason that it must be the same way with the underground dwellers. Dam hadn't met a member of their kind who hadn't been gracious and polite.

Over centuries, they had adapted to living in the sunless underworld, but they weren't so different from aboveground people. The ways that they *were* different were actually better. The Old Ones didn't have a noble class and a poor class. None of them were highborn or lowborn. They were just born. Everyone was treated the same, and everyone was provided for.

Their city plan was strange by aboveground standards. They didn't have the normal byways like streets, alleys, or canals. Their storage houses, factories, homes, and garrisons were built up in quarried stages. From the outside, it resembled a giant ziggurat like the temples of Lemuria. From the inside, it was like an enormous hive with a mazelike network of interior and exterior stairwells, corridors and footbridges. Traveling around was a hellish trial for the legs, disorienting until the route markers from here to there became familiar. Lifts powered by giant, stone cog watermills moved goods from one stage to the other. Boys had taken to catching rides on them, and Dam had done so from time to time.

When he reached the quay on the city-side of the tunnel, Dam boarded a lift piled with musty ore for the smithies. It would take him up to the precinct for the evacuees. That trip gave a view of the tall succession of berths that comprised the city. When Dam, Aerander, and Lys had discovered the place, it had been conquered by the New Ones. The city had been demolished into rubble. Besides their lifts and aqueducts and scores of smelt works, the Old Ones had built up tiers of granite houses for the Atlanteans. The boys called it "the Honeycomb." The complainers among them called it "the Cells."

At night, the Honeycomb stood out from the rest of the city with its many gas-lit lamps. That was another bit of ingenuity the Old Ones had introduced to the evacuees. Underground gases could be harnessed for fire, and they burned better than oil or coal, with less smoke and stench. The Old Ones used that gas to fuel the furnaces of their smelting factories. They didn't need it to make light for themselves. Their eyes could penetrate the depths of night, and they could generate light into their hands when they needed to lay bare their surroundings. During the day, the radiant Oomphalos, installed in the city's tallest watchtower like a lighthouse, showered everything with its strange luster.

In the evacuees' precinct, some of the highborn boys had etched the walls and floors with drawings, both decorative and bawdy. They didn't have gilded columns or bunting with family crests to make the place more like the homes that they had once known. Moreover, they didn't have subjects to bow down when they passed by or to bring them tribute of fine wines and delicacies from their country provinces.

But they still found ways of maintaining the ranks. The New Ones' freed slaves who had survived the liberation of the city had the below-houses. They were one hundred common men who had been bartered to the serpent race by the High Priest Zazamoukh. Many of them had been kept alive for hundreds of years through the mysterious energy of the Oomphalos. The lowborn boys and the seven common women who had survived the flood took a middle floor. Naturally, the highborn boys had the top houses.

Dam climbed a stairwell to the middle-houses. When everything had been built, he could have taken a home at the top level with his cousin. Due to some intermarriage with Aerander's family, House Atlas, Dam's father had owned a parcel of land where he had bred horses. When Dam's father died, he had left that land to Dam. But Dam had only been a baby. Aerander's grandfather, the Governor of House Atlas at the time, had taken Dam in as a ward.

Raised in the Citadel palace, Dam had grown up feeling more noble than country burgher though he had been precisely neither. He and Aerander had been born a month apart, and they had shared nursemaids, baths, and even a bed since the time they had crawled on all fours. The difference between them had become apparent when they turned thirteen and Aerander began his training for the Panegyris. Dam wasn't going to be feted with snippings from the vine, contests for victory fillets, and a parade of chariots. He had no father to sponsor him as Aerander had. Aerander had been the family's gilded legacy. He had been his father's only son, and after his grandfather had died, he had become prince regent.

That summer of their thirteenth birthdays, Dam had left the palace to make his own way as a priest. Despite Aerander's protests, Dam decided to live among city folk after the evacuation. He wasn't destined to be a military general, or a champion of the games, or a politician of renown like the highborn boys with their proud family names.

His place in the world had always been obscure. He held the deed to his father's stables, but they had fallen into disrepair. It would have taken resources Dam didn't have to restore them. Dam hadn't been suited for professions that required hard labor or skill, and he had no interest in them. The priesthood had offered room and board and wages after five years of service. That hadn't seemed like a bad way to earn the coin he needed to take up his father's trade, not that Dam had known anything about breeding horses.

The only interest that had ever captured Dam's imagination was finding that special person he belonged with. Maybe that was because he never had a mother or a father. It shamed him to remember how he had waddled after boys like an abandoned duckling as a child. His aunt Thessala used to tell him that he needed to grow into his own heart, which was so big and yearning, it made him follow whoever happened to touch it. But Dam had changed since then. He had been boarded and schooled with the priesthood's novices, which turned out to be more like stockade living than apprenticeship. The novices had all been orphans and throwaways who had no better prospects than serving the priests. That cured Dam of his delicate nature and taught him how to look out for himself.

Dam hoped to sneak in quietly, but gas-lighting shone out in warm haloes from the adjacent houses. He heard voices here and there. When he reached his home, the house lamps burned at half-fuel.

His roommate Hephad, a former novice priest as well, was awake, and their friend Attalos had come over to visit the survivors' greatest pride, the kittens. When Hephad went below, he had grabbed one of the stray cats who hung around their dormitory. He didn't know that she was carrying a litter. The birth of the kittens—three orange and brown tortoiseshells—had brought about the most excitement the Honeycomb had seen. Even the highborn boys came down to the middle house to bring the cats scraps of fish from their suppers. They had named the mother Pleione after the ancestral Mother of Grace, and they had named her little blind tabbies Alcyone, Electra, and Maia after three of

Atlas' daughters, the Pleiades, who were emblems of virtue and hope. Happily, the kittens were all growing healthy and strong.

Dam made his way directly toward his bed in the far corner of the room. Then he noticed that Aerander's boyfriend, Lys, was sitting on his pallet. Like lightning shot from the sky, Aerander materialized in front of Dam. Everyone's eyes were upon the two.

"Where did you go?" Aerander said.

"The bathing lake," Dam said. He walked past Aerander to the clothing shelves. His tunic was soaked through in places. The evacuees hadn't had time to grab belongings before coming underground. They were left to rewash what they had been wearing or to dress in rationed garments. Dam stepped into a pair of scratchy trousers and wrestled out of his tunic.

Aerander stared at him, somehow appearing to be genuinely baffled. He wore the bone amulet given to him by the heavenly princess Calaeno before they had all evacuated Atlantis. That bit of regalia plus his bossy manner gave him the credentials he needed to lead the survivors. He told Dam, "You know how dangerous it is."

The backcountry was dangerous, with boiling geysers, tremors that rattled through the land every now and then, and fire scorpions the size of bulls. But Dam knew his way around better than most. He wasn't about to tell Aerander about the confrontation with Calyiches. That would rile up Aerander and Lys, making him look even more like the helpless cur that Calyiches and his friends thought he was.

"Why are you checking up on me?" Dam said.

"Someone has to do it."

Hephad squirmed a bit as he sat cross-legged with the kittens on his lap. Aerander had that effect on people. Even the kittens didn't mew. Dam sat down on Hephad's vacant pallet, kicked off his sandals, and examined his feet. He had been meaning to trim his nails. Like his hair, they seemed to grow twice as fast underground.

Aerander hovered in front of him. "I asked you to respect the rules. You want everyone to go running off on their own whenever they please? People will be losing their way in the backcountry or breaking a leg and getting trapped in a gulley. You could get killed by something out there."

Dam retrieved a coring knife from beside the pallet. It did a fine job stripping off overgrown nails. He started working on his big toe.

"You're selfish."

Dam said nothing.

"Do you want to get yourself killed?"

Dam carved an arch of white from the nail of his big toe. The rest of his nails hadn't grown out too bad. A file would do the trick better than his coring knife.

Aerander's voice rose, quavering. "For crying out loud, Dam, you're all I have."

Dam looked up from his trimming. Aerander had lectured him before about family obligation, but something about the way he said it this time pressed the meaning deeper. Aerander had lost his father, his stepmother, his half sisters, and everyone else to the flood. So had all the boys except for a few who had made it underground with a brother or a cousin.

Dam had become a bit cold to that. He had lost his mother and father years before. His father had been orphaned at a young age like him, and he hadn't known his mother's side of the family. He had heard that they were poor, which was why Aerander's grandfather had plucked Dam from the countryside, stowing him away to protect the family land.

He noticed that Lys had turned his gaze to the floor. It hadn't been the best thing for Aerander to say in front of his boyfriend. Dam felt bad for Lys sometimes. He was monumentally in love with Aerander, and Aerander didn't give him much in return.

"You can't keep me like a pet on a leash," Dam said.

"You're so dramatic."

Dam looked up at Aerander sharply. "I'm back now. You can get some sleep."

Aerander heaved a breath. It seemed that he didn't have the fire in his belly to push things further that night. Dam noticed that his cousin looked more pale and weathered than usual. Living underground had taken its toll on everyone, though no one more than Aerander. He had taken on the responsibility of the welfare of the evacuees. Not only did he manage complaints from the others—their quarters, the food, petty fights, the health of the aging men in the below-houses—he also dealt with the constant questions of when they would be able to return aboveground.

The amulet he wore was enchanted. Somehow, it forged a bond

between Aerander and the goddess who was sworn to be his guardian. Calaeno would tell him when the sea had pulled back and it was safe to come above. Every day, many times a day, Aerander checked in with her. Days had stretched into months with no good news. That had to weigh heavy on his cousin. Dam thought Aerander ought to take worrying about him off his list of troubles.

They exchanged a quiet glance. Aerander turned to go. Lys followed him, looking at Dam on the way out. That made Dam feel terrible. He would help, but what was he supposed to do? Aerander wanted him to keep the boys in line, but that wasn't what Dam was good at. He wasn't much good at anything except sneaking around on his own. He'd look like a phony reminding people about rules, not to mention that no one listened to him. The ones that caused trouble, the highborn boys, treated him like dirt.

Distantly, he was aware of Hephad and Attalos moving toward the doorway. Aerander left a thick wake of guilt in the air, and everyone was best off packing it in for the night. Hephad and Attalos were probably making their farewell with hand gestures they had made up to communicate. Before the flood, the High Priest Zazamoukh had cut out Hephad's tongue so he would never speak properly again.

Dam went over to his own bed. Attalos left, but then Hephad went over to the doorway again. Another visitor? Dam glanced over. Hephad had gathered the kittens into his arms, and he was greeting Hanhau.

Dam suddenly felt very exposed in just his trousers. A pulse of light shone briefly from Hanhau's face as he noticed Dam. He grinned handsomely. The underground warrior had helped Aerander, Dam, and Lys defeat the New Ones when they had first come below to evacuate the kingdom. Since then, Dam and Hanhau had become friends.

"I saw your lights. I figured you were awake," Hanhau said.

That voice was nice. Everything about Hanhau was nice, and Dam felt shy. He managed to nod. Hephad retreated with the kittens to the margins of the room.

"You said you'd like to see the Glowing Cataracts," Hanhau said. "I thought I'd show them to you."

Now?

"It's the best time to see them. Before the faults shift. It happens once a night, making a crack in the riverbed. After that, there's not much more than a trickle until the fault shifts back again."

Dam wedged his feet back into his sandals and stood. Why not? He wasn't sleepy. In fact, he was itching to move again after Aerander's latest scolding. Thankfully, he had just washed and probably didn't stink. Dam gave Hephad a warning look not to tell Aerander. He followed Hanhau out to the terrace of the middle-houses.

CHAPTER THREE

They went by foot on a winding route down the city stages to its basin and out the tunnel. Dam had to push himself to keep up with Hanhau. The underground dwellers were built for hiking great distances. They could take mountains of stairs without stopping for a breath. Besides, Hanhau stood a head above Dam.

Once they were outside the city tunnel, Hanhau led a path that skirted to one side of the dead lava fields. The underworld was a boundless cavern scooped out from the pith of the earth. It had its own mountain ranges and steppes and seas and climates.

Hanhau knew every fingerbreadth of the region around the city. Before they had reclaimed their city, Hanhau and his people had moved from one backcountry camp to another. They had to hide from the New Ones, who had split off from their kind many ages ago to horde the Oomphalos. By the ancient artifact's strange power, those dissidents had become grotesque giant serpents. The Old Ones had once been a race of many thousands. Over centuries of being hunted down, they had dwindled to some thirty score.

Hanhau had been through raids. Like the other warriors of his tribe, his upper arm was scarred to show his conquests in battle— five hatch marks for the five giant serpents he had killed. He had seen hundreds of his tribesmen die. Hanhau had told Dam that his people had relocated more times since he was a little boy than he could remember.

Time and age meant something different to the Old Ones. They didn't count months or years the way they did in Atlantis because no moons or seasons were underground. Instead, they accounted for generations. Hanhau had said it was easy to follow because they couldn't afford to have their women carrying babies too frequently. Men and women made babies when they found land that was plentiful with food and water and hidden enough so that they could stay for a while. In that way, their children all tended to be born around the same time.

Hanhau had told Dam that he was from the Dung Beetle generation. That had made Dam smirk until he had seen Hanhau was being serious. He said it was an honorable generation. It had produced a fine leader of their kind, the warrior-queen Ysalane. The children had been named after the dung beetle because their camp had been infested with the pests at the time. Now they took those disgusting little creatures as a portent of good fortune. The Dung Beetle generation had grown up to achieve their greatest victory in ages, the defeat of the New Ones. They were held in great esteem by their people.

Hanhau had explained that the Dung Beetles were his people's youngest generation. As best as Dam could figure, that meant that Hanhau and his warrior kin were around the same age as Dam, which made him feel rather unaccomplished in comparison. Since the Old Ones had rebuilt their ancient city, they had decided that it would be safe for birthing again. The next generation had already been named the Children of the Resurrection. They would be the first of their kind to grow up in a time of peace since the New Ones had laid claim to Agartha many centuries ago.

Dam and Hanhau seemed to be headed forever into darkness. Dam's feet were tired and sore, though he didn't want to complain. The air had turned damp, suggesting a water source somewhere near. Dam hoped it was the Glowing Cataracts.

Hanhau halted. He gazed around, seeing and hearing things in the backcountry that Dam couldn't detect. Hanhau made a funny chirping noise, calling over two giant saddled snails the Old Ones used for climbing steep terrain. Dam had dubbed them slug-sledges.

Hanhau helped Dam hoist himself up to the iron saddle soldered to the giant snail's shell. Dam didn't have any reins to hold on to, but once Hanhau was saddled, he led the way. By chirping and clicking his tongue, he communicated to his slug-sledge which way to go. Dam's sledge followed.

It was a smooth and easy ride until they came to a tall slope and had to mind gravity and balance. They were climbing a great height. Dam couldn't see it too well, but he felt it in his stomach. Falling back meant crushed limbs and a cracked skull. Dam held on tight to his metal saddle with one hand and his torch with the other. The slug-sledges could travel terrain that was nearly vertical.

They crested a broad shelf with little pools of muddy water in the ground. Things smelled earthy and fresh. The sound of rushing water chimed through the air, becoming louder and louder as they went.

The cast of Dam's torch revealed a towering slag of bedrock ahead. Hanhau led them around that. The sound of rushing water pitched even louder. Hanhau and his sledge disappeared around a bend. When Dam's sledge lazily cornered that high wall of rock, Dam's jaw fell open. They had found the Glowing Cataracts. It looked like shafts of light descending from the heavens. It was a staggering palisade of rock streaked by water chutes as bright as moonbeams. Dam could just see the height of the waterfalls when he stretched his neck back and kept a firm hold of his saddle.

Some of the cataracts were thin and misty. Some were robust and rippling like the impossibly long beard of a god. They glowed for sure, though Dam couldn't guess how that was possible.

Hanhau led onward to the mouth of the falls where the water frothed and eddied and many teeth of jagged rock jutted from the surface. Mist pecked at Dam's face. He wondered if Hanhau would want to go swimming, and his shyness came back to him. Hanhau dismounted at a ledge of rock that stretched out toward the pool. He came around Dam's sledge and stood ready to catch Dam when he climbed out of his saddle. Dam handed down his torch. Hanhau held him as he slid down the side of the shell. Dam turned, and they were face-to-face.

"Do you like it?"

Dam grinned, the answer apparent. "I tried to picture it in my head," Dam said. "But it's even better than you described."

"I told you this is one of my favorite places in Agartha. I used to sneak away here all the time." He pointed to the height of the falls. "When I was little, I thought it was a river from the above-world, bringing light to us below."

Dam could see why. He'd seen nothing brighter underground, except for the Oomphalos. He looked at it from all directions.

"We have many legends about it. They say a warrior who washes here will be unstoppable in battle. Others say that it's a trick of the Master of Light."

Dam's brow pinched up.

"That must be one of the few folk stories I haven't told you," Hanhau said. "Supposedly, in the olden days, a couple had a pair of very unusual twin boys. They were always playing tricks on people and bothering the tribe about learning magic. They wouldn't let anyone rest for a moment while they went on about it. The tribe fell on hard times, and they decided to send the boys away. Food was scarce. They had too many mouths to feed, and their enemies were tracking them. Besides, the boys were such a nuisance. The tribe sent the boys into the backcountry to fetch salt crystals from a crater lake, and then they moved on before the boys could return. The legend is the boys discovered magic after all while they were out there.

"One learned to command the glow of fire. He became the Master of Light. The other boy learned to command every noise of the underworld. He became the Master of Sound. That's why we say that when you see or hear something that isn't there, it must be a trick of one of the twins." Hanhau roped the slug-sledges together with a heavy chain.

"What happened to them?" Dam said.

"Most people think they were make-believe. If it's true, it was probably just a story that passed down from generation to generation, and it got exaggerated so that the tribe wouldn't seem so horrible for abandoning the children. There's usually an ordinary reason for legends." Hanhau looked to the waterfalls. "Like this. That cliff behind the falls is a lode for a special sediment. The water passing over it activates it in some way, like scratching at flint. But that much water is like one continuous spark. There's talk of quarrying the spot. That sediment could be used to light our aqueducts and lifts."

"They want to dig into the cliff?"

Hanhau nodded.

"But then the cataracts would be destroyed."

Hanhau's face brightened. "I don't like that idea either. Fortunately, neither does Ysalane." He looked toward the base of the waterfalls. "Let's go for a closer view."

They ventured to the extremity of the ledge where the roar and the crash of the falls surrounded them. Hanhau pointed out a platform of rock that was reasonably dry and flat and made for a good spot for sitting. Dam suddenly felt like they were cocooned together in their remote spot.

Dam picked at one side of his sandal where the leather had frayed. He could feel Hanhau's warm look upon him. Hanhau's eyes were always on him when they were alone. Boys had looked at Dam that way, and nothing good had ever come of it. Though Hanhau was a whole lot different than any boy Dam had ever met.

That private moment was hard to reckon because Hanhau wasn't exactly a *boy* either. He was a different race who had grown up in a world that Dam had never known existed until very recently. In some respects, Hanhau looked like any person from aboveground. The Old Ones had a darker tone of skin, like a chestnut bronzed from the fire, and their hair was inky black and very fine and silky. In Atlantis, they could have passed for Lemurians, the far western peoples, who were said to be very ancient themselves.

But Hanhau's chest made scale armor instead of hair all the way down to the metal hoop at his hips from which draped a short, chain mail skirting. He could make light glow from inside him when he was happy or he was mad or he just wanted it that way. Dam supposed Hanhau found him strange in ways too, though he never showed it. He felt like his brains would burst out of his head if he thought too much about the interest they had taken in each other. They were people from entirely different worlds. But was there anything wrong with that?

"Ysalane is holding a feast to celebrate the completion of the city's last monument, her Great Hall," Hanhau said. "Everyone will be invited. I wondered if you would come with me."

"To the feast?"

"Yes."

No one had ever invited Dam to anything like that. It scared the words right out of him. He wished he could answer Hanhau like a normal person.

"I'm sorry, Dam. Maybe our ways are different," Hanhau said. "I thought because I like you, and if you like me—"

Dam's words came back suddenly. "Why?"

Hanhau's glance danced around. "For my people, when two people like each other…in that manner…they might…do things together."

"I mean, why do you like me?"

Hanhau grinned, understanding. He scooted up a bit closer.

"Because you're brave. Because you do what you want without caring what other people think. Because you're very handsome."

A snort rushed out of Dam's nose.

"I think you're even more handsome because you don't even realize it."

Dam looked up at Hanhau. He had always been honest and kind. But boys had only been nice to him when they were playing a mean trick or looking for an easy target to romance. When they got what they wanted, they went back to ignoring him, like it had never happened.

Dam had gotten used to that. But he felt like it would bother him if it happened with Hanhau.

Hanhau leaned toward him and pressed his lips against Dam's. Dam shut his eyes and pressed back for more of the kiss. Hanhau held Dam's face with his hand. That was awfully sweet. The echoing, rushing water made him feel like he had plunged into some magical realm where everything was beautiful and right.

They broke their kiss. Dam hung his head and kept his eyes shut. He was breathless and his head was rattled, though not unhappily so.

Hanhau spoke. "Why?"

Dam's eyes popped open. "Why what?"

"Why do *you* like me?"

The question was harder for Dam to answer than to ask. He glanced at Hanhau's face. Every one of his features was a divine wonder—his dark eyebrows, the curve and the broadness of his nose, his full lips, and his eyes that lit up like sapphire gems. The fact that he could make light aroused an even deeper fascination. Dam looked at the teardrop swaths of armor that grew from Hanhau's chest. Before Dam knew what he was doing, he reached out to touch them. He caught himself, wondering if he was being too bold.

"You can feel them if you want."

Dam felt one of the scales with his finger. It was tough but supple, like the petals of an artichoke, though Dam had seen that they were much stronger than that. The New Ones' fangs couldn't penetrate those scales, and the scales could withstand a battery of rocks. Each one was about the size of Dam's palm. Close up, in the ethereal glow from Hanhau's face, Dam could see that each one could open and spread a bit to air his body or close up tight to shutter it from attack. Beneath, the skin was nutty and smooth like Hanhau's arms.

"Do you think it's ugly?"

"I think it's nice."

Dam ran his hand down to Hanhau's lap. The metal hoop around his waist was held together with a double pin that could be opened to free him of his chain mail skirting. Before Dam could do that, Hanhau stopped him.

"Dam, I can't do that with you."

Dam's face burned. But then what had the kiss and all the buttery words been about?

Hanhau brushed a stiff lock of hair away from Dam's temple. "It's not that I wouldn't like to do that with you. But for me, for us—*my people*—that's something you can only do when you've twined your heart in iron to another person, as the saying goes." He shifted a bit and looked away from Dam. "It's a delicate thing. We leave ourselves very vulnerable when we're with another person in that way. You'll see once the courtship season starts."

Dam had next to no idea what he was talking about, though he supposed that "the courtship season" signified the underground men and women getting together to make the babies of their next generation. But what did that have to do with anything?

Hanhau muttered, "How to explain?" He twisted up his face and went through a series of glows and dims. Despite the awkwardness from before, Dam grinned. Whatever Hanhau was trying to say, it was cute and funny seeing him so bothered. He spoke the aboveground language perfectly. Many of the Old Ones did. They had been taught it by Calaeno when she had ventured below many centuries before, and they had passed down the knowledge through generations.

"If I…when we…" Hanhau started. His mouth opened and closed. Then he breathed out a sigh. "When we give our bodies to someone, there's a change that happens." He looked down at the scales on his stomach. "We lose our armor."

Dam's mouth fell open.

"It's like a shedding. The scales grow back, but for a while, we're defenseless. You can understand now why mating is very sacred for my people."

Dam didn't know what to say. Then a question popped into his head. "Does it hurt when they fall off?"

"What? No." Hanhau added quickly, "So I've been told."

Dam's eyes widened. "You've never?"

Hanhau shook his head.

"But you would, with me?"

Hanhau's complexion darkened. He grinned and nodded.

That boggled Dam's mind. Out of all the boys who had come underground, he never would have guessed that he would be the one who interested Hanhau in that way. Hanhau was a celebrated warrior. From a foreign race. Dam's worries snuck up on him again.

"I'm sorry if I gave you the wrong impression bringing you here and giving you that kiss," Hanhau said. "For my people, showing someone a place that's special to them and sharing stories is a way to get to know them better. That's all I wanted. For now. Do they have such traditions in Atlantis?"

They did, for other people. Like Aerander, who had been romanced by Calyiches and then Lys. All his life, boys had invited Dam's cousin to sit at their side at feasts. They didn't only ask him to meet up after dark. Dam just nodded. "What about the courtship season, and raising children? Don't your countrymen expect you to take part in that?"

"I suppose some of them do. But not all men are made for courtship with women. When the children come, we all take care of them. It doesn't matter who the father or the mother is as it does with your people. We're all parents to them. That helps in case someone gets sick or injured in battle."

The thought of parents being interchangeable was strange to Dam. In Tamana, where Hephad was from, the desert tribes had a tradition of men taking several wives, but what Hanhau was describing sounded even more complicated. "Did you ever want to know who gave birth to you and who your father was?"

Hanhau's brow narrowed. "Not really. I had many fathers and mothers looking after me. I'm grateful for every one of them. Just around the time I came of age, our tribe fought through one of the worst raids in our history. Most of the older generation was killed protecting the young ones. I wouldn't be able to find who fathered me if I wanted to."

While Dam digested that, Hanhau posed his own question. "You never told me about your parents. They must have been very important to you."

Dam looked down at his feet hanging off the edge of their rock. "I never knew them, really. They died before I can remember. Not in a war or anything like that. There was a fire. I was outside in a crib under a shade tree while my father was bringing his horses out of the stable to exercise in the yard." Dam's voice went flat. "Lucky for me, I guess. My father rushed inside to save my mother when he saw smoke coming from the house. One of the bricks had burst in the hearth, and the fire spread. The roof fell in. They didn't make it out." He brought up his foot to pick at his sandal again. "That's what I was told."

Hanhau slid closer. "I'm sorry. It must be nice that you have friends and family who made it to safety before the flood."

"I have Aerander."

The pounding of the waterfalls ate up the silence for a moment. Dam had told the story many times before, but telling it always seemed to peel back an achy layer of his heart.

Hanhau clasped his shoulder and brushed the hairs at the side of Dam's head. "You also have me. And you never gave me an answer to my invitation to the feast."

Dam curled his neck into Hanhau's shoulder. "What will your countrymen think?"

"Some will probably be unhappy. Others won't care much. None of that matters to me."

A smile overcame Dam. *Very handsome*, Hanhau had said. He felt handsome when he was with Hanhau.

"What will *your* countrymen think?" Hanhau asked.

"What do I care?"

"Then—?"

"I'll go with you to the feast."

They held hands and talked and gazed out at the waterfall for a timeless spell that went too quickly all the same. It was, Dam realized, his first real courtship with a boy, not just sneaking off to fool around and never speaking of it again. This was something anyone would call honorable.

CHAPTER FOUR

Back at his home, Dam buried himself beneath the mossy blanket on his pallet. A swarm of things buzzed inside his head. His life had been a foul heap of horseshit before the flood had wiped out everything aboveground. While everyone else was homesick and hated the underworld, coming below had brought the possibility of a new beginning for Dam. Could the Fates have planned all along that happiness was waiting for him in a world buried beneath his feet?

Dam almost chortled. He sealed his mouth and tucked his head into his neck. Dam didn't want to wake up Hephad, who was asleep across the room. Dam turned over on his side, trying very hard to keep still while his face bloomed with an enormous smile.

Hanhau was handsome and kind and smart. He was honorable, and he made Dam feel honorable too. Their differences had worried Dam at first, but he was certain now he didn't need to worry about that. He liked Hanhau. What did it matter what other people thought? Most everyone had long ago made up their mind about Dam anyway.

If Calyiches and his friends decided to make fun of his relationship with Hanhau, Dam vowed he would set them right, and not just with words but with his fists. Aerander would no doubt have an opinion about it. Hephad would as well. He held on to the teachings of the priesthood like an anchor amid the chaos of the evacuation. Hephad thought Dam had displeased the gods already by giving up his vocation. Giving his heart to a foreigner who disavowed the gods completely was a further desecration. But Aerander and Hephad could be reasoned with, or at least persuaded into resignation. The advantage of being an outcast was it didn't leave you with many people to argue over how you led your life.

One thing bit at Dam, however. What if Hanhau found out what had happened with Leo and Koz? From the years when Dam had been a novice priest, that topped a list of things he wasn't proud of.

Dam could chalk it up to survival and spite. He had discovered early into his apprenticeship that no one left the priesthood with his earnings. The novices were broken down like lowly dogs with beatings, lockups in a cellar pen, and lectures about how derelict they were. By the time they reached five years of service, any thought of bettering themselves had been crushed out of them. All that was left was the desperate hope that they could be vessels of the gods who wielded a brutal authority over men and granted occasional kindness to the most devout. Dam doubted that the priests ever paid out their charges' rightful wages anyway. Everything they had was stripped away, including their bodies. At full dark, they were sent out to the city's quarter-temples, where grizzled old men dropped a few tin coins at the fetish altars for a grasp of pleasure with one of the boys in a shadowy back-room recess.

Dam had been spared from that humiliation. He wasn't a temple whore. Aerander's father had used his influence to assign Dam as an attendant of the High Priest Zazamoukh. If Calyiches had half a brain, he would have known Dam had been confined to the priesthood's mainstay, the Temple of Poseidon.

But the threat of being sent to the city's seedy shrines used to give Dam night terrors. And being under the charge of the High Priest hadn't been much of a privilege. Zazamoukh was a miserable old cur who delighted in suffering. Dam had never known true evil until he had met that man.

Dam's privileged position had been a double-edged sword. Outwardly, the other novices had to respect him, but no one had wanted to be his friend beside Hephad. When their superiors weren't around, Dam used to get tripped and shoved. Bedtime at the dormitory had been the worst. Dam had kept a pocket knife in his pallet, and he had gouged one of his roommates in the ribs pretty bad when the boy had wrestled on top of him one night. He felt like no one in the world cared about him. Certainly no one had cared that he needed his earnings to claim his father's stables. So Dam had started doing immoral things.

He didn't regret stealing from the temple oblations. People left coin at the altars, hoping it would speed their prayers to this or that patron god. But it all got scooped up and wheelbarrowed to the High

Priest's treasury so he could build more temples and collect more coin while no one got paid for their labor. Maybe pocketing the spoils of a thief made him no better than the thief himself, but Dam hadn't gotten rich from taking a galleon away from the priest every now and then. If he had been smart about it, he would have stowed away enough to break out on his own. But he hadn't had the pluck to do that. Where would he have gone? What would he have done?

Nor did Dam regret sneaking out of the precinct at night. The priests preached segregation from the commoners, but getting out of the precinct had been Dam's only freedom. Sometimes he would stake out a spot on the street across from an inn house, hoping that a kind and decent man would take an interest in him. That was the only way he could figure that he would get out of the priesthood. Men had stopped to talk to him, but they were scoundrels and drunkards who had just wanted a sloppy romp in an alleyway. That went against his vow of purity of body besides being dangerous as heck. But Dam had been like a falcon diving from a cliff. He had figured that it didn't matter much if the wind caught his wings or he was pounded into pulp on the rocky shore.

All of that was plenty bad enough for Hanhau to find out about, and still the worst part was how Dam had ended up hurting other people. Could the story get back to Hanhau? Should he tell him before he heard it from someone else?

❖

It had happened at the Panegyris during the strange blur of days before everyone had come below. The island city was overfilled with people from the country's ten kingdoms. Everyone was wild with national pride. No one anticipated the disaster that was coming, though people spoke of omens.

The seaborne wind was unnaturally blustery and cold, and the heavens poured down drenching rains. A military crisis had broken out overseas. In the frozen wilds of the north, a barbarian army with warriors mounted on battle-trained mammoths had trampled the Azilian front and pressed into the country's borders. The Governors Council had scrounged together nearly every able-bodied man to sail across the North Atlantic Sea and hold back the barbarians.

Still, that hadn't done much to dampen people's spirits. No one believed that any misfortune could touch the island of Atlantis. It had been the seat of the world's greatest empire for a millennium.

Games and fancy feasts took place on the walled Citadel Hill. Dam had received an invitation from Aerander's father. Over the years since Dam had left the palace, he and his cousin had grown apart. It had mostly been Dam's doing. Dam had avoided his cousin's letters and visits to the priest's precinct. Aerander just got tired of trying to see him, Dam supposed. Dam had had a foolish idea that he would return to the palace one day when he had made something of himself. In the meantime, the priesthood had made him decrepit. Even if he had washed up and dressed in fancy clothes, Dam imagined his cousin could see and smell that awful change in him.

When the invitation to the Panegyris arrived, Dam shook off the fading embers of his pride. After three years of living with the priests, he would have taken up an invitation to attend the pitching of the stalls at the circus to get out of the precinct for a while. Besides, his uncle's invitation gave him a fistful of salt to grind in the High Priest Zazamoukh's face. The sadistic old man couldn't stop Dam from going. Aerander's father was the governor of House Atlas. Dam cleaned himself up, went down to the agora to buy a wooden figurine of a soldier as a gift for his cousin, and traveled to the Citadel for the first day of the festival.

That was where Dam had met Leo.

Of everything that Dam regretted, it was the simplest of things that he wished to the gods he could erase from history. It would have been so easy for him to continue on his way to the backhouse benches of the dining pavilion, dismissing a lingering gaze from a highborn boy as a curious compliment and nothing more. Then nothing bad would have happened. But Dam returned that gaze. Leo had invited him with a wave, and Dam meandered over to Leo. sitting at a table decked with silver trenchers and the garnet standard of House Eudemon.

Leo was a lesser legacy from the clan that held sway in the kingdom's Fortunate Isles. His cousin Lys, now Aerander's sweetheart, was Governor Eulian's son. Leo wasn't the most handsome boy Dam had ever met, but he grabbed Dam's fascination fast. He wore the costume of nobility with a bit of sloppy irreverence, his cape askew and his *chiton* thrown on casually. He had a crown of perpetually sleep-tossed hair, which was as red as a blood orange. His lopsided smile announced his cynical view of the world.

To anyone who would listen, Leo trumpeted that he was an actor bound for a storied career in House Eudemon's court of players. Dam had thought that was rather brilliant. Traditionally, boys of noble birth became politicians or military officers. They looked down their noses at the common men who entertained a House Governor's court. No one bothered Leo about it. If they tried, he cut them to the quick with a few biting words.

Leo wasn't much for the traditions of the Panegyris: the lawn hockey games, the martial practices, and all the parties where boys showed off for girls. Instead, he had an entourage of admirers and aspiring players. His younger brother Koz counted as both. The two put on parodies of their athletic trainers and the granite-muscled and granite-brained champions of the games. In front of a crowd, Leo shone like the sun itself.

At night, he led his friends to stake out a darkened corner of the palace courtyard. The jumble of boys would splay out on blankets. No one treated Dam any different because he was a priest and only marginally affiliated with the Poseidonidae. Sometimes Leo would draw Dam near so they were shoulder to shoulder and leg to leg while they joked around, drank the finest wine in the kingdom, and made up bawdy verses for the patriotic anthems that the boys had been taught to sing.

Leo had lots of questions about the priesthood. He said he was working on a play where one of the characters was a priest, and he needed to know their habits and their rituals. Dam had been skittish about that at first. It had been drummed into his head not to speak about those sacred things. Leo had been relentless. He even offered Dam gold coins if he would take him into the priests' precinct. That was barter Dam could use. More so, Dam had wanted Leo to like him. He was no longer an abandoned duckling waddling after boys, but a place in his heart longed for someone to love him. Leo could be that special person. In his head, Dam had imagined the two of them would be together for a lifetime.

There were secrets Dam had discovered while wandering around on his own at night. He knew he should keep them to himself, but he wanted to impress Leo since Leo had brought him into his group of friends. Dam didn't have much of anything that could impress a House Governor's nephew. So Dam told Leo a big secret.

He had found an underground passage in the ossuary beneath the

Temple of Poseidon. It led deep beneath the earth, and if you followed it to the end, you found a hidden gateway to the Citadel wood that opened and closed through some kind of enchantment. Dam hadn't been able to explain how it worked at the time. He just said it was an old tunnel that must have been dug out as an escape route when the Citadel had first been built. He understood things now. The New Ones had used the magic of the Oomphalos to create portals to the surface so they could kidnap men as slaves.

Dam could use the passage to sneak Leo into the priests' precinct without anyone knowing. They made plans to meet up at a spot in the woods at moontide. Though Dam told him not to tell anyone about it, Leo brought his brother Koz.

Dam led the two through the passage and showed them the temple's crypt. Leo and Koz thought the creepy place was the best discovery in the world. They chased each other around the bone-walled passageways, pretending to be corpses risen from the dead. It was a risky game with the High Priest and all the heads of the precinct bureaus just above them in the temple quarantine. Dam tried to get the boys to keep their voices down, but he was happy to have shown Leo something that he really liked.

Later, Leo and Koz caught up with Dam in a dead end of one of the crypt's narrow veins. It was a dark alley barely traced by torchlight. Leo had a strange, grim look on his face that made Dam suddenly aware of their proximity. Leo drew up flush to Dam, nuzzled against his neck, and asked Dam for a special favor.

Dam felt funny about Leo's brother hanging around. But he did like doing that with boys, and he wanted to do it with Leo. He stooped down and gathered Leo's tunic above his waist to give him that special kind of kiss boyfriends gave each other. When he was done, Leo pressed two gold pieces into Dam's hand and asked him to do the same thing to Koz.

That hadn't been right. But Dam's head had been jumbled at the time. Maybe it was normal in the place Leo was from. He even thought, idiotically, maybe it meant both Leo and Koz wanted to be sweethearts with him.

Afterward, he had shown the boys back to the Citadel, and the shame of what he had done crushed down on him with the weight of the sky. They were silent all the way, and Dam could feel something had changed. Dam had not foreseen just how terrible it would be.

The next day, Dam came round the dining pavilion for the afternoon feast just like any other day. When he approached House Eudemon's table, Leo and his friends nudged each other and laughed at him. Dam didn't have to ask why. It poured over him like tar. Leo and Koz had told everyone what he had done the night before. They all thought he was dirty and a fool.

Looking back, Dam should have let things be, especially after Lys cornered him in a stairwell threatening to crack open his skull if he didn't stay away from Leo. But that flipped something inside Dam. If people were going to treat him like a derelict, he decided he would show them just how derelict he could be.

Dam started pocketing little things around the palace: fancy bronze clasps left unattended while the boys changed outfits for their athletic practices, silverware sitting idle on the dining hall tables. Dam even stole a jewelry box from Aerander's younger sister while passing by the ladies' parlor. He couldn't rationally explain why he had done it. It just felt good to hold something over the people who thought he was nothing special. Taking the jewelry box had been a really rotten thing, but it seemed to Dam Aerander's family was part of the high society that laughed at him.

A few days later, Leo caught up with him in the palace while he was minding his own business on a deserted breezeway. Leo said he had to pretend they weren't friends because his family had found out he had broken curfew with Dam the other night. Leo told Dam he really liked him. He said he would make things up in coins, and he promised he wanted just the two of them to be sweethearts. Leo asked to go back to the priests' precinct. He told Dam he had to bring his brother Koz along, but it wouldn't be like the last time. Dam just needed to find one of his priest friends for Koz.

Like the biggest idiot who had ever lived, Dam agreed to meet Leo and his brother after dark in the woods again. He wanted to believe Leo really meant what he had said. Besides, his reputation had been so blackened from the last time, he figured it didn't matter what happened anyway. Dam had learned that night the gods could always come up with even worse ways for mortals to suffer.

He persuaded Hephad to meet them at the ossuary, thinking he and Koz might like each other. But after traveling through the underground tunnel, Leo announced he was interested in something different. He wanted Dam and Hephad to show him and his brother Zazamoukh's quarters. Like many of the boys in the Panegyris, they thought it would be brilliant to get one over on the gory old priest who was always telling them they were a sorry show as legacies of the Great Poseidon.

That was really gutsy. Hephad got cold feet and went back to his room. It was crazy to try to smuggle two strangers into the High Priest's chamber. If Dam was caught, he would get one hell of a beating or possibly get thrown out of the priesthood to fend for himself on the streets. But danger dangled in front of Dam like a gem. It was a chance to show Leo how bold he could be.

He stealthily led the boys on a route through the priests' quarantine. Dam had a key to the High Priest's room, but he figured that it would be barred from the inside being so late at night. With some luck, he would sneak the boys back down to the ossuary unseen. They could say they had broken into the forbidden quarantine of the priests, and they would be done with their adventure for the night.

When they arrived at the threshold to the High Priest's room, Dam opened up the pin lock on its outer latches with his key, and he felt give on the other side. His heart lurched up to his throat. Zazamoukh must have stepped out for some sort of business. Leo and Koz pushed open the door and traipsed inside.

Dam stood at the door, stricken to stone, while they went through the High Priest's robes, his collars of bone, and his gory fetishes: snippets of hair, bloodstained figurines, and his putrid collection of animal parts. They found Zazamoukh's bull's horn, which he wore around his neck and used to anoint boys who had come of age with blood from the sacrifice. Moments after Leo and Koz had stuck their fingers into the horn and smeared their foreheads, enacting a parody of temple service, they fell to the floor drained of life.

Dam couldn't reason what from what. He wasn't sure how long he stood there, debrained by the dimensions of his predicament. He heard a sly, quick footfall behind him. It was Zazamoukh. He snarled at the discovery of Dam trespassing in his room, took account of things, and shut and bolted the door behind him.

He clamped Dam's ear with his cold, bony hand and bullied him down to the floor where the boys' bodies lay. He told Dam he was an abomination. He said Dam had betrayed his trust, dishonored Poseidon by bringing laypeople into the sacred quarantine, and the boys had been struck dead in retribution. The Governors would hang him for treason. The only way for him to hold on to his life was to help Zazamoukh bring the bodies to a sacred place underground.

What could Dam do? He followed the High Priest's orders and raced to the storehouse to empty two sacks of grain. He brought the empty sacks to Zazamoukh's chamber, and they stowed Leo and Koz inside, dragging them down to the ossuary and through the secret passage. In a vault below, Zazamoukh went through a strange ritual preparation with a salve and strips of cloth that he wrapped around the boys' bodies from head to toe. He said it was to purify them for burial.

Seeing how deliberately Zazamoukh handled the bodies, Dam had an eerie premonition. He broke away from the priest and hid from him in a shadowy alcove of the passageway. If Zazamoukh found him, Dam was certain he would be killed and bound in cloth as well. Thankfully, Zazamoukh didn't have much time to search for him. He couldn't be absent from the temple in the morning.

Meanwhile, Dam discovered a well that throbbed with an otherworldly glow. A magical source of light came from deep below the passage. He returned to the vault to gather Leo's and Koz' bodies, and he witnessed the greatest terror of his life. Two giant serpents trundled into the vault and swallowed Leo and Koz whole.

Gradually, Dam made sense of the bizarre mystery. The boys had been poisoned by some vile concoction in Zazamoukh's bull's horn, but they weren't dead. Zazamoukh was using a paralyzing venom to kidnap boys and barter them to the New Ones as slaves. His payment was basking in the magical power of the Oomphalos. Its brilliant, hypnotic energy had kept the priest alive for centuries.

Even after Dam had helped to break them out of the prisoner camp and worked with Aerander and Lys to clear the way for people to take refuge underground, boys still thought Dam was a thief and a whore. And Leo and Koz blamed him for being sold to the snakes. While Dam had run away, Zazamoukh had interrogated Hephad and maimed him so he couldn't speak of Leo and Koz having come to the temple. That was Dam's fault. He had brought Hephad into their late night scheme. He had made Hephad a mute.

❖

Dam tucked his legs up to his chest. That history had stained him ugly. When Hanhau found out about it, what would he think of Dam? Dam couldn't imagine that Hanhau had ever done anything so dishonorable.

One of the cats pounced on his foot and climbed up to Dam's hip, stepping gingerly across the side of his ribs on clawed and padded feet. By the cat's weight, Dam figured it had to be Pleione. She came purring up to his shoulder, looking to horn in for a cuddle. It was good timing for some comforting. Dam stretched his arm and brought her close to his chest.

Pleione had never visited him in bed before. She was more attached to Hephad. Dam stroked the back of her neck and opened his eyes to look at her. He did a double take. He saw by the glow of the room's altar lamp that it wasn't Pleione. Her muzzle was brown with one thin strip of orange down the line of her nose. The cat luxuriating against him looked like Alcyone. She had an orange spot around one eye and a brown spot around the other. But the kittens were barely weaned from their mother. Alcyone had grown as big as Pleione in that short span of time?

That curiosity didn't amount to much that night. Dam had bigger troubles on his mind. He gently closed one arm around the cat, shut his eyes, and tried to sleep. At least the cat didn't shun him for what he had done in the past.

CHAPTER FIVE

Dam woke up to movements around him. When he opened his eyes, he noticed first that Alcyone had left the cradle of his arm. The red light of the Oomphalos washed into the room from the doorway. That strange radiation was vibrant. Its intensity meant it was well into the height of the day.

Hephad and Attalos were laying out clothes on Hephad's bed. They had tracked in wet footprints from washing up, and they looked very serious about their task. Meanwhile, the kittens scampered back and forth across the floor attacking the two boys' ankles.

Those three kittens had grown big for sure. They were playful like young ones, but they were the size of house cats. Dam spotted their mother in one corner of the room. She was cleaning her brown face with the scoop of her paw. Dam pushed up on his elbows. He wondered again how her babies had become as large as her so quickly.

Dam called out, "What's the grand occasion?"

Hephad had kept to the habits of a priest with a shaved scalp and a single hair braid at the crown of his head. He scowled at Dam like he was dim-witted. Attalos was short and scrappy, and his overgrown brown hair was damp from washing. He answered Dam more helpfully.

"Ysalane's feast. Did you forget?"

Of course Dam had forgotten. He felt itchy from head to toe. How much time did he have to get washed and dressed? He was going to the feast with Hanhau.

"Hephad can't decide what to wear," Attalos said. Hephad shot him a baleful look. But he hardly had much to decide. It was either a shift and trousers or the novice kilt that Hephad had worn the night he had escaped the flood. Hephad was partial to his traditional outfit, but his kilt was dingy from many wearings.

"Pick a pair of trousers," Dam said.

Attalos smirked at Hephad. "Told you."

Hephad picked up a pair of laced trousers from his pallet and frowned at them. That made Dam grin. Hephad had always been fussy about dressing, though he supposed he should allow his friend some give. They hadn't had a reason to dress up for anything since they had come below. Dam's stomach twinged as he remembered he had decided to talk to Hanhau about his past. Should he ask for Hephad's and Attalos' opinions about it?

Those two were preoccupied by something. Attalos was making hand gestures. A bashful shadow passed over Hephad's face. Attalos' gestures turned more emphatic. He put his hand on Hephad's shoulder and spoke. "Show him."

Hephad dragged himself over to Dam's side of the room. Attalos quickly retrieved an oil lamp from the floor and lit it with a flint. Hephad sat down next to Dam on his pallet while Attalos stepped around the two with the lamp trying to get a good reflection of light on Hephad's face. Dam had no idea what it was he was supposed to be looking at. Hephad stretched his mouth open wide as though Dam was a physician ordering an examination of his teeth. Dam stared into his friend's mouth keenly.

He blinked in disbelief. By the light of the lamp, he saw an enlarged stub of pink flesh that had grown from the blackened wound where Hephad's tongue had been cut out.

"It's twice the size as yesterday," Attalos said. Hephad closed his mouth and smiled.

Dam knew about lizards and possums that grew back tails, but he had never heard about body parts growing back on men. He looked at the overgrown kittens. Maia and Electra were pouncing on a pair of trousers on Hephad's bed while Alcyone had dragged a pair onto the floor. The red crystalline light of the Oomphalos shone upon them from the terrace like a heavenly shower.

Dam surrounded Hephad's skinny frame with his arms and pulled him into his chest. Everything suddenly made sense: his toenails growing so fast, the kittens maturing so quickly, and now Hephad's tongue regrowing. Tears welled in his eyes. It was the miracle of the Oomphalos.

❖

While Hephad and Attalos went around the middle-houses to show the other boys Hephad's regrown tongue, Dam grabbed drying cloths and a sponge. He headed to the yard below where the spigots for washing were. Ysalane's feast was to begin at dark, when the Oomphalos was cloaked completely in the pinnacle gallery of its tapering granite tower.

Already, Dam could see and feel that the stone was at least half-shuttered. The tower rose above the city's highest stages. Housed in its pinnacle, the Oomphalos was like a fragment of the sun caged in stained glass. That monument was both a tribute and an impenetrable keep for the Old Ones' prized artifact. An elite corps of warriors managed the shuttering and unveiling of the stone in its slotted gallery, and a pair of guards was always on watch at the tower's sole gateway. Rumor had it that inside, intruders would find a winding stairwell engineered with traps. Even if a thief managed to get past the guards and sidestep the deadly triggers on the steps, the climb to the pinnacle gallery was long and grueling, with plenty of time for the guards to summon reinforcements. They could surround the tower well before anyone made it to the top. A thief would have no way out, unless he wanted to leap from the gallery and splatter his guts on the cobblestone square below.

Dam reached the ground-floor yard. He was grateful that he had the place to himself. Everyone else must have washed up earlier in the day, and that gave him some precious privacy. With some luck, he wouldn't have to worry about Calyiches and his friends strutting into the yard and claiming their territory.

Dam headed to a spigot in one corner of the yard. He slipped off his trousers and set them aside. He gave the spigot lever a few creaky pumps to get the water flowing. Dam knelt down and doused his head to rinse the salty lake water from his hair.

His breath caught in his throat, and goose pimples scored his arms and chest. It wasn't like the water from the bathing lake. The yard spigots drew down icy, freshwater from wells higher above the city shelf. Dam turned his head so that the water flow spilled over his open mouth. It was brutal to bathe in but deliciously quenching.

Since waking up that morning, Dam kept slipping in and out of believing that he was really going to Ysalane's feast as Hanhau's guest. The memories from the night before jangled, and he felt like he had been spun around and blindfolded, fumbling around to make his way. If he'd been dreaming, he wouldn't have to tell Hanhau his shameful secret, but he knew he had to own up to it. His armpits were damp, and he was sure he would be sweating and possibly stinking no sooner than he had dried off. Dam scrubbed himself and rinsed and scrubbed and rinsed until he worried that he was scraping blemishes into his skin.

The water tapered off from the spout, and Dam was startled to notice that he was no longer alone in the yard. Some paces away a pair of elderly men made their way to a spigot.

One of them was frail and older. His companion supported his weight on his shoulder while he limped along. They were freed prisoners of the New Ones, and two of the most weathered of the lot. Some of those men were centuries old. They had been kidnapped by Zazamoukh and had spent an unfathomable lifetime mining a precious substance called mori-mori to feed the evil serpents.

The one man managed to bring the other to the spigot. The older man hunched down to his knees. He looked like he was barely able to hold himself upright. His companion struggled to free him of his tunic. Dam quickly patted himself dry, stepped into his trousers, and traveled over to help.

With just a glance to confirm their cooperation, Dam lifted the older man's arms while the other rustled to pull the tunic over the older man's head. The old man's arms were so delicate, it felt like the bones could break in Dam's hands. Naked, the man was horridly pale and shivering. No wonder—he didn't have an ounce of fat to keep him warm. His head bobbled like he was continuously catching himself drifting off to sleep.

Then Dam remembered. The man's name was Silenos. He had helped Aerander solve the riddle of the Lost Daughter, the Seventh Pleiade, which had released Calaeno from her exile in the heavens. Silenos was the oldest prisoner from the New Ones' slave camp. He had been stolen underground a millennium ago when Poseidon's first-born son Atlas was emperor. He was so old he had known Atlas' daughters, the Pleiades, himself.

His companion gave Dam a kind look. He was aged and gaunt but held himself proudly. It had to have been one hell of a labor bringing Silenos to the yard. The old men kept their own schedule, washing in the yard early in the morning, well before the boys woke up in the upper houses. Some of the highborn boys complained, wanting a separate washing yard for the young and the old. Dam wondered why the two men had come out so late.

"Got to get him ready for Ysalane's feast," Silenos' companion said, a twinkle in his eye. Dam was stunned. He hadn't considered that the prisoners would be going to the feast. Then again, why shouldn't they? Hanhau had said that everyone in the city was invited. Dam realized it was presumptuous of him to think the old men would be left out.

Dam lowered Silenos' arms to his sides and stooped down to brace him from his armpits. "You want me to hold him while you get the pump?" Dam said to the other.

The man pshawed. "You'll get yourself all wet again." He crouched behind Silenos to take over supporting the old man's weight. Silenos' head bobbled just inches from Dam's chest. He was a skull with a few long spindles of white hair barely rooted to his scalp.

"I know you," Silenos said.

The old man raised his bony hand and fumbled it over Dam's chin and lips. That was awkward and unpleasant. But it felt like it would be impolite to shove the man's hand away. His eyes were clouded by milky cataracts.

"The second prince," Silenos said. "You saved us from the snakes."

"No sir. I'm Damianos. You're thinking of my cousin Aerander."

The old man's face shrank up irascibly. "I know Aerander. And I know you. You're twins, but never have two different boys been born from the same mother's womb." His mouth hung open, and he wheezed to regain his breath. "How are the emperor's girls? Still living in the apple orchard?"

Dam grinned. He glanced at the man's companion, who smiled knowingly. Supposedly, Emperor Atlas had kept his six daughters in a secret apple grove to protect them from suitors. That was ages ago. The old man's mind was so eroded, he couldn't distinguish the past from the present. When they had first met, Silenos had thought that Aerander was the emperor Atlas himself. Now he thought that Dam was Atlas the Golden's twin, Gadir?

Dam gently redirected the man's hand from his face. "The girls are fine, sir."

The old man nodded or bobbled. Dam wasn't sure.

"Good," Silenos said. "You keep them safe. You keep yourself safe too. There's more adventures ahead of you, second prince."

His companion had a good hold on Silenos from the back, so Dam carefully released the old man and turned to the spigot pump. It seemed cruel to subject Silenos to the frigid water, but that was the only way to wash him. He cranked the pump, drawing up a vigorous gush. The other man ducked Silenos' head beneath the flow.

Silenos barely budged. He was too weak to put up a fuss. He could only quiver his lips as the cold water gushed over his head. The man should have died hundreds of years ago. It was the Oomphalos that kept his corpse-like body still breathing and pumping with blood. A frightful shiver ran down Dam's spine. How long could the Oomphalos keep Silenos alive?

❖

As Dam made his way upstairs, red daylight was eclipsing, and the gas lamps around the Honeycomb had sparked on. A commotion hailed from the upper houses. The highborn boys were getting rowdy in anticipation of Ysalane's feast. It reminded Dam of the clamor in the palace courtyard when the boys had waited to be ushered to some event for the Panegyris. Dam picked up his pace.

Entering his house, he smiled at the sight of Hephad dressed in trousers and a tunic. Then he spotted Aerander in the middle of the room. His cousin had fixed his hair in sculpted waves with some sort of concoction and put on a fancy *chiton* that draped from one shoulder down to the middle of his calf in the style of a statesman. It was spun from elegant silk, and its seamstress had embroidered hems across the top, the single sleeve, and around the bottom in the indigo hatch mark pattern of the House of Atlas.

Calaeno's trident amulet hung proudly on the outside of his clothes. With his shadow of a beard growing in, Aerander was looking more like his father by the day. The only thing missing was a gilded lariat for his head. Dam glanced around for Lys, but he was nowhere to be found.

"Naturally, you're the last one to get ready," Aerander said.

"I overslept."

"You wouldn't have that problem if you got to bed at a normal time."

"What happened to your hair?"

That left Dam's cousin chuffed for a moment. His hair didn't actually look bad, but a mischievous little ember inside Dam glowed.

"It's a special oil they get from fish," Aerander said. "But it doesn't smell. See?" He bowed his head, inviting Dam to take a sniff.

"No thank you."

"A lot of the boys are using it. I brought some for you."

Dam stepped past him to pick out some clothes. He needed a dry pair of trousers and a clean shirt.

"I brought you an outfit too."

Dam followed Aerander's gaze to his bed. There was a *chiton* laid out there. It was the same style that Aerander was wearing. All the highborn boys must have requested noble clothes for the occasion. He was supposed to wear a *chiton* to the feast while Hephad and Attalos were going in plain shifts and trousers?

"There'll be two head tables," Aerander said. "One for Ysalane and her people, and one for us."

Dam skirted his glance. He felt like a cold shadow had descended on him from above.

"Go on," Aerander said, glancing at the bed. "We have to get over to the hall."

"I made plans for the feast."

Aerander twitched his nose, and then he grinned as though Dam was putting him on. Of course, Dam wasn't. "What do you mean?"

"Hanhau asked me to go with him as his guest."

"Hanhau?"

Dam nodded.

During the long silence that ensued, Attalos came to the doorway dressed for the feast. Hephad hurried over to leave with him, and they waved good-bye. The oversized kittens must have been out exploring the Honeycomb. Their mother, Pleione, was the only one left in the house. She had a firm eye on the conversation between Dam and Aerander from her comfortable sprawl on the floor at one side of the room.

"I thought—" Aerander started to say. He grimaced. "It's a public occasion, Dam. People are supposed to sit with their family."

"You'll have Lys and Dardy and Evandros." Dardy and Evandros were Aerander's best friends. They were from House Gadir. But they were all so close, they called each other brothers.

"They're friends. Not family," Aerander said.

"It's just a dinner. We'll all be in the same room."

"It's not just a dinner. It's diplomatic. You knew that, and you made plans without even talking to me about it."

"It only came up last night."

"How could you do that to me?"

Dam winced. He pushed on. "Hanhau asked me to go with him, and I told him would. Because I want to."

"Because you *want to*. Did it ever occur to you that *I* need you at the feast? I'm representing everyone. Is it too much to ask that my only flesh and blood could sit beside me?"

Dam looked at his cousin helplessly. Ever since they had been reunited by the disaster, they were like lost pups who rediscovered each other in the wild. Aerander pushed too hard, and Dam nipped and clawed back. He needed time to go back to the way they had been with one another.

Aerander's face was flushed and trembling. Dam stepped near.

"I'll be there to support you. Does it matter that we're at the same table?" He reached to clasp his cousin's shoulder. Aerander jerked away from him.

"What did I do to you to make you treat me like such a shit?"

Cold irons sank into Dam's chest.

"Why can't we be brothers, the way we used to be?"

Aerander had lost his birth mother when he was a baby, just like Dam had lost both his parents. They had been raised together by nursemaids in the Governor's palace. They had both been taken into a household where they didn't belong, which made them feel like they belonged to each other even more.

"When the flood came, and I couldn't save my family, all I wanted to do was bury myself in my bed and die," Aerander said. His eyes were watery and haunted. "You pulled me out of that. You told me that people needed me to give them something to believe in. You said we would stand together. Just like I took your side when everyone thought you double-crossed Leo and Koz, I might need your help someday."

Dam stared at Aerander, frozen. "It's only a feast."

"Is everyone right about you?" Aerander said. "You lie and steal, and you only care about yourself?"

"Aerander, don't."

He eyed his cousin steadily. If Aerander wanted to have a conversation about the past, they could start with Aerander's family brushing Dam aside like a domestic to clear a gleaming path for their one and only rightful legacy. Maybe Aerander couldn't have done anything to intervene, but at least he could admit that it was House Atlas that had abandoned Dam, not Dam abandoning them.

Aerander drew a breath, and his diplomatic airs came back to him, albeit strained. "Do what you want," he said. "There'll be a seat at the table if you change your mind."

He glanced at the *chiton* on Dam's bed, and then he stepped out of the room.

CHAPTER SIX

Dam couldn't help feeling like a traitor after his cousin walked out of the room. The fancy outfit he had commissioned lay on Dam's bed as though it was the funerary clothes stripped from Aerander's own father. Dam supposed he could live with his cousin thinking he was selfish and disloyal. He had lived with worse things said about him.

But it wasn't fair.

Aerander acted like Dam naturally had a place at a statesman's table, but did he care to acknowledge that Dam spent the last three years as a penniless servant of the priests, far beyond the grandeur of the Citadel? Dam wondered why sitting together at the feast was so important to his cousin. Did he truly want him there, or did he need him as a prop for the House of Atlas? If Aerander thought he was worthy of the Atlas name, why did he treat him like a wayward child who needed constant minding?

But Aerander was the leader of their countrymen and a far better leader than any of the other men. He had risked his life clearing the way for their evacuation. He had made friends with the Old Ones for everyone's benefit, and he believed in putting country first rather than the self-serving interests of his fellow Poseidonidae. He had rallied Dam to join his mission to retrieve the Oomphalos against impossible odds. That was why, when Aerander had been lost in grief after the flood, Dam had begged him to break out of his seclusion and show himself standing strong in order to pull the survivors together. Dam knew he ought to take Aerander's side on that principle alone.

But it was so hard to do.

Dam wished he could skulk off to some remote spot to sort things out, or maybe just to let those things settle and sink away to some forgotten place. But the feast awaited him. He dressed in clean trousers, a tunic, and his sandals, and he washed his mouth and teeth in the basin in the corner of the room.

Just as he was wiping off his face with a cloth, Hanhau arrived at the house. That normally would have lifted Dam's spirits, but he was in such a fog, he just managed a glance at Hanhau and headed to the door so they could make their way to the hall.

Hanhau held his place. Dam noticed he had darkened his eyes with kohl. He was dressed in formal trousers tailored snugly to his long, powerful legs and studded like armor at the seams. His body armor was robust and shiny like oiled leather. He wore metal armlets and anklets, and his silky black hair had been braided on the sides in a martial fashion.

He hid his hands behind his back, then brought one out, showing Dam the metal bracelet in his palm. "For you," he said.

Dam took the bracelet. It was a simple wrought iron loop that fit perfectly around his wrist.

"There's writing on it," Hanhau said. The room was dim with just the glow of hanging gas lamps at the corners of the walls. He brought over an oil lantern that Hephad kept by his bed so Dam could see the bracelet better.

Dam wiggled it off his wrist. The outside was engraved in an arcane script. Hanhau's people didn't have books like they did in Atlantis, but Dam had seen their strange, cuneiform markings etched on the sides of caves and around town on totem guideposts pointing out the byways to this or that section of the city. On the inside of the bracelet, he saw a single word in Atlantean letters: "Dam."

"Now you know how your name is written in our language," Hanhau said. "There's no precise translation. Since you came down here with your cousin, you have been known as 'the second son.' And 'One of three who banished Ouroborus.'"

Dam studied the scripted characters. Ouroborus had been the Snake Queen, the leader of the New Ones who Aerander had killed with Lys and Dam's help. Silenos had called Dam "second prince." The similarity was eerie.

"Do you like it?" Hanhau said. "I was never good at metalcraft, but one of the smithies gave me a hand."

Dam slipped the bracelet back on his wrist. "Yes." He felt

idiotically empty-handed. He had nothing for Hanhau. Hanhau must have forged the bracelet in the early hours of the day, while Dam had slept and thought nothing about a gift for the occasion. So he gave Hanhau the only thing he could think of giving. He stepped up close, stooped to Hanhau's height, and pressed his lips against Hanhau's. Hanhau reached around Dam's shoulders and held him.

Telling Hanhau about his past was not going to be easy.

"I didn't know what to wear," Dam said.

"You look fine."

Dam wasn't so sure. Hanhau was dressed for ceremony. He had thrown on rationed garments like a peasant.

"It's a celebration for the people," Hanhau said. "You wear whatever suits you." His face darkened shyly. "You're handsome to me no matter what you wear."

That made Dam feel a little better. For a moment. Dam looked at the *chiton* that Aerander had left for him on the bed. A blink of light from Hanhau's face showed that he noticed it as well.

Dam told Hanhau about his visit with his cousin. He shared how terrible he felt about disappointing Aerander, and equally how terrible he felt about having to act like Aerander's noble brother when that wasn't the case. It was easy and natural telling Hanhau these things. In fact, Dam would have been plenty happy to stay at his house with Hanhau while the feast went on without them.

"You should sit at the table with your cousin," Hanhau said.

"It's just a feast," Dam grumbled.

Hanhau wiggled his eyebrows. "That's true. It's just a feast."

Dam dropped his head. He understood what Hanhau was getting at. He was being stubborn. It was just a feast that meant a lot to Aerander.

"You won't be mad?" Dam said.

Hanhau gently lifted Dam's chin and kissed him full and deep again. He broke away and held the side of Dam's cheek. "We'll just have to plan to do something else together."

A huge smile sprang up on Dam's face. "When?"

"We'll have our own feast, after the feast."

"Tomorrow night?"

"Whenever you want. Wherever you want."

A thought popped into Dam's head. "The Fire Canyon?" Hanhau had told him about a place with lava channels and geysers that burst up from crater islands.

Hanhau interlaced his hand with Dam's. "The Fire Canyon," he said.

Dam would have liked another kiss, but he noticed the commotion outside had disappeared like a receding tide. Everyone had moved on to the hall. He looked to the *chiton* on his bed.

"I can't wear that. It's too fancy."

Hanhau gave him a reproachful smirk. A woeful weight descended on Dam. He supposed he had no choice. Dam stepped over to his pallet to try on the *chiton*. Just then, one of the kittens trotted in and her sisters bounded after her.

That first cat had something in her mouth. Dam stared at her closely. She had caught some sort of lizard that was two-thirds her size. Dam had seen animals of that sort in the underworld. They were tough-skinned and quick-moving, and they hung around the rubbish bins outside the city's dining hall. The cat dropped the lizard's lifeless body in front of her and sat up proudly.

Dam could swear the kittens had started to look more like cubs than cats. Their bodies were stout and thick with downy fur. Their paws were nearly as big as fists. Dam glanced at Hanhau. He appeared to be adding things up too.

Chapter Seven

They walked through town together to the core of the city where an expansive yard had been cleared for Ysalane's Great Hall. It was the first time that the building had been seen. At night, pipe scaffolding and tarpaulins had been draped around the construction site. For a fortnight or more, it had just been a dusty, fenced-in worksite on a plot of rock adjacent to the Oomphalos Tower.

Passing through the totem gateway to the yard, Dam halted in awe of what the Old Ones had created. It was now one monumental square—the hall and the tower together—surrounded by the terraced stages of the city like an arena for men the size of giants.

Between the two grand buildings was a rectangular reflecting pool with the biggest fountain Dam had ever seen. It was an otherworldly marvel. Beneath the pool, beams of light shone up from the water, and a rainbow arc stretched across the cascading spouts. Dam gathered the Old Ones had devised some invention of gas and gaslight, like a lighthouse beam, under the pool. The fountain chutes reached halfway up the height of the tower.

Across the water, the hall stood majestic in black, shiny onyx. Spires on its massive roof surged with higher peaks of gas-fueled flames. Like most of the underground people's buildings, the hall's ornamentation was spare. They didn't decorate walls with friezes or erect sculpted plinths in public squares to please the gods like they did in Atlantis.

Dam and Hanhau crossed the square to the hall's grand portico, where stairs led up to an archway nearly the staggering height of the building. The double doors of studded bronze were open and posted at the sides. The entryway could accommodate a whale. A sea of voices from inside echoed as one indecipherable commotion.

Beyond the hall's vestibule, Dam saw a single, dizzying room with infinite gas-lit candelabrums hanging from the ceiling. Dam knew it was an illusion, "a trick of the Master of Light," as the Old Ones said. The bordering walls were plated with shiny, reflecting silver. The room was built from looking glass, giving it even greater dimensions. A broad promenade extended between two banks of benched slate tables, and two head tables stood at the far end, as Aerander had said there would be.

The façade beyond the head tables shone with many lanterns, and it bore the room's only art. It was a sweeping mural Dam gradually recognized as the creation story of the Old Ones. Their Creator God had made three races of men: the ones who lived above the earth, the ones who lived on the earth, and the ones who lived below the earth. In shades of red ochre and cobalt blue, the mural showed the sky world, the earth world, and the underworld, representing all of the races welcome in Ysalane's hall.

Between the head tables, a tall fount presided over the room like a ceremonial torch. The Old Ones had filled it with red, glowing mori-mori, the most precious substance in Agartha. They mined it from a lode in the hills near the city. They called mori-mori "the blood of the earth." Its nature was mysterious, and it was said that the Oomphalos had been forged from mori-mori during the olden age of peace.

Dam's pace dragged at the end of the promenade. It was time for him and Hanhau to part ways. Ysalane sat at one long head table. Her long black hair was braided and pinned up high on her head like a crown, and she wore the bronze collar and crimson cape of tribal chief. The warriors sat at that table, men and women all dressed the same as Hanhau. Their eyes were all darkened with kohl, and only the broadness of the women's scale-covered breasts distinguished them from the men.

At the other table, Aerander was in his indigo House Atlas *chiton*, Lys in his garnet *chiton* representing House Eudemon, and Dardy, Evandros, and a half dozen of their cousins, uncles, and nephews in the emerald robes of House Gadir. They hadn't looked so noble since the days of the Panegyris. Dam felt strange about joining them. The royal *chiton* he was wearing felt like it belonged on someone else.

Aerander looked at Dam and the space on the bench beside him.

Hanhau squeezed Dam's hand, gave him an encouraging grin, and stepped over to Ysalane's table. Dam made his way next to Aerander.

The other boys greeted Dam warmly, and Lys collared him and patted his back in a brotherly way. Aerander's friends were all decent people. Dam had no gripe with them as he did with Calyiches and his pack of goons. But the formal occasion reminded him of the Panegyris, which he had been trying to forget.

When he sat down on the bench, a chortle broke out in the room, and Dam could see it had arisen from Calyiches' table where he and his friends were smirking at him. The highborn boys had taken seats at the front of the hall directly across from his table. They counted about seven dozen in total and were a fairly even distribution of boys from the royal houses: the boys from House Mneseus in purple *chiton*s, Elassipos in amber, Azaes in gold, Diaprepos in persimmon, Autochthonos in copper, Mestor in silver, and Amphisos in aquamarine.

Farther back was a table for the common boys and the surviving women where Hephad and Attalos were seated. The freed prisoners sat at tables stretching all the way to the back of the hall.

Dam searched for Silenos, hoping the frail man had made it to the feast, but there were too many people and they were too indistinguishable from his distance. The prisoners outnumbered even the highborn boys, and they were all old men with white or gray hair wearing the same common man's apron.

Scullery workers in bibs and trousers wheeled metal carts into the hall with the first course of the feast. They fanned out through the room, bringing each table a steaming trencher of soup, a ladle, and a stack of bowls.

The highborn boys nudged one another and snickered about the martial style service. They were so unfathomably rude. The Old Ones didn't make men slaves so they could stand at tables and fill other people's soup bowls. Those boys ought to have been grateful that they were getting fed at all, but naturally, they clanged about sloppily with their ladles and sniffed at the soup as though it might be foul and poisonous. Dam served himself and drank his soup, a rich, tasty broth with smoky clams and snails.

Afterward, they ate from platters with many kinds of fish and mushroom steaks and a ribbony, undersea vegetable like black seaweed. Other sorts of foods were too exotic for most of the boys' tastes: slimy jellyfish and brazier-charred lizards whose bellies needed to be picked open. Each table had a pitcher of chilled water.

Dardy, a stalky, straw-haired boy who had the curse of pimples, brought up how much he missed eating meat. Everyone around the table joined in to reminisce about the banquets from the old days. They missed wine. They missed bread from the oven and honeyed cakes. They even missed the bland porridge in winter.

Dam missed those things too, though he had lived with a lot less than Aerander's friends. In the early days of their asylum, a few of the boys had stopped eating completely. They were sick with grief, and they couldn't stomach the foods they had underground. The highborn boys had been raised to be statesmen and military *strategoi*, but beyond their lush palaces, they could be remarkably frail.

"I miss girls too," Dardy announced. That brought grins to his companions' faces. Everyone had heard Dardy's story about Palmdyra, the pretty girl he had been courting, but he told it again and no one complained. Dam noticed some boys looking at the women who were far aloft in the middle of the hall. They were common folk who Dam and Attalos had rounded up from the Temple of Poseidon on that awful night when the sea had overtaken the city. The women had been kneeling at the foot of the grand cella of Poseidon with budded boughs from the sacred cypress tree, making prayers to the god to spare the city.

Those women kept to themselves. Dam supposed it must be even harder for them to adjust to living underground than it was for the boys. While Aerander's friends gazed at the group, Dam wondered how long the traditions of segregation by class and gender would hold the boys back from the stirrings of nature.

The conversation brought up another private thought. Hanhau had said that Dam would see for himself what happened when his people went through "courtship season." Glancing around at the men at tables on Ysalane's side of the hall, Dam noticed a few men whose scales had molted off their back or chest, revealing patches of fresh, tawny skin. And some of the women had bound their breasts with bolts of silk, which was entirely unusual.

Dam bowed his head and grinned. What must it be like to have one's private business open to be seen by everybody else! He glanced at Hanhau at the head table across the aisle. Sultry thoughts overwhelmed

Dam's brain. Aerander gave him a strange look, and Dam shook those thoughts out of his head.

Ysalane stood. The chatter and the clang of cups and utensils throughout the hall receded into silence. The chieftain of the Old Ones spoke some words of welcome, first addressing her people in her own language, then in Atlantean to the other half of the hall.

Two warriors marched down the central aisle, carrying a metal box on chains and hooks between them. They halted in front of Ysalane. Their Chieftain called Aerander to stand beside her. He came over, and Ysalane opened the lid of the box, bringing out a gilded gauntlet. It was simple in craftsmanship but splendid. Ysalane presented the gift to Aerander and spoke out to her people first, then to Aerander's.

"To the one who slayed Ouroborus and brought peace to our kingdom. May this armor forever remind us of his strength and bravery."

Aerander took the gauntlet. The Old Ones stomped their feet as was their custom, and the old men in the back of the room cried out: "Hear, hear!" as was theirs. Aerander raised the prize above his head. Dam and Aerander's friends cheered and beat their fists on the table. The response from the front tables was timid.

The fracas died down, allowing Aerander to speak. "This gauntlet shall be tribute not only to our victory over Ouroborus but also to the men and women who gave their lives for our freedom." He looked to Ysalane's side of the Hall. "To our new friends I say, we shall always remember the losses of your warriors. May they live on in our hearts and in the sagas of your people. You have taken us in as your own. For your generosity, we are forever grateful."

The stomping of feet erupted again. Dam had to admit that his cousin had become a good speaker and a politician in short time. Gradually, the stomping trailed off, and Aerander turned to the other side of the Hall.

"To my countrymen I say, this gauntlet is dedicated to our fathers and all our kin who cannot be with us today. We have lost much. At times, that sorrow carves us empty as shells, and it feels as though it is too much to go on. But our promise to the ones who came before us, the ones who built a mighty kingdom across lands and seas, that promise is as unbreakable as the ore from which this armor was forged. We will return. We will restore Atlantis to its glory. In remembrance of our loved ones. To show the world that Poseidon's legacy lives on. As leader of our people, this I vow to you. Every man and woman born of our country will have a place in that new world. Every one of you in this Great Hall will have land and freedom."

There was a finer point to make about how Poseidon and his legacy had achieved their glory. As Dam and Aerander had learned from the Old Ones, the Oomphalos had cleaved the island of Atlantis from ice during an age when titan gods clutched the world in an eternal winter. The stone's life-giving energies had turned the land fertile so that people there could thrive. From that prosperous city-state, Poseidon and his heirs had claimed colonies in the frozen continents where barbarian races had eked out primitive settlements from the stingy earth. When the Oomphalos had been returned underground, centuries ago, the above-world had gradually been set off balance. Ultimately, the thawing of the land had made the sea rise up and swallow the island.

No matter. The response to Aerander's speech was deafening. It began with the freed prisoners in the back of the room taking to their feet and hollering, and then everyone was standing, cheering and throwing up their fists and calling out Aerander's name. Dam stood and gazed at his cousin with pride. Aerander had managed to include every person in the hall in his speech. He had been an emblem of hope since the evacuation, but in that moment, he had earned his right to lead.

The cheers went on for quite some time. Aerander bowed his head again and again, and then he started back to the head table. A murmur from the crowd dispersed abruptly. While everyone had sat down, Calyiches remained standing.

Dressed in princely splendor, Calyiches was even more arresting than usual, the embodiment of the handsome hero from the adventurous tales of his martial clan Mneseus. Calyiches looked to Ysalane, awaiting a chance to speak.

"I have something to say to our fine new leader."

Aerander halted on his way to his seat. He raised his eyebrows, bidding Calyiches to go on.

"Your speech was apt," Calyiches said. He glanced at his companions. "As legacies of the royal Houses, we are, of course, dedicated to restoring glory to our kingdom. But let us not forget that our country was founded by sacred laws. 'Ten kings for one kingdom.' Such was the decree of Father Poseidon.

"We, who are all that is left of the confederacy of ten kings, have a duty to spread his dominion over every realm of the earth. Yet we remain refugees in a foreign country. What glory is there in that?" Calyiches looked to Ysalane, disarming as always with his artful smile. "I mean no disrespect to you and your people, Your Grace. You have sheltered us with the utmost generosity." He turned to Aerander. "But the time has come for us to make our own way. We are sovereigns, and we want a sovereign land."

Dam could not believe his audacity. Raising a complaint right after Aerander had been feted for saving his skin and ridding the underworld of their greatest enemy? On a night that was supposed to be a celebration for Ysalane's people? Calyiches' friends egged him on. The better part of the hall was silent.

Aerander answered him. "We will have our sovereign land when it is safe to return to the surface."

Calyiches' companions hemmed and hawed. Their spokesman grinned cleverly, and then he launched his voice above the fracas. "How long must we wait for an answer from that amulet of yours? There are lands beyond this city that we could claim as our own. There are passages to the surface that we could explore."

Besides the portals to the city of Atlantis, there were rumors of a passage far away in the backcountry that led to the mountains of Mauritania where the highland might still stand above the sea. But even the Old Ones could not confirm that such a portal existed. An expedition to find it could be a colossal waste of time, not to mention extremely dangerous.

"Calaeno has promised to give us the signal as soon as the sea relents," Aerander said. "We must be patient, and we must stand united. We have men among us who are not fit to leave the city."

Lys called out, "Hear, hear!" and Aerander's friends joined in. The highborn boys from the other tables grumbled and sneered.

"Your fellow Poseidonidae do not agree with you," Calyiches said. "We have the right to vote on our country's future. In point of fact, it is the tradition of our fathers that our leader shall be chosen by a council of ten Houses. Yet we have been given no such privilege. In the meantime, you allow your kingship to be bought by a foreign race."

Lys, Dardy, Evandros, and all the others at Aerander's table stood from their benches, readying for a brawl. Dam had never been part of any sort of group tussle, but at that moment, he felt quite ready to try his fists against Calyiches and any one of his arrogant friends. How dare he twist things around to embarrass Aerander and insult the Old

Ones? They had been nothing but gracious to Calyiches and his band of ingrates.

Aerander looked over his companions, steady and temperate.

"You are right, Calyiches. My place as leader has not been put up to a vote as law prescribes. This will be done. But not tonight. This is an evening of celebration."

Calyiches turned to his friends, and they spoke to one another quietly. Calyiches came back quickly with a response. "In two nights' time then. We need just one to draw up a balloting procedure and another to cast the votes. We see no need to delay things any further. And I herewith announce my nomination as Governor-Magistrate."

Dam gazed helplessly at his cousin. If electing a leader was up to the royal Houses—one Governor-Magistrate to preside over their council—Aerander was doomed. He had his own House and Dardy's on his side. Lys was House Eudemon's leader by birthright, but even that third House's endorsement was not assured with Leo and Koz from his clan cozying up to Calyiches. Calyiches had seven Houses in his pocket. He would easily oust Aerander. His cousin stepped over to consult with Ysalane.

Aerander returned to give his bearing on the matter. "It is agreed, in two nights' time," he said. "As we have no proper statehouse, Ysalane has offered this hall as the place where the vote can proceed." He looked broadly across the room. "But we are no longer the same kingdom that we were aboveground. We have no protectorates to allot, no armies to raise, no trade to manage, not even a spare penny to start a treasury. We are two hundred and twenty, and every one of us arrived here with no more than the clothes on his back. We need every one of us to build a future for Atlantis. For that reason, I motion that for the vote in two days' time, every man and woman born of our great country shall have a chance to cast a ballot. Every one of us shall have a say in Atlantis' future."

Calyiches raised his voice to challenge him. Dam could not believe himself what Aerander had said. Common folk casting ballots for a king? It would be the end of centuries of House rule. It would make the claim of birthright meaningless.

It was genius.

The boys in the front tables shouted Aerander down. Calyiches tried to speak over them, but he could not be heard over the din. Then a thunder even greater rose up from the back of the hall. The freed prisoners, ten dozen strong, pounded their fists on their tables. They shouted in unison, "A vote for every man."

Dam stared at the commotion. It was a savory dilemma for the highborn boys. They couldn't very well bully back the freed prisoners. Not if they expected to win them over as subjects. Dam fastened his gaze on Calyiches. With his clever smile, he played things off like he was taking them in stride. He had to know that Aerander had bested him. What was Calyiches plotting for his next move?

CHAPTER EIGHT

The next morning when Dam awoke, his mind spun rapidly. In one day's time, a vote would decide the leader of a new Atlantis. It would change everything he had known about his country. It would dissolve the tradition of sovereignty by bloodline. Effectively, it would make Dam equal to any other man, though believing that boggled his mind.

Calyiches and his highborn companions would fight hard to maintain the old ways. If the vote didn't go the way they wanted, which seemed assured, the rift could divide the survivors nearly in half. Dam realized Aerander needed his support, and he felt very selfish for having given his cousin a hard time about sitting at his table at the feast.

Dam was also going to a "feast after the feast" with Hanhau later that day. That thought made his stomach cramp up nearly as much as thinking about tomorrow's vote. Dam set it adrift as a worry for later. He pulled on a shift and washed his face in the basin in his room. Hephad still slept, so Dam tried to be quiet.

Red morning bled into the house. It was still quite early. Most everyone in the Honeycomb had to be sleeping. They had all stayed up late after the feast. They had so much to talk about: trying to figure out how many votes were assured for Aerander, guessing at the schemes Calyiches might try to influence the outcome, and going through scenarios of victory or defeat.

One thing was certain, the boys in the middle houses were thoroughly behind Dam's cousin. Aerander promised them land and freedom when they returned to the surface. Hephad's friends, Callios and Heron, had big dreams of building homes and reviving the trades of their fathers. They would be unfettered by tariffs and guild masters setting rules and taking commissions for their trade.

Those thoughts were dazzling, though Dam had no idea what he would do with land and freedom. A son's duty was to take up the trade of his father, but how was he to make a living raising horses? He had never had a father to teach him.

In any case, Aerander's vision for a new Atlantis shone splendid and true. The refugees were all descendants of Poseidon one way or another, so why shouldn't they all come together to rebuild their country? It didn't matter who was noble or peasant. Dam had lived as both, and he didn't see how some men were better suited for owning land and gold than others based on their heredity.

He left the house to catch up with his cousin and see if he could do anything to help on the eve of the vote. He hadn't seen the overgrown kittens since the previous night—a mild curiosity—and he went on his way without investigating that. They were probably out hunting for those lizards. Dam took a stairwell to the upper tier of the Honeycomb and traveled to the house that Lys and Aerander had taken as their own.

At the early hour, things were desolate on the terrace of the upper tier. Dam moved along briskly. He would be happy to make it to his cousin's quarters without running into anybody. The highborn boys had marked up the outer walls of their houses with their clan emblems. They needed those reminders of where they stood in society even though it was quickly becoming apparent that no one else cared. Coming around the side of the terrace where Aerander and his friends lived, those markings had been washed and rubbed away. A single doorway had been embellished with drawings of twin columns and a crowning arch with engraved lettering.

Here lives Aerander, slayer of Ouroborus, and the new King of Atlantis.

The gas lamps lit up a thin aura in the interior, and the partially shuttered light from the Oomphalos Tower didn't help Dam anticipate what he was walking into. Aerander had always been an early riser. Dam was counting on that habit. He stole into the house and glanced around, trying to penetrate the shadows.

A body came at him quickly and forcefully. Before Dam could back away, someone trapped him with two powerful arms and held a sharp blade at his throat.

"Who goes there?"

Dam recognized the voice. "Lys, it's me."

The blade fell away. "Sorry, Dam. You ought to announce yourself." Lys went to a gas lamp at the wall and turned up the fuel.

Light laid bare the small, sparsely furnished room. Aerander's imposing boyfriend stood in front of Dam in a pair of silk trousers. His fair hair was sleep-tossed. Lys was martially trained and built in proportions to wrangle an ox. He was a good friend to have on one's side.

"If you're looking for Aerander, he's down at the polyandrium."

The boys had built a yard with grave markers for their families. Aerander used to go there every morning, and Dam realized he still did.

"How's he doing?" Dam said.

Lys shrugged. "Fine. We had company all night. Dardy and Evandros wanted to stay over in case Calyiches had any bright ideas about sabotaging the vote. Aerander wouldn't let them. He said it wouldn't look right to be surrounded by bodyguards all the time."

Dam smirked. Lys smirked back. Either one of them could have told Aerander that having some protection was no dishonor. But Aerander had his pride and his stubbornness. They were family traits.

"Has Calyiches tried anything?"

"Not to speak of. The lot of them cleared out of here early. Who knows where."

That had left Lys to guard the house like a fighting dog. Methodically, he looked back to the doorway. His broad shoulders were tense and alert. When they first met, Dam had a touch of a crush on Lys. He was a celebrated athlete from the Eudemon clan, which was known for its hearty sea captains who fought off barbarian raiders in the fearsome North Atlantic Sea. Standing face-to-face, alone, with the older boy half-clothed, that little crush bedeviled Dam for a moment.

But they were friends now. Lys had once wanted to crack Dam's skull open when he had thought Dam had been corrupting his cousin Leo. Their lives had been interwoven when they each joined up with Aerander to journey underground and clear the way for evacuees from the flood. That adventure had made their differences seem petty. When they found the prisoner camp of the New Ones and roused a rebellion with fire bombs of niterbats, Lys had kept Leo and Koz in line, battering back their unkind words about Dam.

"You think he wants to be alone?" Dam said.

"I don't think he ever minds seeing more of you. You're family." Was a hint of a grudge in that statement? Dam wasn't sure. He sympathized with Lys in any case. For a long time after the flood, Aerander hadn't had the will to get out of his bed. Aerander gave Dam credit for bringing him out of that, but Lys had been the one who had spent day and night with him, keeping after Aerander to drink and eat. Since Aerander had taken on leading the survivors, Lys had stood loyally at his side. It couldn't be easy being Aerander's boyfriend. Aerander put his duty as a politician ahead of everything.

Dam glanced at the two pallets in the room that had been pulled together into one bed. "You're family too," he told Lys.

Lys gave him a tight half-smile.

"I know he doesn't show it, but he really does care for you an awful lot," Dam said.

Lys looked askance. He put up a good front, but he was struggling with his emotions. That made Dam antsy. What was he supposed to do if his cousin's boyfriend broke down in front of him?

"I'll go check up on him," Dam said.

Lys gave a quick nod. Dam figured Lys wanted to be alone. It made sense. He would have an easier time pulling himself together in private. Dam turned back to the doorway and headed out to the stairwells.

❖

The polyandrium yard was on the basin of the Honeycomb, on the opposite side of the bathing yard. It had been started by a young man named Kaleidos, who had built a pile of stones to signify a marker for his family some days after the boys had come underground. That gesture had caught on. Boys had gathered rubble from the construction sites and staked out spots in the yard to represent the graves of parents and siblings who had perished in the flood.

They had built a low perimeter wall twice as long as it was wide. In short time, the yard filled with many mounds, and the boys had taken great care to inscribe each stone with the name of one of their kin. They didn't have honey or wine to sanctify the gravesite, but they collected the most precious things that they could find—silvery, polished shells from underground pools—to leave at the foot of their memorials. Altogether, the yard looked something like a potter's field and something like a trawled beach. No matter. The boys took great pride in it. Amid the city of tiered bedrock and gas-fueled torches, they had created a place that they could call their own. The grounds sparkled in the blossoming light of the Oomphalos. Dam spotted Aerander easily. No one else was in the yard. In the middle of the space, he knelt at a collection of rocks laid out like a trident spear encircled by an oblation of shells. That was meant to symbolize the channel around the mounted Citadel of House Atlas.

Dam charted out a careful path through the polyandrium's narrow lanes. He didn't want to displace the stones, or gods forbid, knock a mound to rubble with a careless step.

He arrived behind his cousin. Aerander wore a short traveler's cloak over his tunic. His head was bowed. He appeared to have his eyes shut, making silent prayers. It was strange peeking in on his cousin's private life, but Dam worried that they might not have another chance to talk that day. He waited for Aerander to stir a jot from his prayers. Then he spoke his name softly.

Aerander turned. Tears scored his face. In a moment, his eyes beamed and a smile crept up on his lips. He gestured for Dam to sit beside him. "Come."

Dam stooped down and smoothed out his shift over his knees.

Aerander pointed out the different stones in his construction. "There's Father. And Thessala. Alixa and Danae. I could have used Thessala's help. She knew every bit of the family's genealogy. I did the best I could."

Dam was amazed by what his cousin had created, and a bit self-conscious about the fact that it was the first time he had seen the memorial. Aerander had etched the names in each one of the stones by hand. Thessala had been Aerander's stepmother. Alixa and Danae had been his younger half sisters. Dam didn't recognize some of the names of lesser relatives he had never known. There must have been close to one hundred stone tokens. Dam noticed the name Sybilia. That had been Aerander's birth mother. Somehow, that triggered an ache of sorrow in Dam's heart.

Aerander stared at a large stone at the top of the spear's middle tong. Pylartes.

"Father loved you like a son," he said.

It hadn't felt that way to Dam. Pylartes had been a good patriarch of his House, and generous with him to an extent. But Pylartes had never adopted him, which had left Dam to earn his own way while Aerander had been spoiled and feted as a prince.

"What's that look for?" Aerander asked. "If you hadn't left the palace so young, you would have come to know Father better," he said. "He might have found you a place as a bureaucrat in his court."

Dam kept his mouth shut, though it was getting harder for him to do.

"Do you think he's proud of me?"

Dam said nothing.

"He used to visit me in my dreams. He was angry, telling me I should have made it back from the underworld in time to save my sisters." Aerander face turned stricken. "I haven't dreamt about him lately. It's like they've all gone farther away. So far they can't visit me anymore. Do you think they know we're still here?"

It was a better question for Hephad, who had been much more serious about their novice training and still asked the gods for knowledge of the spirit world. Hephad had made a household altar with stones and shells for fetishes. He used an oil lamp for its eternal flame, and he made daily sacrifices of spilt blood for his prayers of obedience to Poseidon, asking Him to pull back the sea so they could return home. Dam wasn't sure that he believed such things made a difference. It hadn't helped to pray to Poseidon before the sea had turned against Atlantis. As best as Dam could figure, the gods kept their own counsel on when and how they would intervene in the fate of mortals. Having cursed Dam as an orphan, they certainly hadn't shown him any partiality.

If Aerander's father wasn't visiting Aerander in his sleep, Dam counted that as a good thing. Maybe it was disrespectful to Pylartes, but Dam didn't want to see his cousin haunted by death as he had been when they had first come below.

Aerander perked up. "I almost forgot to show you. Look there." He pointed to a middle section of his trident monument where two stones were tucked together. Gaios and Eunike. Dam's father and mother.

Dam used to visit the family cemetery on high holidays to wash his parents' steles beneath which their physical remains had been buried. The stones that Aerander had picked out for them shone before his eyes like diamonds.

He nudged Dam with his elbow. "See, everyone belongs here,"

Aerander said. "When we return aboveground, we'll build a grander memorial. And there'll be feasts of the bull, and wine, and horses to race under the full sun of the countryside. At night, we'll look up at the sky and see the faces of our family in the stars."

Dam smiled, imagining that. Then he glanced at the bone amulet around his cousin's neck. That ancient heirloom bothered Dam. He couldn't explain it rationally. The amulet was a link to the goddess who had helped people escape from the flood, but the gruesome necklace looked like a cursed relic of the dead. He asked Aerander, "Have you heard anything from that?"

"Calaeno says it's still too early. We could swim up from the portals, but there isn't any place to go. The highlands would leave us scalded in the sun, not to mention, there's no food or water there nor any place to build and farm. We have to be patient and wait."

"What about the passage to Mauritania?"

"Calaeno's heard of it. She knows every part of Agartha. She said that it would take at least two fortnights to get there, and the way is very dangerous. We can't have the old men trying to make that kind of trek."

"When the old men come aboveground, they won't have the Oomphalos to protect them," Dam said. "They'll be coming home to die."

"I've spoken to them. They'll do it so they can feel the sun and breathe the air of their country once again. Besides, they want to be buried in the place of their births."

"What if Calyiches doesn't abide by the vote? He and his friends could go off on their own."

"They'll be traitors to their country."

"I don't think they care much about that."

Aerander said nothing.

"They could rouse a mutiny before the vote even takes place. You ought to have Calyiches locked up so he can't try anything."

"I can't do that. It would prove his point that my leadership has been forced on everyone. We need the vote."

"What if he rallies his friends to overpower you? He's got seven dozen allies from the other Houses." Dam thought about the weapon Lys had held to his throat. "They could be making short blades from metal scrap. They could take you prisoner when the vote takes place. Have you at least asked for Ysalane's help?"

"She's offered. I refused. We can't have the voting place filled with her warriors. They'll claim it's put on to intimidate people."

Dam sighed. He didn't agree, but pushing things with his cousin only made Aerander push back harder.

"You realize what you're giving up by letting everyone have a vote?" he said.

Aerander looked at him quizzically. Dam gestured to the stone-laid memorial. "All of this. There'll be no more line of kings. You'll have nothing to give your heirs."

"I thought you'd approve of that. Aren't we all 'stuck-up, coddled ingrates'? Isn't that what you used to say?"

Dam smirked. "I do approve of it. But it is a lot for you to give up. And Lys and Dardy."

"I'm not giving up the family tradition. I'll be a politician for as long as the people need me," Aerander said. "Times have changed. You can't lead a country when you don't have a country to lead. Most of the Poseidonidae understand that. Our duty is to rebuild Atlantis, however we can."

"You really mean everyone will have land?"

"Why shouldn't they? When the sea pulls back, there'll be more than enough to go around."

"Good. Let's make sure you win the vote tomorrow, then. What can I do to help?"

Aerander grinned and brushed his shoulder against him. "You've spoken to Hephad and Attalos?"

"We were up all night. They're all behind you. Everyone in the middle-houses. The women said it wouldn't be proper for them to vote, but Attalos and some of the other boys are going to work on them."

"Then there's not much to be done. Just keeping people calm. Keeping to a routine. Making sure that everyone shows up tomorrow night."

"I don't think that will be a problem." Dam remembered something. He brought it out all at once. "I'm going to see Hanhau tonight."

Dam studied his cousin's face in the silence. He could tell when Aerander disapproved of something. He got flushed and shifty like a little boy. Like he was at that moment.

"What's the point, Dam?"

"What do you mean?"

"I mean, it's like with Leo. You get yourself attached to someone, and there's no future in it."

A furnace of heat rose up in Dam. "You'll never forget that, will you? Makes you happy to bring it up, does it?"

"Why would it make me happy? You're so sensitive."

Dam tried to swallow his anger. They had just spent a private moment together without fighting, and the important thing was keeping Aerander safe through tomorrow's vote. But Dam couldn't stop his anger from breaking through.

"You don't know anything about me and Hanhau."

Aerander rolled his eyes. "We're really going to talk about this?"

"Why shouldn't we?"

"What do you think is going to happen, Dam? We're going home. You'll never see Hanhau again. Then I'll have to deal with you being moody and forlorn all the time."

Dam pinched his shoulders up tight. "Suppose you didn't have to deal with me. Suppose I stayed down here."

"Here we go—"

"I'm not your charge to look after. You ought to mind your own personal life instead of interfering in mine."

He was referring to Lys, and he knew his cousin would catch that. Aerander glared at him, grim and forceful. He looked away and poked idly at the rocks on the edge of the mound. When he spoke, his voice had mellowed. "Why are we always doing this? I didn't mean to put you down. Can we call a truce?"

Dam stood. The conversation was hardly finished, but it was no time to be at each other's throats. He reached his hand to pull Aerander up. "Truce."

They walked back to the Honeycomb together, barely looking at one another and not talking.

CHAPTER NINE

D am felt like the rest of the day hurtled toward meeting with Hanhau for their feast-after-the-feast. Dam washed and dressed. He went down to the dining hall with Hephad and Attalos for their midday meal. They joined up with the other boys from the middle-houses: Callios, Heron, Tibor, and Deodorus. Dam sat at the far end of the table while they all drank their fish soup. He tried to pay attention to their conversation instead of the jumping beans in his stomach.

Attalos talked about his meeting with the women. They were still undecided about voting, and a visit from Calyiches and his gang earlier that day had made them even more timid. Attalos' speculation was that Calyiches had given them a lecture about tradition. Women belonged at the family hearth. Matters of country were the province of men. Whether or not that advice was compelling, coming from a foreign prince who was half the age of most of the women, it had likely been delivered with enough heat to recommend staying out of the contentious business of selecting a leader for their people.

Boys had spotted Calyiches campaigning in the below-houses as well. No one thought that the old men would be impressed. What could Calyiches promise them that would win their vote?

Still, it was news to be minded by the group. Attalos and Callios had been merchants' sons, and they knew how the city's politics used to operate. The Citadel gave bribes to the guild masters to keep their people loyal. Shop owners who didn't march in lockstep had their storefronts demolished overnight. If that didn't keep them in line, they got harassed by thugs. Some had their houses burned down. It wasn't the Governors' sentinels doing any of that dirty work. It was mercenaries hired by the guild masters themselves.

Hephad, Dam, and the other two novice priests, Tibor and Deodorus, knew about the dealings between the priesthood and the Poseidonidae. The High Priest Zazamoukh had curried fat patronage from Aerander's father for preaching to common folk about the divine sovereignty of House Atlas.

The boys were skeptical about Aerander as well. He was Poseidonidae. He had been raised with the belief that he stood above all others and had inherited a divine right to lead. Would he really keep his promise to recognize everyone as equals when they returned home? That pulled Dam into the conversation.

"Aerander wouldn't have said it if he didn't mean it."

His companions glanced at one another around the table. No one said anything. Dam never had to defend his cousin to the boys from the middle-houses. He realized what a trap it was. In their eyes, Dam's association with House Atlas made his opinions suspect even though Dam lived among them.

Attalos piped up. "No offense, Dam. We all know we're better off casting our lot with Aerander than Calyiches."

The others quickly raised their voices to agree.

"You stick with what you know, don't you?" Callios said.

"Won't be following a king from House Mneseus," Heron said. "All those foreign clans are contemptuous and arrogant."

Dam drifted to the background of the discussion again. He wondered what things were said when he wasn't around. In the new country Aerander envisioned, Dam wondered where he would fit in.

❖

Later, when the light of the Oomphalos eclipsed, Dam left with a torch to meet Hanhau at the quay outside the tunnel. It was time for their excursion to the Fire Canyon.

Hanhau was waiting for him. He was back in his chain mail skirting, and he had a pack of provisions strapped to his back with a metal harness. They trekked out of the city and crossed the dead lava fields heading in the opposite direction of the Glowing Cataracts.

They had lots to talk about and plenty of time to do it as they hiked across the darkened landscape. But all the while, Dam couldn't bring himself to speak quite yet.

They took slug-sledges for the last leg of the trip. It was a descent to a shelf of rock below the zone of the dead lava fields. Heat rose up, and traces of burning sulfur filled the air. Dam noticed a shadowy swarm of niterbats above them, and he listened keenly as the creatures fluttered away.

After a long lope downward, they came to a ledge where the Fire Canyon spread out in front of them with an infernal spit and cackle. Dam dismounted his sledge to look out at it from the lip of their perch. Glowing rivers of lava crisscrossed the earth like latticework. The parcels of lands in between steamed like baked coals. Here and there, a jettison of water shot up from them, hissing and crackling as it rained down on the red, molten flow. The canyon was like a war zone, entirely impassable, and so broad its extent was beyond Dam's sight.

Dam sat down with Hanhau who was unpacking his cargo of smoked eels, dried morels, and a canteen of water for the two of them to share.

"It's not the feast from yesterday," Hanhau said.

Dam grinned. "It's better."

Each of them tucked into the food. Hanhau was unusually quiet, which worried Dam.

"Calyiches and his friends are idiots," Dam said.

Hanhau said nothing.

"What they did, in the middle of a nice occasion…it wasn't right." Dam was having trouble putting words together. Apologizing for the behavior of his countrymen was strange. Dam didn't know how much needed to be said, and he didn't want to say it in a way that would insult Hanhau. "Calyiches only speaks for his group of snobs. You know that I…the rest of us don't feel that way."

Hanhau smiled. "I know."

Dam relaxed. "He's not going to win. When the vote happens tomorrow night, he'll have to shut up. Either that or go off on his own."

"It must be hard, being so far away from your home."

Dam glanced at Hanhau's face. Was he was getting at something?

"I don't mind. Things weren't so great for me up there."

"Still, it is your home. Like Aerander said, you will restore your country to its former glory. Aerander is a good leader. You will all have better lives when you return."

Things weren't turning out the way Dam had imagined. The feast-after-the-feast felt all at once like a farewell party.

"No one knows when that will be."

"That's true. But eventually, your world with retake its natural course." Hanhau gestured to the canyon. "This all started as one big eruption in the shelf. Pressurized heat is still pushing up the rock and the water, and then the lava that rises up eats it away. It's happening very slowly, but over time, the canyon is sinking. Centuries ago, it was the height of this ledge. One day, it will cave into itself and open up into a giant dead pit."

Dam gazed below. It had to be fifty yards or more to the bottom. As he stared, he could imagine the crisscrossed lava channels carving deep into the floor and everything collapsing like corroded iron webbing.

"You're saying it could take ages for the sea to pull back."

Hanhau took up a tiny rock from the ground and flicked it over the edge into the canyon. "To pull back completely, at least. But there are already parts on the surface fit for resettling. That's what our men who study these things say."

Their elders interpreted the climates of the backcountry and the minerals of the earth to judge conditions in the surface world. Dam hardly understood how that worked, but he didn't doubt that their kind had accumulated learnings well beyond the knowledge of his own people.

"Then Calyiches is right. They ought to be looking for other portals."

"Once your countrymen come together behind Aerander, Ysalane will commission a search party to scout for those portals. When we've figured out a route to a good passageway, she'll lend Aerander the Oomphalos so that the old men can make the journey home."

Dam wasn't sure what to think or feel.

Hanhau grinned at him. "I thought this would make you happy."

"Ysalane wants us to leave?"

"That's what everyone wants, isn't it? For your people to have your own country."

Dam's head was muddled. Why was Hanhau telling him all of this on a night that was supposed to be special for the two of them?

He drew his knees into his chest and veered away from his companion and the laid out meal. "You didn't have to go to all this trouble. You could have told me when we were back in town."

"Told you what?"

"That there's no future for us. That you've been sorting out reasons to get rid of me."

"I think you misunderstand. I don't want you to go, Dam. But that's not my decision to make. You have a family and a country. That will always come before our friendship. I ought to have thought about that before. I realized it last night when I saw how much your cousin needs you." His voice mellowed. "I guess I didn't want to think about it."

Sadness pressed in on Dam from his temples. He wanted to be with Hanhau more than anything. Now everything had fallen apart in the passing of one night because of the feast and people talking about going home and creating a new country. A country where once again Dam wouldn't fit in anywhere.

"It's my decision to make. What if I didn't leave? What if I stayed down here?"

Hanhau didn't answer for a while. "How long would you be happy, Dam? Being so far away from your family and your friends?"

"I don't know. I never knew much about being happy anyway."

Hanhau slid up close. He encircled Dam with his sturdy arms and drew him into his body so that they sat together snugly chest to back. "Does this make you happy?"

Dam reached his arms around Hanhau's, buttressing the warrior's embrace. "Yes."

"It makes me happy too," Hanhau said. "If you stayed, I'd be even happier. But I need to know that you've thought it through. You would be forsaking your cousin and your people. Those are enormous things to give up to be with someone you've only known for a short while."

"Why does everyone think they know what's best for me?" He shifted around so his face was tucked into the crook of Hanhau's neck. His lips nearly touched the warrior's skin.

Hanhau brushed his hand through his hair. Dam cocked his head to look up at Hanhau, then they kissed even longer than the night before. Dam held Hanhau's side with his hand, pressing against his leathery body armor. He felt something funny. One of the scales was loose. Like a wobbly tooth, it could break off in his fingers if he jostled it a bit.

The change was happening inside Hanhau, and if they kept doing what they were doing, his chest and his back would be laid bare. That was a tantalizing proposition, but another impulse warred inside Dam. Hanhau losing his armor was a sacred thing. He had never been with anybody before.

Dam broke the kiss. He cleared his throat. "You should know some things about me."

Hanhau gazed at him. His eyes were bright and eager. Unfortunately, it wasn't a pleasant story.

"I'm the reason Hephad lost his tongue," Dam said. That was the worst of it, and he circled back to the awful business with Leo and Koz. It was easier to say than Dam had imagined. He wasn't sure how Hanhau would take it, but Dam knew that he wouldn't be mean. When Dam finished the story, Hanhau's arms were still wrapped around his sides. That was a good sign.

"It wasn't your fault," Hanhau said.

"Of course it was. If I hadn't gotten Hephad involved, Zazamoukh wouldn't have made it so he couldn't speak."

"Zazamoukh stole the lives of hundreds of men. All so he could live forever through the energies of the Oomphalos. He would have hurt anyone who got in his way."

Dam had thought about all of that before. He still felt like a villain.

"You said Hephad accepted your apology. You saved his life bringing him down below while millions of others perished."

"I thought you'd be disgusted."

"We have an expression. 'Let the past roll back like the current of the river. It's a man's deeds today that matter.'"

Dam imagined his past drifting away. It would be like tossing an ugly clump of mud into a rushing stream, turning the water cloudy and brown. But as the stream carried it on its course, it would dissolve and break apart. Eventually the water would run clean again.

"I've just told you the most embarrassing thing about my past," Dam said. "And it's not fair. I don't know anything embarrassing about you."

A little glow flushed from Hanhau's face. "C'mon," Dam said. "There's got to be something."

Hanhau leaned back behind him while he considered. "You remember the warrior Backlum?"

Dam nodded. Alongside Hanhau, Backlum had led the charge to rid the New Ones from their city. He was the tallest and the broadest of Ysalane's warriors, and each of his arms were scarred from his many kills.

"When we were young, I was jealous of him," Hanhau said. "He was stronger and better at the crossbow and with swordplay. He was everything a warrior is supposed to be. Disciplined and reserved. The elders used to tell me that I talked too much and asked too many questions."

Dam could picture that. It made him grin.

"They told me I was better suited to be a *nikwah*. To your people, that's something like a nursemaid. Keeping the children fed and clothed. Showing them right from wrong. Teaching them words and letters until they're old enough to be sorted into a trade. Being a *nikwah* isn't dishonorable. Everyone in the tribe has a role to play. But I wanted to be a warrior like Backlum. We wouldn't have even had any children to look after until the women of my generation came of age for birthing."

"We had something called the Day of Challenges when boys and girls were called into the elder circle to square off in spars. It was my last chance to show I was meant to be a warrior. So I told the others if they got matched up with me, they had to let me win. My future depended on it.

"The Day of Challenges came, and I drew Backlum for my challenge. I thought for certain he would honor my plea. The elders had already pronounced him the best of our generation. For him, losing to me would be a small sacrifice. He had already proved himself.

"We drew pikestaffs for our battle. We had barely squared off in stances before he came at me and walloped my staff right out of my hands. Then he struck me low and knocked my legs out from under me. As I lay on the ground clutching my knee, everyone laughed. They all started chattering about how I had begged them to play weak so that I would win that day."

Dam knew it was a story that was shameful to Hanhau, but he found it encouraging that Hanhau's people could be as cruel as his own. And that history was fascinating. Hanhau's body looked like it was sculpted from iron. He bore the weight of chain mail and heavy manacles and anklets just to go about his everyday business. He had slain giant serpents.

"How did you become a warrior?"

"Not long after that day, everyone had to fight in a raid, and it turned out that when I was pushed to defend myself, I could hold my own. We took many losses. The days of sorting boys and girls into trades were over. The tribe needed everyone to be warriors."

Dam picked at the frayed part of his sandal.

"Does that make you think less of me?" Hanhau said.

"How could that make me think less of you? You turned out perfect."

"I don't believe that. I became a warrior by necessity. Now that times have changed, it's possible I could follow a different path. I wonder sometimes if the elders were right about me."

"You want to be a *nikwah*?"

A shy grin passed over Hanhau's face. "Maybe. There'll be children soon enough, and we'll need people to take care of them." Dam smiled. Children would love Hanhau. He was handsome and patient, and he loved telling stories.

"What do you think will become of me?" he asked. "I was lousy at being a priest. I have no idea how to take up my father's trade. Even if I knew how to raise horses, I don't even know if I would want to."

"Do you like children?"

Dam's face shrank up gruesomely. "Not particularly."

Hanhau sat up and tucked Dam into his body once again. "You're a hero. You've earned the right to do anything you want."

Dam remembered the engraving on that bracelet Hanhau had given him. *One of three who slayed Ouroborus.* That hero's epithet felt misplaced on him.

Hanhau's statement was enticing in a different way. If he had earned the right to do anything he wanted, there was definitely something that he wanted to do at that moment. He turned his head and reached for another kiss.

Chapter Ten

On the day of the vote, it seemed like everyone had gone mad. Dam awakened to what sounded like the hue and cry of a vicious brawl. He gathered his bedsheet around his waist and scampered from his pallet toward the commotion coming from the terrace just outside his room.

What he discovered was a very ordinary scene. Some boys had set up a lane for bowling. Attalos stood at one end and Callios was at the other, aiming for the stone markers in the middle. The two had assembled teams behind them: Hephad and Tibor with Attalos, Deodorus and Heron with Callios.

Callios launched a rounded stone toward the markers, and Attalos hurled a bigger one down the lane, trying to block Callios' throw. Each team hollered bloody murder, and when the stones collided, an ear-splitting, triumphant screech came from Attalos and Tibor.

Dam looked over the group, baffled. He didn't begrudge their right to play the game. But why did they have to do it on the terrace when they had plenty of space in the yards below? And why were they so keyed up about it? By the half-light of the Oomphalos, it was awfully early in the day to get excited about anything.

When they all went down to the dining hall, the place was a typhoon trapped inside four walls. Cups were being hurled around the room for sport. Sparring matches had broken out in the corners of the room. Boys were hoisted atop the shoulders of other boys. Some ran around the room playing a version of tag where they tried to rip off each other's loincloths. Others had climbed on top of tables and stamped their feet and linked arms to swing each other around in the style of a martial dance. Everywhere, people were shouting. Some clamored for more soup from the food line, where a grim scullery worker was trying to keep up with the traffic. Dam's friends dove into all of that as though they were leaping into the surf of the ocean.

Dam stood off, watching, not understanding. Attalos and Callios clasped hands with two boys from House Gadir like they were old friends. The fellows from House Gadir shouldered the two to their table in the center of the room and called the rest of their group over to join them. The table farthest from the food line, where Dam's friends normally sat, was empty.

Overnight, it no longer mattered who was middle-house or upper-house? Not only that, boys from different clans were mixed together, wrestling under tables and tossing their soup bowls to each other. When had the rivalry between Calyiches' friends and Aerander's friends fallen away? Dam scanned around. It looked like the only people missing were Calyiches and his closest friends, and Aerander and Lys.

A whistle knifed through the din. Heads turned to a young man standing on a table with a goblet in his hand. His emerald-colored robe was barely hanging from his shoulder, and it had come untucked in more places than not. He raised his cup. "To Aerander. The new King of Atlantis."

A boisterous bellow rose up from the room. Fists pounded on tables. Boys turned over their bowls on their laps and beat them like drums.

When Dam got back to his house with the other boys from the middle-houses, Hephad threw himself down on his bed and started bawling. Everyone drew up around him, asking him what was wrong. Attalos interpreted his hand gestures. Hephad was certain that something dreadful had happened to the cats. They hadn't been seen since the day of the feast, though Pleione still bedded herself on Hephad's pallet.

They could have gone a thousand places, and they had shown an interest in hunting lizards. Dam tried to tell Hephad that they should leave out some scraps of fish by the door that night, and the trio of cats would return. Hephad shook his head. Attalos insisted that they needed to find the kittens then and there. The others agreed, and Dam was outnumbered. They were determined to search every part of the Honeycomb and to fan out into the city from there.

They started with the upper-houses, where more boys volunteered to join the cause. A herd of boys tramped down to the below-houses and spread through the old men's quarters asking questions and calling out the kittens' names.

Dam followed them around halfheartedly. They were going about it all wrong. The nature of cats was to skitter away from commotion. They should have sent one or two people into the below-houses to search instead parading through the rooms where the old men slept. But nearly every boy in the Honeycomb had taken up the search as though an untold disaster awaited them unless the cats returned safely. The cats didn't turn up in any of the houses, or the lavatory, or the yards around the staged apartments. A crowd of boys ended up in the polyandrium. Attalos fought through their noisy chatter to pick out groups to canvas the various districts of the city.

That was when Dam spotted Calyiches and his crew headed to the stairwell of the Honeycomb. Gods knew what they had been doing all day. They halted and wandered over to the gathering.

"What business is this?" Calyiches called out. Over the past few days, Calyiches had become reviled by many, but by his proud, patrician bearing, he still was a halting presence.

Attalos explained to him that they were searching for the cats.

Calyiches shook his head woefully. "Someone must have kidnapped them, if they haven't eaten them already. You should try interrogating the prisoners. If nothing comes of that, investigate the Old Ones. They don't like things that aren't from their own world. They'd want to take those cats just to spite us."

Dam saw red. The crowd around him quieted. He could sense that Calyiches had planted worries in the other boys. Many of them were still distrustful of the Old Ones because their ways were different from their own people.

Calyiches' hands and face were streaked with dark smudges, and his friends were smudged as well, as though they had been digging in coal. No one else seemed to find that strange. They were hell-bent on finding the cats, and they headed out to their assignments.

Dam stayed back, and he looked for Aerander. He remembered the smell of niterbats when he had run into Calyiches' crew at the bathing lake. They needed to keep an eye on those boys. They should see if someone from the upper-houses knew something about their plans.

Neither Aerander nor Lys was home when Dam arrived at their

house. He traveled around the side of the upper-house terrace, drew up to the corner of the wall, and peeked down at the bathing yard. Calyiches, Perdikkas, Mesokantes, Boros, Leo, and Koz turned up to wash the black dust from their faces, arms, and legs.

They were awfully quiet about it. No joking around. No complaining about the water from the spigots being ice cold. There seemed to be barely any conversation between the boys at all. Somehow, that signaled more danger to Dam than if they were boasting about the scheme in their heads.

❖

It was nearly dark when Hephad, Attalos, and their friends returned home. Dam could not believe it. They really had to get a move on to make it to the vote at Ysalane's Hall.

Everyone looked weighed down by defeat. They had searched up and down the stages of the city for the kittens to no avail. Hephad hand-gestured to Attalos that he wouldn't go out to vote. He would stay back in his room in case the kittens came home. Everybody turned their attention to talking him out of that melodrama. Dam tried to tell the boys his suspicions about Calyiches. Attalos, Callios, and Heron had been part of the prisoner rebellion. They knew what niterbat cinders could do, but they were only mildly interested in Dam's story.

"What would be their plot?" Attalos said. "Attack the hall so nobody can vote? Guess we'll know if they don't show up. But they won't get within throwing distance with all the warriors posted around the square."

Dam supposed he had a point. Firebombs were a rather conspicuous strategy for sabotage. They would need to load up a wheelbarrow to bring enough to do damage to the hall. How would they sneak that through the city?

"Leo and Koz were probably just showing them some tricks in the backcountry," Callios said. "Someone would have snitched if they saw them bringing that stuff back here. There's no private place to store it."

That made sense as well. Dam felt a bit relieved. He would talk to Hanhau about it after the vote. The warriors could keep an eye on Calyiches. Dam left out with the others to make their way to the voting assembly.

❖

When they reached the hall, the mood in the meeting room was serious and restrained. Everyone from the highborn boys to the freed prisoners was there. That included Calyiches, Perdikkas, Mesokantes, Boros, Leo, and Koz. Seeing that suspicious crew took a weight off of Dam.

No one spoke while they waited for a straggling group of old men to take seats. Glancing around the hall during that uneasy silence, Dam was suddenly struck by the significance of the occasion. No one in their assembly had been asked before to give his say on how their country should be run. Even the highborn boys had deferred to their fathers, grandfathers, or uncles to make those decisions for them. They, the survivors of Atlantis, had become their country's politicians. They had assembled to vote not by privilege but by duty. Maybe it had taken Dam longer than everyone else to appreciate the importance of that night. He had been too busy worrying about Hanhau, his own problems and what else. But at that moment in the hall, the meaning soared above Dam's head like a pinnacle stretching toward the sky.

Ysalane and her head consort, a tall warrior girl named Ichika, were the only Old Ones present. They sat at one of the head tables while the candidates and their sponsors sat at the other. The voting procedure had been negotiated by Aerander and Calyiches. Each candidate needed two sponsors to oversee the balloting. That also provided a way for the candidates to show who among their countrymen endorsed their candidacy. Aerander had used that strategy to a greater advantage.

Aerander had chosen as his sponsors one of the women named Pyrrah and one of the freed prisoners named Markos. Calyiches had chosen his brother Oleon and Leo. Dam marveled at his cousin's ingenuity. Aerander must have spent all day convincing the women to participate, and one had even agreed to help with the voting procedure. Those sponsors showed that he had a lock on every faction of their countrymen. Meanwhile, all Calyiches had was the sentimental choice of his brother and Leo, who might be popular enough to split off some votes from House Eudemon.

Calyiches looked bemused by the proceedings. He had to know that the vote was a forgone conclusion, but it was his nature to disguise any chink of vulnerability. Dam caught his cousin's gaze and smiled. He had never felt so proud of Aerander.

The sponsors stood and scanned the room, counting heads. People stood clear back to the doors, so the four conferred until they finally agreed on a number. They looked to Ysalane, and she stood. The warrior chieftain had been appointed to announce the procedure of the vote.

The candidates would each address the body of voters, and then the ballots would be distributed—a black disc for Aerander and a white disc for Calyiches. Each voter would come up to the slotted box on Ysalane's table and select his candidate by depositing either black or white and exit the hall.

"The discs will be counted by each of the candidate's two sponsors. When all the sponsors are in agreement on the number, the body of voters will be called into the hall and the results will be read."

Ysalane swept her proud, decisive gaze across the room. "The vote of the people will be final. Let no one dispute it or the penalty will be exile." Some halfwit in the middle of the room cheered. He was heckled and shushed by everyone around him.

Ysalane handed Aerander the privilege of speaking. A flurry of clapping and hurrahs broke out. Aerander stood up in his blue *chiton* and short cape and waited patiently for the room's enthusiastic clamor to ebb.

"My friends, we know each other. From the august days of the Panegyris. From the rebellion at the prisoner camp where we won our freedom. From the hollow wake of the evacuation, when our world was torn from us, and there were no words to describe the agony of losing so many people we loved. We have been each other's comfort, and we have persevered.

"I ask for your vote because our country needs a leader. The way ahead for us will be hard. We will need courage. We will need hope. We will need each other. I do not want tyranny. I want us united. If you believe that we are better together, beneath one standard for two hundred, I ask you to place a black coin in the box. I will lead us ahead, and I promise that I will see that every one of us returns to the country of our birth. We will see the sun and gaze upon the stars. We will gather our dead for the rites of burial. And we will build homes of lumber and plow fields and gather snippings of the vine in the season of springtide so that our world may start anew."

An outburst of cheers and pounding came from the tables. Three-quarters of the room took to their feet. From the front bench, Lys and Dardy chanted Aerander's name. Dam joined in. The boys from the middle-houses joined in, and the freed prisoners cheered as well. Soon, the hall filled with chorus of voices for Aerander and his slogan, "one standard for two hundred." Dam shouted until his throat was hoarse and dry. The commotion dwindled. Aerander retook his seat. It was Calyiches' turn to speak.

The handsome, golden-haired boy stood and scratched at his beard as though Aerander's speech warranted thoughtful rectification. Some jeers broke out around the room, but they were hushed down.

"It was pretty, wasn't it? A rousing speech from our country's hero." He turned to his rival. "We know each other as well, don't we? *'From the august days of the Panegyris.'* When little romances bloom in boy's hearts." He looked back at the hall. "He has forever been a sweet speechmaker and a generous sweetheart."

A gust of laughter fluttered through the hall. Dam stared Calyiches down. He meant to make an issue of Aerander's honor? Lys, who stood across from the candidate's table, looked like he was ready to launch at Calyiches with his fists.

"I cannot claim the great deeds of Aerander," Calyiches said. "As we have all heard, many times, it was by his will that the way was cleared for us to leave our country, taking refuge in this dark and barren world, at the mercy of a foreign race. I cannot stand before you and vow that when we return, our sacred lands, bequeathed in trust by Poseidon to his sons, will be parceled up to each of you like spoils of war." His face turned hard as granite. "This is not what our fathers would have wanted. This is not what the people of Atlantis would have wanted. This is treason."

Murmurs of disbelief warbled around the room. Dardy, Evandros, and every boy from House Gadir shot up to their feet hurling curses at Calyiches like a *hetaroi* defending their general. Aerander glanced over them, urging forbearance. The fracas calmed. Calyiches resumed his speech.

"What do we truly know about what happened when Aerander disappeared from the Panegyris on a supposed mission to clear the way for our evacuation? We know that an alliance was forged between him and these people's warrior queen. We have yet to understand what promises were exchanged. We do not even know the cause of our country's downfall. It is told to us as a consequence of their magical artifact being retaken from our world." Calyiches looked over the hall gravely. "This is a place of dark magic. These barbaric people, by their own account, were banished from the earth in a hail of fire from the gods. They tell us that they are our saviors. But this tale does not stand to reason. These are a people damned to a sunless, craven existence. I say what is far more plausible is that they used their sorcery to wash our world clean so they can take it as their own. This is the pact they have made with Aerander. This is his betrayal."

Voices roared to declaim him. Lys swaggered toward Calyiches like a charging bull. It took four of his friends to hold him back. For a moment, Dam wished they would let Lys at Calyiches. Dam would have happily given the boy a kick to his face and his ribs after he was pummeled down to the floor. But by the riot Calyiches had created, Dam gradually recognized that this was not a candidate's speech intended to persuade and gain him votes. Calyiches was like a prisoner at the gallows taunting a mob.

"Who shall you be led by?" Calyiches shouted. "A deserter who sold our country to barbarians? A man whose only supporters are shells of men who would bargain their own fathers to hold on to their wasted lives for another day?"

The prisoners stood and chanted "Slander" to overwhelm him.

Calyiches lashed out at them. "I am Calyiches of the honorable House Mneseus. I stand for tradition. I stand for justice."

Dam joined in with the prisoners' chant to defy him. He glanced around the hall. All the boys and the women had taken to their feet. They were an army, riled up to take the battlefield.

Calyiches strained to be heard. "This vote is a sham. You can have your traitorous leader. I will not bear it. I leave tonight to make my own way. Let any man who stands for tradition join me. The rest of you shall perish when Poseidon's mighty fist brings thundering justice to this wretched place."

He looked to Oleon and Leo. They stood up from the table and followed him down the aisle. Mesokantes, Perdikkas, Boros, and a half dozen boys from House Mneseus fumbled through the crowd to follow Calyiches. Those were his only supporters. Even Koz stayed back. The crowd booed Calyiches while he made his way to the doors.

As soon as the group left the room, a triumphant cheer swelled up in the hall. Lys and Dardy rushed up to Aerander and hoisted him on their shoulders. Dam ran over to him too. Soon, a sea of people surrounded his cousin and hollered to proclaim the new leader of their people. The vote was over before it had begun.

CHAPTER ELEVEN

Everyone stayed at the hall to celebrate. Ysalane called for a banquet to be brought in, and warriors showed up with kettledrums. While a group of them played the instruments, others did a fighting dance with iron batons atop the room's head tables. The boys wove a *choreia* through the promenade, and they broke out with verses they had been taught at the Panegyris.

Dam pushed Hephad along to the front of the hall to watch Hanhau performing with the dancers. The troupe was made up with war paints on their faces, arms, and legs. Their only other covering was thigh-length kilts. They showed off martial stances and leaps and airborne somersaults. Dam could have watched the performance for hours, but plenty more was going on with the celebration. He grabbed Hephad by the hand and pulled him into the dancing circle. They went galloping and swinging their arms along with the others.

When the circle split off for food and drink, Dam searched for his cousin. Earlier, Aerander had been paraded around and swung around the *choreia*, and Dam had lost track of him. Winding through the crowd, Dam spotted Aerander in a cluster of boys.

Dam gained up on his cousin, hugged him, and lifted him off his feet. "You did it."

Aerander grinned. "You did it too. We all did it."

Dardy pushed a goblet of water into Dam's hands. "Wine would be better, but what the hell?" Dardy said. He launched his goblet above his head. "To the new king."

There was a hearty "Hear, hear," and they all swigged down some water.

Then Lys lifted his cup. "To Calyiches, stumbling his way into a den of fire scorpions."

Evandros piped in, "Or getting his head blasted off by niterbats."

They all laughed. Lys glanced at Dam grimly. "You don't know how much I wanted to murder him. Twisting things around, as though we didn't risk our lives getting the Oomphalos so people like him wouldn't be taken prisoner by the snakes."

Worries crept back to Dam. "What do you suppose he's going to do?"

Dardy snorted. "Besides skulking away in defeat? What else can he do?"

Dam glanced over his cousin and the others. A dreadful feeling had suddenly sunk into his bones. "He was awfully angry, and he's been awfully private lately." Dam told them about seeing Calyiches and the others washing that suspicious black dust from their hands and faces earlier that day.

Dardy scoffed. "How would *they* know how to use that stuff? They suddenly think they're alchemists?"

Lys locked eyes with Dam. "No," Lys said. "But Leo and Koz would."

"Where's Koz?" Dam said.

They all craned their necks to look around the hall. There were so many people, and they were dispersed helter-skelter. Dam stared at Lys. If anyone had an account of the boy, it should be him.

A blood-curdling blast shattered the commotion in the room. The floor shuddered beneath their feet and sent people cowering into each other. Something had happened outside the hall. It was as though Calyiches' threat had come true: Poseidon's fist of justice thundering from the sky through leagues of rock to demolish the underworld.

❖

Dam pushed through the startled crowd to get to the gates of the hall. Aerander, Lys and Dardy, and Evandros followed close behind. They were like minnows fighting through an eddying stream. People shifted in all directions. Some stood immobilized by shock. Others pressed toward the doors from either side of the room, creating a bottleneck. Dam spotted the warriors ahead of him, though he couldn't distinguish Hanhau in the crowd.

A low bass horn resounded from outside. Dam had never heard it before, but it had to be a call to arms for the Old Ones, probably coming from the top of the Oomphalos Tower. Dam managed to push and squeeze his way into the vestibule and onward to the gates of the hall. Out in the open air, the sharp smolder of saltpeter filled his sinuses.

He ran down the stairs to the square. The fountain pool was a dusty void. Its underground lamps had been squelched, and many of the streetlamps surrounding it had disappeared as well. It was a dark and disorienting sight, but Dam gradually saw the pool must have cleaved and buckled from an underground explosion. He halted to get his bearings. Across the darkened expanse, a swarm of warriors headed toward the tower. Aerander grabbed Dam's shoulder. They stood together, judging the situation.

"I don't think anyone was hurt," Aerander said. "We were all inside the hall."

"Why would he blow up the pool?" Dam said. *He*, of course, was Calyiches. No one else could have been responsible. He tasted bitter bile in the back of his mouth. Holes ate through Dam's heart. He should have tried to stop Calyiches. He should have insisted they confront him days ago.

At the base of the tower, there was an ear-splitting crack of bedrock and a fiery flash of light. Black columns of smoke belched from the ground. Dam jumped into Aerander. He ducked his head and covered his ears, which were throbbing from the blast. Everything was muted, as though he had been plunged underwater.

He regained his balance and stared at the tower. At its foot, the lighted guard post was gone, and the yard was a smoky lake, concealing the extent of the explosion. A silhouette of the tower rose up from the smoke. Mercifully, it still stood. But the warriors had been headed into the blast. Hanhau might have been among them.

Aerander turned Dam by his shoulder. Lys and Dardy had caught up with them, and Aerander was mouthing something. For the first time in his life, Dam felt his father's blood coursing in his veins. His father had shown no fear rushing into a burning house to save his family, so Dam would lead a charge toward the explosion. Another blast could happen, engulfing anyone who had been hurt by the last one.

Dam sorted out an approach across the square with Aerander, Lys and Dardy close behind him. Now Dam understood the point of destroying the pool. Calyiches had ruptured the shelf between the hall and the tower to delay anyone trying to intervene. He jogged through spaces where the ground was even, climbed over buckled rock, and stepped carefully over jagged fractures in the square. The smoke and dust was choking. Still, Dam cried out hoarsely for Hanhau. He prayed that Hanhau hadn't been part of the first wave of warriors who had tried to reinforce the tower watch.

They made their way to a bleak scene. Bodies were strewn on the buckled ground. Dam raced to one of the fallen warriors. His friends spread out to check on others. How many could they drag to safety? How quickly?

Dam recognized Backlum. The mightiest of the warriors had been thrown onto his back from the explosion. Dam knelt down and investigated him gingerly. As a novice priest, he had been taught the basics of healing. A head injury would be the worst. Dam didn't see any blood. Backlum winced and strained his shoulders to lift himself from the floor.

The warrior might have injured his back, paralyzing him, or he might have been crippled by shock. If he had broken bones, his injuries could be worsened if Dam displaced him, but Dam didn't have time to take a careful account. Dam couldn't let Backlum lie there, waiting to be thrown or swallowed by another underground explosion.

He shuffled behind Backlum's head and wedged his hands beneath the man's shoulders. "I'm going to help you," he told him.

Backlum grasped his arm with unexpected force. "The tower," he sputtered.

"It's all right," Dam said. "We've got to get you out of here."

That strength in the warrior's hand was a good sign. Dam heaved Backlum up from beneath his arms so that his back was upright. He released the warrior and Backlum held his posture, just slumping a bit. Dam came around to pull him up to his feet. With his arm slung around Dam's neck, Backlum was able to limp a bit. Dam helped him toward the borders of the square.

"Was Hanhau with you?"

Backlum didn't answer.

That didn't mean one thing or the other, Dam told himself. All of Backlum's concentration was focused on withstanding the pain that racked his body. They made it some fifty paces from the tower. That seemed like a safe distance. Hanhau could be among the many others lying helpless from the blast.

As though he had read Dam's mind, Backlum's arm sloughed free from his shoulder. "Go." The warrior limped forward at a snail's pace, but he was making his way on his own.

Dam started toward the tower.

He felt a rumble underground before the most horrifying sound that Dam had ever heard, like the solid curtain of the world had been split open by an axe. The floor around the tower erupted in a hail of stone. The massive shadow of the tower budged to one side—clinging to its majesty for a moment—and then it slid downward into its lacerated foundation. Dam's breath halted in his throat. The solid flanks of the sacred monument shed from its core as it declined. Beneath, the angry crater stretched wider, swallowing hillocks of ruptured bedrock and everything else in its circumference.

Aerander. Lys. Dardy. Hanhau.

The tower crumbled away to its pinnacle gallery. In the dust cloud of its wake, the crater settled, bearing the weight of the tons of stone that had collapsed inside it. Red light diffused through the dense screen of smoke. A familiar rhythmic energy thrummed through Dam. If he hadn't known that it was the Oomphalos, he would have reckoned it was the very heart of the tower, shucked from its shell to bleed in brilliant color onto the square.

Dam coughed out the dust that he had inhaled and pulled up the collar of his shift over his nose and mouth. Smoke and pumice still hung in the air. His eyes burned, and everything was a cloudy blur. Dam staggered toward the center of the eruption. He was still much better off than a lot of people, and those people needed help.

He heard a distant cry. Dam's heart leapt from his chest. That voice was Hanhau's. Dam's legs took on new life. Hanhau sounded strong, in charge. Dam stumbled, nearly blindly, to the lip of the cratered tower yard. He couldn't decipher what Hanhau was shouting about, but Dam had to reach him so Hanhau would know that he had made it through the catastrophe as well.

Hanhau's cry roused more shouts of alarm. Dam scouted the valley of rubble beneath him. Illuminated in the ethereal red glow of the Oomphalos, he saw a band of hooded boys climbing down into the wreckage. They were making their way to the remains of the pinnacle tower where the Oomphalos lay reefed and unprotected. A group of warriors fought through the crevices of boulders to intercept them from the other side, but they had too much ground to cover.

Attalos and Heron came up behind Dam, bringing torches to help locate survivors. But now that the tower had been razed, the Oomphalos illuminated their dire surroundings in watery, crimson light.

Dam turned back to the wreckage pit, and all three boys stared at the thieves closing in on the prize they had brought down from the tower. Dam and the others were stuck at the lip of the tower crater. It was a ten-yard drop to get down there, and even if they sorted out a better place to descend, they had no time to close the space to the Oomphalos shelf. So they shouted at the thieves. Attalos and Heron took up stones from the ground and tried to pelt the boys from an archer's distance. Below, warriors scrambled through rocks and ditches to try to overtake the bandits. One of the thieves grasped the gleaming artifact and stuffed it in a satchel.

Darkness engulfed the crater. No one could stop the thieves from making their way into the shadows of the besieged city with the Oomphalos cached in their bag. Their only hope was that the robbers would be stopped by the guards at the tunnel to the lava fields. Dam was torn by an impulse to rush after them in that direction and a duty to attend to the many people who had been thrown and possibly buried by the explosion of the tower.

Vaguely, he was aware that Attalos had taken account of something below. The boy shuffled with his torch to a jagged foothold to the floor of the crater bed. Heron guided Dam along to a perch above the spot where Attalos had landed. Attalos crouched over a body and swept his torch above his head like a standard bearer on the battlefield.

For a moment, Dam was overcome with disbelief. He knew scores of people had been near the tower when it had collapsed. But where had been the gods sparing mercy for the righteous to even out the evil of the bandits? Emotions flooded him. He scampered down the bank of ruptured bedrock by hand and foot.

Aerander lay on his back with one arm twisted under him and a leg turned over at a frightening angle from his hip. One side of his head was dark with blood. He wasn't moving.

PART TWO

Chapter One

In Atlantis, hoary, honey-skinned women from the desert tribes of Tamana were said to have been gifted with the knowledge of palmistry by the witch goddess of the Amazons. They wore cloaks of many layers and veils for their faces, and they set up stalls at night in the alleys around the harbor. It was a district of rowdy tavernas and whorehouses, and Dam supposed that it was a good place for the witchy women to find men who were drunk or dumb enough to pay them for a glimpse of the miseries the Fates had in store.

Before Hephad had disavowed the practices of his native peoples, he had shown Dam some of the arts of palmistry, for it was known and held in great esteem in his country. A hairline furrow nearly the length of Dam's palm signified his life's trail, and it was traversed in places by finer wrinkles that heralded obstacles to overcome. Looking at that long groove etched across his palm, Dam understood his life as segmented by disasters. Each crosshatch closed off the past and ushered in a new journey.

The first trial had been the death of his parents, a stitch in his skin barely past the start of the line in his palm. The second trial, a fingertip's distance farther, was the betrayal of House Atlas on his thirteenth birthday, which had sent him on a new course in the priesthood. A melon seed's length from that, the third trial, in a long, crooked slash, had been when the world was washed asunder.

Those three trials had been plenty, and Dam hadn't troubled to tempt some mischievous god to turn supposition into truth by guessing what the next crossing in his life's trail could mean. He understood now. It was the night when lightning and thunder had burst up from the floor of the underworld, and the Oomphalos had been stolen. The life he had known was lost to him. A new path had begun.

As soon as Dam had heard the news that a house had been set up for the wounded, he volunteered to help, as did the other novice priests, Hephad, Deodorus, and Tibor. They had none of the convalescent herbs or salves they had been taught about in their training, but they had water to wash the grime from the men's wounds, rags to bind the skin to stop the bleeding, and water-soaked compresses to ease the men's fevers. They had chamber pots, and they knew to cover a man with a sheet so he could relieve himself with dignity.

Three dozen people had been recovered from the collapse of the tower, half of them dead. They had been thrown and crushed by the eruptions in the square, and some had deep, charred welts in their flesh from the bursts of fire and scalding smoke. The fallen had included the two warriors who had been at their posts by the tower gates when the second explosion had ruptured the yard. The rest had been mostly Old Ones who had arrived soon after to try to save the Oomphalos from the attack.

In the underground dwellers' tradition, they washed the bodies and set them on a pyre of coals so that they would not rot. While the bodies had smoldered down to bones and ashes, they had scored a plot of rock with giant concentric circles. The largest had been forty strides across. That represented to them nature's eternal cycle, and in the inner, smaller circle was the cycle of man. There, they had used their pick axes and hammers to dig out a shallow grave in which to place the bones. They mounded high the communal grave with the rubble from the tower yard. They were a people born from stone and returned to stone, as Hanhau had told Dam.

Of the Atlanteans, only two had died. One was a boy named Hiero, a thirteen-year-old cousin of Dardy's. He had been swallowed by the tower's sinking crater while trying to pull a warrior to safety. Both had been buried in the merciless fall-out of stone. They discovered Koz in the fissure of a crater bed. The boy had been blackened with the dusty fuel that he had used to burst open the floor beneath the tower.

An explanation had come together. After Calyiches and his friends left the hall, Koz snuck away and crept into the work-shafts beneath the square. They stockpiled their fuel of niterbats in the underground passageways for managing the fountain's system of beacons and water ducts and appointed Koz to set it off with flints while everyone had been celebrating Aerander's victory in the hall.

Had Calyiches told Koz he could scuttle out of the tunnels after the blasts, or they would come and fetch him? Had Koz been dumb enough to believe that? Could his own brother Leo have been so cold-hearted as to let him die?

Koz would never be able to answer those questions. His body had been burnt and blistered almost beyond recognition. The circumstances slightly modified the abomination of his deeds, indicating Koz had been a pawn of the others. They had razed man and monument to steal the Oomphalos, sparing no loyalty to their accomplice. Koz had been given the rites of burial and a crumbled, fire-scorched stone as his marker in the polyandrium. Calyiches' party had overpowered the tunnel wardens that night and made away into the backcountry.

Pyrrah and the other women helped out in the infirmary, as was their nature. They spooned broth into men's mouths and sat with them to calm their fears. Those women were brave and devoted. They didn't hesitate to visit even the most mangled and bloodied of the wounded, always with a smile and kind words for each man about what he had done to protect his countrymen. Dam wondered at times if they had taken up the wounded as surrogates for the husbands and the children they had lost in the flood.

Some underground dwellers were able to set bones with metal stints and braces so they could heal. Most horribly, surgeries had to be performed with saws and fire-stoked cautery prods to remove festering limbs and prevent the rot from spreading. The patient's screams were scalding and lingered in Dam's head like echoes.

It occurred to Dam from time to time that if they had the Oomphalos, it would speed the course of the men's healing and spare them some agony. It might even save the lives of some who were sallow and wasting with fever. But the magical artifact was gone. They had only the tools of rudimentary care to keep the wounded alive.

Dam had not prayed since he had left the priests' precinct. What he had learned about the High Priest Zazamoukh sent his faith adrift and made him ashamed of having served as an accomplice to his treachery. But one night when he and Hephad returned to their house to sleep, Dam joined Hephad at the altar his friend had set up in a corner of the room.

He remembered Aerander's question when they were at the polyandrium. Dam had wondered about many things since the disaster at the tower.

"Do you think the gods of our world hear us down here?" he asked Hephad.

Hephad nodded. Even after he had been so cruelly punished by the High Priest Zazamoukh, his faith was unwavering. Others would say that Atlantis had been abandoned by Poseidon or banished by Him. For Hephad, that was all the more reason to keep up his ritual devotions and push those traditions on the other boys. He had chiseled stones into fetishes—their patron Atlas, his mother Pleione, and the Great Poseidon—and set them on the altar shelf. That night, Hephad's faith no longer seemed foolhardy. Dam sat down with Hephad at the altar like they had so many mornings before when they had been novice priests.

They made oblations of snippings of hair and let them burn in the altar's tin lamp. Dam shut his eyes and asked Pleione, the mother of mercy, for miracles. That men who bled from their bowels might be brought back from the edge of death. That the freed prisoners who had clung to life by the radiance of the Oomphalos might survive until the relic was recovered. That Lys, whose hand had been shattered by a fallen boulder, might make it through without an amputation. That Dardy, who had broken his leg in two places, might walk again.

Most of all, Dam prayed to the goddess to grant mercy to Aerander. Many nights had passed and still Aerander could not raise himself from his pallet. Worse, he shivered awake at times with cries that rang through the infirmary, grasping out for someone to explain why he couldn't see.

"Dam." A voice called Dam's attention away from his prayers. Someone had spoken his name. Dam realized that tears were running down his face. He wiped his eyes with his apron and looked to Hephad.

"Dam," Hephad said again. His voice jolted Dam for a moment. Hephad turned his head to hide a grin.

"When? How long have…"

"Since the day we found the kittens."

That was some time ago—the only bright spot since the night of terror. The kittens had been discovered locked in a vacant storage vault in the lower warehouse district of the city. Calyiches and his friends must have lured and trapped them as a ploy to cast suspicion on the Old

Ones and to distract people from voting. The kittens had grown even bigger. Like leopard cubs, they could stand on their hind legs and reach their paws to Dam's waist. Whatever enchantment the Oomphalos had cast over them hadn't worn off when the magical stone was taken away.

So it was with Hephad's regrowing tongue.

"Why didn't you tell me?" Dam said.

Hephad frowned. "It didn't seem right."

Dam tried to retrace time since they had found the kittens. Everything blurred together in his head. Their routine a cycle that had repeated too many times. They woke. They went to the infirmary house. They split off to opposite sides of the room, emptying chamber pots, changing dressings, changing the bedding of the soiled pallets, and sponging off the men who coughed up blood and turning them on their sides. Dam recalled one, maybe two times when he and Hephad had taken a break together to drink some soup at a bench outside the house. When Deodorus and Tibor had come by to relieve them, Dam discussed the men they were most worried about, but Hephad never said anything. Then Dam and Hephad dragged themselves to wash up in the yard and lay down on their beds. Each night, sleep had overwhelmed them quickly.

Dam poked Hephad in the ribs. "You should tell Attalos, at least."

A blush blazed across Hephad's face. Dam and Hephad had never talked about it, but it had become pretty obvious that Hephad and Attalos were more than friends.

"Already did."

That earned Hephad two pokes in the ribs and a pounce on the shoulders. Dam hovered over him. "Did you tell Attalos like this?" He opened his mouth and lashed his tongue lewdly.

Hephad giggled. "Stop."

Dam pinched at his sides, and then he gave Hephad a reprieve. A thought occurred to him.

"Tell Aerander tomorrow. He'd want to know."

CHAPTER TWO

The theft of the Oomphalos had taken away any sense of day or night, and everyone around the Honeycomb seemed to drift like ghosts consumed by their private worlds. They slept until they didn't need to sleep any more, and they rested when their bodies ached for it. When Dam next awoke, by some rhythm of nature he felt it was time to relieve Deodorus and Tibor at the infirmary, just as he had felt it numerous times before. Dam looked across the room, cast in the flickering flame of the altar, and he saw Hephad stirring with a yawn. They made their "morning" oblations at the altar, dressed in clean aprons, and headed to the infirmary.

The stench of urine and bile was hard to manage each time they first arrived. But as Dam swam into the fug of the infirmary, his nausea always subsided, and he scarcely noticed the foul odors after a while. He took account of the rows of pallets like every other day. An empty pallet could signify hope or tragedy. A few of the men with milder injuries had gotten better and been moved to their homes. A few had been removed for funeral rites.

That day, he noticed the empty space where a warrior named Teochin had been languishing after the amputation of both of his legs. Lately he had complained of an agony gripping his abdomen. That was a very serious stage of affliction, Dam had learned. Deep flesh wounds, like the kind soldiers incurred in battle, could lead to a disease of the intestines. When those organs were afflicted, the man could not be nurtured with food or drink. The end of the warrior's suffering struck Dam as merciful. Amputations were always chancy. It was hard to tell whether or not the bad blood in the lost limb had already traveled deeper into the body, causing the organs of the gut to rot.

Before they started their routine, Dam led Hephad to the far end of the room, where Aerander had been laid out for care. Lys lay on a pallet beside him. Dardy was on the other side. They were the only boys left in the dormitory. Dardy's brother Evandros had been well enough to limp out on metal crutches with his leg in a brace some time ago.

Lys noticed Dam and Hephad's approach. He propped himself up gingerly with his good arm, and he called out to Aerander. Aerander struggled to raise himself up on his elbows. The crown of his head was wrapped in cloths down to his brow. His unseeing eyes worried around the room.

It hurt Dam to see his cousin's complexion so pale and the boyish roundness of his face wasted away from the strain of his injuries. But there were encouraging signs that day. Aerander looked more alert and more aware of his surroundings. Pleione had bedded herself at his feet. Hephad had brought the cat to the infirmary to lift the men's spirits. For her to take to Aerander that way, he must have eased off from his waking fits.

Dam nudged Hephad forward, and he knelt beside Aerander. "Good morning, Aerander."

Aerander's face shrunk up. He turned toward the voice. "Hephad?"

Hephad grinned shyly. "Yes." Aerander reached out to him, and Hephad pressed their hands together. Dam drew up on the other side of his cousin, near Dardy, who cocked his head to take part in the visit. Both of Dardy's legs had been fitted with metal braces.

The five boys talked about the miracle of Hephad's healing. Lys and Dardy wanted to see his tongue, so Hephad showed them his mouth as though he had caught a prize fish in there.

"You look better," Dam told Aerander.

"I feel a bit more so. The nightmares haven't been as bad. That's the only time I can see—when I'm dreaming. Last night, Father visited me."

Lys broke in. "The medic says the sight sometimes comes back even in the worst of cases."

"Of course it does," Dam told his cousin. The medic was their most knowledgeable healer. Her name was Sacnite. She was a white-haired woman from the oldest generation, the Children of the Aerie. She had been setting bones and sewing up wounds since before Hanhau's parents had been born.

"Father said he's looking over all of us," Aerander told Dam. "He wants us to know that Hiero is doing fine. He's joined his father and his mother and sisters now." Aerander winced and lay back on his pallet. The others quieted. Dam craned over him.

"He gets dizzy after a spell, that's all," Lys said.

Hephad looked to Dam. "We should let him have his rest."

Aerander's hand fumbled around at his side to touch Dam's hand. "It's all right. Dam, stay with me for a bit." Dam glanced at the others. Hephad nodded and went off to do his rounds. Lys and Dardy lay back down.

Dam gathered together the bedding beneath Aerander's head so it would be more comfortable for him. The shredded cave moss was damp with sweat. It could have used refreshing, but it seemed cruel to bother his cousin with that while he was laid out so feebly. "You don't have to talk. We'll just sit together for a while."

"I need to talk to you," Aerander said. He swallowed and cleared his throat with some effort. "Dam, we have to get the Oomphalos back."

Dam squeezed out a wet cloth from a nearby bucket, dabbing it on the sides of his cousin's face. "We will. As soon as you're better."

"No. Not when I'm better," Aerander said. "It will be too late."

"You keep resting and getting better every day, all right?" Dam said. "There's no reason for you to be worrying about anything else."

"Dam, I might never get better. I won't be any use to anyone if I can't see."

"That's not true. You're the King of Atlantis."

"So I am. And I need your help. You've got to stop Calyiches before he gets back to the surface."

Dam sat back on his heels. *Him?* What made Aerander think he could do anything to stop Calyiches?

"Dam, it's our only chance to return home. I promised the freed prisoners. I can't organize an expedition like this. There isn't much time. Calyiches already has a good lead."

Dam bit his lip. He had thought about the same thing in his spare moments. A shameful hope was buried deeper in his consciousness. If they gave up their mission to return to the surface, they could stay in the underworld where Dam knew his place and could be with Hanhau. Dam knew that was selfish. He had been praying for Aerander to get better, but that might not happen without the power of the Oomphalos. He couldn't deny Aerander his help.

But how would anyone find Calyiches? He could be anywhere in the backcountry. He could have found a portal to the surface already.

Aerander's breaths turned shallow. His lips moved weakly. "Promise me, Dam."

Dam squeezed his hand. "I promise. Now rest."

❖

After Dam had finished taking care of the men on his side of the infirmary, he went to find Hanhau. He had a good idea where he was likely to be. Teochin had been taken away for burial rites. The warriors would have gathered to pay their respects.

Dam hadn't spoken to Hanhau since the collapse of the tower. Everything after that had proceeded in such a dazed routine, and Hanhau had been appointed to the city watch since so many of the warriors were unable to serve. After Dam and Attalos carried Aerander from the tower crater, Dam had spotted Hanhau across the smoke-blighted square. Hanhau's face had glowed in recognition, but not more than a reassuring glance had passed between them.

Dam climbed the stairwell to the gravesite with an oil lamp to light his way. The funeral plot had been set up on a tall platform of rock apart from the main stages of the city. Across a dark pool of shadow, dotted tiers of gas lamps outlined the Honeycomb. It was like looking at a harbor village across a void of sea at night.

When he crowned the top of the shelf, the stench of smoking coals scraped at his sinuses. Flames flapped from tall totems staked around the grave mound. Dam had been to the gravesite for the first communal burial. Three more warriors had died since then. The mound of rubble was higher than Dam's head and many times as wide. The yard was deserted.

The gathering for Teochin must have finished some time ago. That was troubling. Hanhau had moved on to who knew where. Then Dam heard voices coming from a shadowy pavilion on the far end of the yard. Dam headed over to search for Hanhau there.

It was some sort of rudimentary meeting house that the Old Ones must have built recently. It had flat slate roof buttressed by squared columns. The foundation was a slate slab as well, and it was broader than the roof, creating a narrow terrace around the perimeter.

As Dam neared the house, he could see the silhouettes of a dozen or so warriors seated at tables, muttering in a grieved tone. White light flashed from their faces. Dam stepped lightly into the house and looked around for Hanhau.

His arrival was quickly noticed. The warriors halted their discussion, looking at Dam warily. Dam recognized Ichika and Backlum, who was wearing a metal collar to hold his neck straight so it would heal. Miraculously, he was only sore from being thrown by the first blast at the tower. Hanhau stood up from a corner of one of the tables and stepped over, drawing Dam aside.

Hanhau smiled, but he was a bit shifty. "Why did you come here?"

"I wanted to say I'm sorry about Teochin. And I need to talk to you. Was that a bad idea?"

"No. Of course not. Come. We can talk over here." Hanhau gestured to a corner of the house's terrace, away from the interior and his warrior friends.

Hanhau's careful behavior warranted some explanation. Dam was acquainted with many of Hanhau's friends. He even thought of Backlum as his own friend. So why was Hanhau taking him away from them?

Had Hanhau's interest in him died with the wrecking of the tower? Were lines drawn since Dam's countrymen had stolen the Oomphalos? The gods had offered Dam few moments of happiness in matters of love. Normally, Dam would have heeded the signs of disaster and gone on his way, sparing himself the hurt of some delicately worded explanation. But he had promised his cousin he would find a way to bring back the Oomphalos, and Hanhau was the only person who could help Dam with that plan.

"Aerander wants me to put together a search party to find Calyiches."

"That won't be necessary."

Dam's brow furrowed.

Hanhau glanced toward the house. He spoke in a low voice. "We're going."

"I'll go with you. There's others who will want to help. Attalos, Heron—"

"Dam."

"What?"

"This isn't a mission for you."

"Why?"

"It will be a journey deep into the backcountry. That's too dangerous for you."

"It's dangerous for anyone."

Hanhau stared at Dam. "Calyiches' crime was against *our* people. Rendering justice is our responsibility and our right."

Dam understood to an extent. Many more warriors than Atlanteans had perished in the explosions, and Calyiches had demolished their sacred monument and taken their prized relic. But Calyiches had done it to punish Aerander and his countrymen as well. They needed the Oomphalos just as much as Hanhau's people. It was the life source for the freed prisoners, and it might be the only thing to heal Aerander.

A troubling thought occurred to Dam as he glanced at the shadowed meeting house. "You were all going to run off to catch him without telling anybody? Does Ysalane know about this?"

Hanhau didn't answer, although that was an answer in itself.

"That's treason."

"Eighteen warriors were killed that night. Twenty others were crippled. That murderer stole the most sacred artifact of our people."

Dam answered fiercely. "You don't have to tell me. I was there. And I've been in the infirmary every night since it happened."

A group of warriors came out to the terrace. Too late, Dam realized he had raised his voice loud enough to be heard from quite a distance. They were an imposing, desperate-looking pack. Their faces were smudged from burying Teochin's charred bones in the rock pile. Their chest armor was dented in places, and their unwashed hair was loose from their braids. Ichika stood at the head of the group. She stared at Hanhau bitterly.

"You told him."

Hanhau looked at her helplessly.

"Don't be mad at him," Dam said. "He wouldn't have bothered telling me unless I dragged it out of him."

"That's not true, Dam," Hanhau said.

One of the men griped, "What is this? A lover's spat?"

"He never should have come here," another cried. "This is sacred ground."

"He should go back with his kind."

Hanhau stepped toward the group, speaking with both his mouth and his hands. The response that returned to him felt like it could ignite into a brawl. Dam had never felt threatened by the warriors before. As much to Dam's surprise as anyone, that danger emboldened him. He pushed his way into the crossfire between Hanhau and the others.

"You say I don't belong here? Guess what? You're stuck with me. Because I don't have anywhere else to go."

Dam's outburst silenced the warriors. Their silence lifted his courage to greater heights.

"I don't know how to fight," Dam said. "I don't know the backcountry. But I've got as much to lose as any of you if we don't stop Calyiches. You go running off to claim vengeance, and what'll you come back to? Mutiny? Terror? You want my people to feel even more helpless than we already feel? We want justice too. You can't grab it all for yourselves."

Some of the warriors came back at him with shouts and jeers. Dam raised his voice to answer them. Hanhau turned and stood between Dam and his companions.

"This isn't your fight," Hanhau said.

Dam searched Hanhau's face. Raw emotion overwhelmed him. It had been pushed down too long so he could do his duty caring for crippled men, so they wouldn't see he was afraid for them, so the broken world might mend itself if he pretended everything was fine and routine and going to get better. But it wasn't getting better, and it never would unless he did something.

"What is my fight? Tell me. Because there's anger burning through my veins, and I don't know what to do with it. I don't know how to make it stop." His hands trembled at his sides. "My cousin was maimed that night, and all he wants is to make good on his promise to the freed prisoners. I swore to him that I would help. What am I supposed to do? You can't leave me here with no purpose. You can't do that to me."

Ichika spoke out to the others. "We can't be held up by surface dwellers following us through the backcountry. We'd be wasting all our time looking out for them."

Words of agreement grumbled from the warriors. Dam fastened his gaze on Ichika. "Look at your city. We're people from above and people from below, and we're all hurting from the same catastrophe. You can't split us off as a burden to be stowed away until we rot. We need to come together. That's how we got the Oomphalos back in the first place."

The faces of the warriors dimmed. Hanhau looked upon Dam with understanding and a glint of pride. While the pack of warriors glanced around to gauge each other's bearing on the matter, Backlum eked his way to a spot beside Dam.

"He risked his life pulling me away from the tower," Backlum said. "I say we hear him out."

❖

They talked things over in the meeting house. With Hanhau and Backlum sitting beside him, Dam was able to get the others to ask for Ysalane's commendation of their mission. If the warrior queen agreed, they would take a small squad of Dam's countrymen along.

One of the warriors called Dam "Stone Badger," and the rest of the group broke out in laughter. Hanhau explained that it was a kind of lizard, small but fierce, that chased men away from its chalky hollows in the high ground of the backcountry.

After a while, everyone's shoulders were heavy, and yawns stretched from the warriors' mouths. They said their good nights and went back to their homes to sleep. They would speak to Ysalane the next day.

That left just Dam and Hanhau back at the house. Hanhau wandered out to the terrace and sat down at the edge looking out to the burial mound, which was painted in flickering light and shadow by the yard's flaming totems. Dam followed him out and sat down at a spot nearby.

Dam was too tired to feel the full force of his indignity from the way Hanhau had first treated him, but the unsettled feeling stirred in his gut. What if he hadn't sought out Hanhau? Would Hanhau have left the city without even telling him?

"I'm sorry," Hanhau said.

Dam picked at his sandal, waiting for more to come.

"I told you I didn't care about what the others thought about the two of us, but I let that bother me tonight."

Dam studied him sidelong. Hanhau's face was tense and embattled.

"I'm ashamed," Hanhau said.

Dam let that pass in silence for a while.

"Good," Dam said. "Then I guess you're lucky that I forgive you." He reached out his hand, and Hanhau took it. Hanhau's palm was rough and calloused from working at the burial site. He squeezed Dam's hand, and Dam squeezed back. That simple touch said more than words could. Their disagreement was forgiven and forgotten. In fact, as they interlaced and pressed their hands together, it roused familiar cravings in Dam from the previous times they had been alone.

There were ways to mend a fight that were much better than talking about it.

Dam slid his hand up Hanhau's arm.

Hanhau cleared his throat. "When we go on this mission, it will be as comrades."

That seemed far in the future and hardly troubling. Now was the time for just the two of them to be together. Dam edged up close, gliding one hand over the smooth skin of Hanhau's shoulder and the scars of victory that bloomed there. His other hand closed over the scales of Hanhau's belly. He reached his mouth to Hanhau's for a kiss.

Hanhau turned his head away. He told Dam gently, "We can't."

Dam remembered the shedding of Hanhau's armor. He would need it to protect himself on their mission into the backcountry. Hanhau ran his fingers through Dam's coarse and messy hair.

"When we come home with the Oomphalos," he said.

Dam bowed his head. His body steamed like doused coals. Waiting until then was going to be awfully hard.

CHAPTER THREE

They came together as a party of sixteen for the expedition to capture Calyiches and return the Oomphalos. Ysalane had granted this privilege to eleven warriors, including Hanhau, Ichika, and eight other volunteers, along with five boys from Atlantis.

Dam had been appointed with the job of raising that faction. He chose Attalos, Callios, and Heron since they had taken part in the prisoner's rebellion and knew a bit about traveling the underground backcountry. A fifth boy, Radamanthes, had presented himself as an unquestionable asset to their cause. Rad was from the martial clan, House Autochthonus. Next to Calyiches and Lys, he had been a formidable athlete in the Panegyris. He was eighteen years old and had trained with his father's infantry, which was renowned for their maneuvers across all kinds of terrain—desert, grassland, and jungle—patrolling the wilds of Tamana. Rad had kept up a routine of exercises in the bathing yard, and between that and his rations of fish, his brawny body had tightened like metal cord. If their mission came down to hand-to-hand combat with Calyiches and his band of traitors, Rad was the one to bet on.

Their party had Ysalane's full sanction with the proviso that they attempt to bring back the traitors alive so they could be brought to trial in front of the people. Word spread quickly, and "Ysalane's sixteen" were hailed as heroes before they had even stepped out of the city gates. The smithies worked quickly to equip them with freshly minted crossbows and lightweight blades. The scullery workers packed up smoked and salted meats for their journey.

Around the Honeycomb, it seemed like every boy who had a lick of martial experience came down to Dam's middle-house to offer advice.

They had all been genuine and encouraging, but Dam understood their lessons were born from an undercurrent of doubt. Dam was a novice priest. He had no training in soldiery like many of the highborn boys. Neither did Attalos, a pawnbroker's son, nor Callios, whose father had run a tannery, nor Heron, who had grown up in a shantytown of orichalcum miners. Yet they had been entrusted to capture the most heinous criminals their generation had ever known, other than the High Priest Zazamoukh himself.

Dam had his reasons for selecting his crew. It had to do with instinct rather than experience. He needed boys who would come together as a company under his advisement, and more importantly, under the command of the foreign warriors. The boys from the middle-houses were used to being told their place. They hadn't been part of their country's venerated noble class, of which Dam sensed the Old Ones were even more suspicious due to Calyiches' treachery. As for Rad, who Dam only knew in passing, he counted on the boy's stolid dedication to a soldier's lifestyle as a favorable disposition to taking orders.

When everything had been settled with Ysalane, Dam had gone to see Aerander. The infirmary's charges had dwindled to about a dozen. Sacnite had sent home any man who could hold down soup and water and cough without hacking up blood. That helped lessen the spread of rot through the air, and it gave those with the most serious conditions more attention from the medic's team of healers. Hephad had been relieved of his duties. He wasn't needed anymore, for which he was grateful. The "kittens" needed boarding and training now that they were half the weight of men and scaling the highest stages of the city. A yard with a high stone wall was set up outside the Honeycomb where Hephad could handle them and temper their wild natures.

Just two boys were left at the infirmary. Dardy had been carried home by his brothers. Lys was in fine condition to leave. The swelling in his hand had lessened, and a healthy pink had returned to his fingers. But Lys would not give up his pallet at Aerander's side. Aerander still could not withstand sitting up for more than a short while before plunging back to a dizzy lethargy. His head was still swaddled in cloths. He remained blind.

While his cousin lay on his back and Lys sat up at full attention, Dardy told them about the expedition.

Aerander smiled weakly. His voice was as thin as paper. "You did it. I knew you would. You're House Atlas. Our ancestors charted the seas and fought Amazons and Minotaurs."

"Don't let the Old Ones claim all the glory," Lys said. He tucked into a boxer's stance to demonstrate for Dam, making play jabs with his good hand. "If you're face-to-face with Calyiches, an uppercut to his nose will stun his senses. Then box his neck to break the bone and artery."

Dam had heard the advice before, but he nodded solemnly to Lys. No one would look after his cousin better. Lys would fight off the demons of death to keep Aerander alive.

Aerander groped for Dam's hand. "I have something for you. Lys?" The bigger boy crept over and knelt behind Aerander. Delicately, Lys grasped the amulet around Aerander's neck and lifted it over his bandaged head.

"If you're ever in danger, talk to Calaeno," Aerander said. "She's promised to help you."

Lys held out the amulet for Dam. Dam stared at the ugly thing. Its ancient chain link was dull and rusted. Three pale bones twined together formed its trident decoration.

It could bridge a mental connection to Atlas' daughter, a Pleiade who had been banished to the night sky. Dam had begun to believe in prayers again, but that possibility left him frozen. The goddess had been obscured from history due to a scandal that Dam only understood in bits and pieces. Her father had raised her as a boy because he had no male heirs, and Calaeno had abdicated her duty, running off with a suitor to the underworld. Later, she had been imprisoned in the heavens by a powerful spell that could only be broken when she was spotted in the night sky and her beholder revealed the mystery of her disappearance. When Aerander had done that on the night of the flood, Calaeno had shone a heavenly light on the portal at the Citadel so people could evacuate during the flood.

"You'll need it more than me," Aerander said.

Lys looked to Dam encouragingly.

"How do you...talk to her?" Dam said.

"You just do. It helps if you try thinking about nothing, and just listen to the space inside your head. Say her name. She'll answer you."

Taking the necklace from Aerander didn't seem right. Strange as it was, the amulet was his cousin's only regalia. He somehow looked weaker, a common invalid, without the ancient heirloom around his neck. But Dam couldn't just sit there with Lys pushing the amulet on him. Dam took it in his hand.

The necklace felt light and delicate, but not special or magical, however something special and magical should feel. Dam pulled the necklace over his head. Nothing happened. That was fine with Dam. "We'll bring back the Oomphalos," Dam told his cousin. "And you'll see again."

❖

The sixteen gathered in Ysalane's Hall on the eve before their departure. The warriors had advice to give the boys. They discussed a rough plan for their route into the backcountry to intercept Calyiches, who, as best as anyone could figure, had headed to the highlands to find a legendary portal to the mountains of Mauritania. They had their last meal in the city, and they all decided to take their rest in the hall that night as one united company.

While they were gathered around a table, finishing off their last course of fish, a weak, emaciated man hobbled into the hall. It was Markos from the below-houses. He had traveled a great distance for a man his age. Everyone at the company stared at him, wondering what news could compel him to make such a journey.

He sputtered it out all at once to everyone at the hall. "Silenos is dead."

CHAPTER FOUR

The expedition embarked on the vigorous wings of hope. They dug briskly into the darkened backcountry, and Dam marveled that Ysalane's sixteen had come together as a formidable force. Hanhau and Ichika took the lead, scouting the way ahead. They were unfettered by supply packs and armed with hiking crooks. Those grapple-headed implements had blades as sharp as a butcher's cleaver. They made for fine tools to scale rock and to batter aside any surprises in their path.

Two pairs of warriors followed them, an archer team and a skirmish team who had tread-handled *kopis* swords. They wore light harnesses on their backs for small packs of provisions, and they were ready to maraud forward as soon as their quarry was spotted. A third pair ferried the heavier packs of supplies for their travel.

Dam and his group followed next. Over their military shifts, they had geared up in metal mesh aprons, which were fashioned from a light but hardy silver ore. Rad had described to the smithies the traditional weapon of their country's legionnaires: the *xiphos*. The smithies forged scabbards to sheathe those short stabbing blades, which the boys had strapped across their backs.

At the warriors' advice, they hiked in twos. Each pair was to be an unbreakable unit, sworn to look out for one another while they traversed the caves and the treacherous gorges of the underground terrain. Dam had paired with Attalos, Callios with Heron, and Rad with an amiable warrior named Blix who was short for his kind and closest to Rad's impressive stature. With a mix of irony and pride, Blix had dubbed their group "the iron belly of the caterpillar." As they made their way through the low-ceilinged, narrow passageways of the underworld, they did indeed seem to Dam like one long organism winding through wormholes of tiered rock. The last of their company were a pair of warriors with one-handed flails. They scouted for danger from behind. Their first objective was to pick up Calyiches' trail. The traitors couldn't have known much about the backcountry. They would have only had the knowledge that a portal to Mauritania was rumored to be somewhere in the highlands beyond the Fire Canyon. At the ledge above the vast, lava-scored gorge, Hanhau spotted their first encouraging sign. Pick-axes and pouches of ground-up niterbats were scattered on the ground. The boys must have thrown them off in order to ford the valley.

Hanhau explained that they could take routes above and around the bed of molten rivers and fire spouts, but they were best off retracing the boys' path to keep pace with their quarry. So they rappelled down the valley's steep escarpment with corded leads. Hanhau and Ichika sorted out a route across the fractured islands of the lava tributaries.

Heat slashed at their feet and legs, and a bilge of sulfurous smoke clogged their lungs. It was nearly unbearable, but the caterpillar soldiered on. They accomplished a route to the ridge at the other side of the valley. Hanhau led the party to a cleft in the ridge that had gradual footholds for ascending. From above, he called out that he had found more signs of Calyiches' team. It was miraculous how well the warriors could penetrate the darkness.

Blix stopped at a little shelf in the ridge and channeled his body's luminescent energy into his hands, which shone onto the pewter-colored ground. Dam and the other boys huddled around the spot.

They saw shreds of burnt fabric. Most likely, one of Calyiches' crew had burned the skirting of his shift while fording the valley. The singed ends had fallen away during his climb. As Dam looked closer, he noticed dried droplets of blood on the granite shelf. More than clothes had been singed. Someone had been burned badly. A trail continued up to the shelf and onward, suggesting a direction. Once the flail bearers climbed to the top, the company plodded onward across a field of bedrock.

Gradually, the floor scaled toward the ceiling. Their progress dragged. Dam worried that they were headed to an impasse of solid rock. A lead warrior's phosphorescent hand sparked from the darkness up ahead, waving the company forward like a miner's lantern. Hanhau or Ichika must have sighted a path.

A narrow gulch was carved into a massive bulwark of rock. They had to take it single file. Dam's heartbeat drummed in his chest, and his lungs shrunk up. They were vulnerable inside the pass. The slightest seizure would crush them, or an enemy could squeeze their line into fumbling havoc by cutting off the way forward and the way back.

Shouts up ahead jangled Dam's nerves even more. As he rubbed his wet brow, he noticed that it wasn't only sweat coating his face. The air was rich with moisture. A cool drop of water plunked on the crown of his head. A few steps forward, Dam heard the chirping sound of a cascade and stepped down on slippery stone.

Water was seeping from the ceiling. Up ahead, it spilled down in a curtain and streamed in the direction they were headed. Dam filled his chest with a full breath of air. That stream would lead out to an opening in the gulch. Each man splashed through the refreshing shower and trudged down the stream. They came to the head of a cataract that fizzed down to a sightless grotto.

The supply carriers brought out leads, and they rappelled down to the floor of the grotto in order. Dam caught Attalos as he splashed down into the water, and the two made their way to a bank to wait for the other pairs. The boys exchanged a sportive grin. Their journey already felt like a triumph.

Dam noticed Hanhau and Ichika investigating the bank of the grotto. When everyone had made it down from the gulch, the two warriors called the group over. Uncloaked in the glow of their palms, they saw a circlet of stones and whitened coals doused with water—a rudimentary campfire. Calyiches must have called his group to rest in the spot.

"We'll camp here as well," Hanhau said. "Ichika and I will go ahead to track the next leg of their course."

❖

They refueled the fire pit with fresh coals and staked their wet clothes to dry. The warriors said that the grotto stream was potable, so the boys filled their flagons with water. Later, they had their first meal of salted fish. The warriors worked out sleeping and watch shifts among themselves and left the boys to take their rest.

There were pallets to unroll around the fire and thin woven blankets to wrap up in. The broad socket of bedrock around the stream was cool and dank like a cellar. The boys sat together arced around the glowing coals. They complained that their bodies ached in funny places from all the hiking and the rappelling. They were tired, but the thrill of what they had been through kept them awake.

"They couldn't have made it much farther," Rad said. "They don't have the experience or the equipment for this terrain."

The others piped in to agree. None of them had traveled so deep into the backcountry either, and they were proud of what they had accomplished that day. Bloodied patches of rock around Calyiches' campsite indicated that the party had struggled. With no way to rappel from the top of the gulch, they must have jumped down blindly. That plummet would have resulted in some twisted knees and ankles, if not broken bones. Still, Dam remembered that they had the Oomphalos, which provided a magical protection.

"What is the Oomphalos?" Rad said.

Dam looked at the boy. Rad was staring right at him. Everyone had been told the history of the magic stone. The Old Ones had forged it to preserve their people. Some of them had turned ambitious and greedy— the New Ones—and revolted to wrest the stone for themselves. The Old Ones had sent the stone aboveground so the New Ones wouldn't use it for destruction. Years later, Zazamoukh had been tricked by the New Ones to bring the Oomphalos back belowground. Their era of terror had lasted until Aerander killed the serpent queen and returned the stone to Ysalane.

But Rad seemed to be driving for something more than that.

"They say it's forged from mori-mori," Dam said. He recalled the glowing founts in Ysalane's Hall. *The blood of the earth.*

"Why can't they make another one?" Rad said.

"They don't know how to work magic from mori-mori anymore," Dam said. "They lost that knowledge when the New Ones drove them from their city, ages ago. Before Aerander killed the snake queen, they were scattered across the backcountry, just surviving, for generations."

Rad reclined on his elbows. "I heard the stone can give you immortality," he mused. "Makes you understand why Calyiches would take it, doesn't it?"

Dam answered with some heat. "It's not meant to be hoarded. The Old Ones used it for everyone's benefit."

"But it's the nature of man, don't you think?" Rad said. "Always wanting a little more for ourselves."

"The nature of *some* men," Dam said.

Attalos pointed a question at Rad. "Weren't you and Calyiches mates?"

His words hung in the air for a while. They had all been wanting to ask Rad about that history, but somehow no one had brought it up until that moment. Rad had been the favorite son of House Autochthonus, and Calyiches had been the favorite of House Mneseus. Some political and athletic rivalry sprang up between the houses, but all the highborn boys sat together in the dining hall. Everyone had seen Rad and Calyiches chumming around the Honeycomb from time to time. Rad had scrounged up rocks from the quarry to practice putting, and he had given Calyiches pointers on the sport.

Rad rustled up from his slouch. "We were mates. But if you think I volunteered to come along so I could sabotage this campaign, you're dead wrong. I want to catch him as much as the rest of you." His self-righteous gaze passed over each of the boys who were staring at him. "I was just trying to have a philosophical discussion. Though I suppose none of you have heard much about philosophy."

"We're not stupid," Dam said.

"Not saying you are," Rad said. "I'm saying it's man's nature to improve himself." He looked over Attalos, Callios, and Heron. "Like all of you. You supported Aerander to gain land and an equal say in how the kingdom is run. But do you think when everyone is equal, we'll all be happy with what we've got? Every one of us with our same square plots of land. How long you think it will be before someone says, 'Your plot's better than mine. How come he gets a grove of trees while I've got to dig up trenches to water my fields?'

"And who sorts out what's fair? If everyone gets a vote, we're all voting for ourselves, and no one gets what he wants. Soon enough, people get smart and join up with people for mutual interest so they can vote as one block. It won't be one man, one vote. It'll be whoever can get the most friends behind him that gets his way. That popular vote could take your land right from under you. So much for Aerander's 'freedom for every man.'"

"If that's what you think, why didn't you run off with Calyiches?" Dam said.

Rad smirked. "Wasn't much of a choice, was there? Tyranny or anarchy. I went with anarchy because I figure things will sort themselves out in the end. Our country's system of ten kings for one kingdom worked. You need an elite class to govern the masses."

"It works if you're one of the ten kings," Dam said.

Rad didn't have a response for that, but he didn't look offended. He was practical, not fanatical like Calyiches. It occurred to Dam that Rad probably spoke for most of his highborn peers. They hadn't been inspired by Aerander's vision for a new Atlantis. They had been resigned to it. He wondered what would really happen if they all made it above the surface.

Another thought entered Dam's head. It seemed so obvious all of a sudden. "Did you know what Calyiches was going to do?"

"Not precisely. But a good lot of us suspected he was up to something."

How couldn't they? The upper-houses had scarcely any privacy. People would have seen Calyiches' crew coming home with blackened hands and faces.

"There wasn't anyone who wouldn't have tried to stop what happened that night if he knew what was coming," Rad said. "What Calyiches did was a betrayal of Poseidon's most sacred commandment, 'Let no son of His take up arms against another.'"

"So that's why you're here? To do justice by the Poseidonidae?" Dam said.

"That's part of it. And I've got the reputation of my House to keep up. Can't leave all the glory to the likes of you. Besides, you might have noticed there's a whole lot of us men, and seven women to go around. Coming back in the shine of victory ought to improve my chances of getting a wife." He glanced up to the heights of the cavern. "Unless there's lots of women left up there, it won't be easy to continue the family line."

Just then, a shriek like seaborne wind and a rumble like thunder echoed through the cavern. Dam's four companions shot up to their feet and stared in the direction of the noise. Not that they could see anything in the dark.

Dam smiled to himself and muttered, "The Master of Sound." He explained to the others the folk tale about the twins. But like Hanhau had said, mysteries usually had ordinary explanations. The underworld had currents of wind, and it had probably been some distant volcanic burst that bounced around the bedrock walls and traveled to their cavern. Nonetheless, the others were rattled.

"There's beasts in these parts, aren't there?" Rad asked Dam.

"Bats, giant snails, fire scorpions. Lizards twice your size."

Rad shivered. "You've seen those things?"

Dam considered lying. He had only seen niterbats and slug-sledges. Hanhau had told him about the other creatures. "You ought to sleep cradling your *xiphos*. Or maybe cozy up with Blix for the night."

The others chuckled. Rad gave Dam a smart-alecky scowl. "I'm to bed. The rest of you should too. A soldier's work requires discipline, and that includes getting a full night's sleep."

Rad crept back to his pallet. Dam, Attalos, Callios, and Heron stayed seated around the fire. They didn't need to be bossed around by a military hero-in-the-making. They exchanged lopsided grins about their new, supremely self-assured companion. They talked about their adventure until their bodies felt as heavy as wet mortar and ached for sleep. Then they took to their pallets with their blankets drawn over them.

Dam noticed that Attalos was rummaging through his traveling satchel beside his bed. He had laid out pieces of something on the ground. They were too far away from the fire's weak light for Dam to see what he had.

Attalos took account of Dam's snooping, and he passed him a strip of some sort of stone as smooth as the inside of a conch shell.

"Black glass," Attalos explained. "I found it in the stream. I'm bringing it back for Hephad."

Dam handed him back the piece of glass. Hephad would like it. He could use the glass to decorate his household altar.

Rad was counting on bringing back a name for himself from their expedition. Attalos was collecting pretty things for his sweetheart. What would Dam have to show for their adventure? He wondered about that for a while, and then sleep pressed down on him like an iron blanket.

CHAPTER FIVE

Dam woke to a rustle of activity around the camp. The fire had gone dark. The warriors were faint blurs of light moving around the perimeter. Attalos and Heron were shuffling around in their beds. Dam got up on his knees and fumbled through the darkness to retrieve his tunic from the stake where he had left it by the fire. The tunic was stiffly dry, and it reeked of smoke. Dam pulled it over his head.

"The iron belly rises," Blix said to the boys as he approached them and handed the torch to Dam. "You can do your business behind those rocks over there. We'll have drink and food by the campfire. Hanhau has news he wants everyone to hear."

Once Attalos, Callios, Heron, and Rad had dressed, Dam led them to the place Blix had suggested to empty their bladders. When they came back, the fire was burning vigorously, and everyone was sitting or squatting around it. Dam wondered if he and his people were a burden to the Old Ones. The warriors certainly didn't need them to manage a camp, but they never gave them a chance to help out.

The group passed around platters of salted fish and a flagon of water. Then Hanhau and Ichika came over. Dam watched Hanhau slyly. His forehead was tensed the same scrupulous way as when he was searching for the right words in Atlantean.

"We charted their trail," Hanhau said. "They followed the grotto out to a lake and beyond into a range of mountains. They camped often to rest their wounded. There are markers like this site all along the way."

Rad stretched into the conversation. "How soon will we overtake them?"

Hanhau exchanged a glance with Ichika. "We can reach the foot of the mountains in one portage. It's a farther distance than yesterday's hike, but it will be easier terrain. We're on pace to gain up with their party in another night or two after that."

Attalos, Callios, and Heron looked to one another encouragingly. Dam could not believe it. They had barely scratched into the backcountry, and they were already on the heels of their target. They might return with the Oomphalos in just five or six nights.

Hanhau spoke out over the boys. "There's more. That pass through the mountains straddles an active fault. There was a seizure just last night."

Dam recalled the echoing thunder they had heard around the campfire.

"How bad was the damage?" Rad said.

"Hard to say. From our location, it appeared to be mild. But we don't know what we'll encounter when we head into the pass. The route could be strangled by fallen rock. There's no way to predict the next time the fault will shift."

"Makes our job easier then, doesn't it?" Rad said. "The seizure could have done the work, burying the bastards. We'd just have to dig them out of the fallout."

"Makes our job harder," Ichika told him. "If the thieves made it through before the seizure, they might have managed to cover their tracks with a solid wall. And it's too much of a risk to bring the entire party through that fault zone."

Dam had a terrible feeling he knew where the conversation was headed. He looked to Hanhau. "There's got to be other ways around that pass, right? One group could follow their path, and another could venture around to the other side of the mountains."

"That's not an option," Hanhau said. "The mountain range is much too broad. You could walk from here to the mountains and back one hundred times before you found another way around."

"What about slug-sledges?"

"The mountains are staggered. The terrain is too difficult for even them."

Rad stood. "Then we all go through the pass. We're wasting time talking about it while the bastards are getting a lead on us."

Ichika glanced at Hanhau. Dam didn't like that look.

"Six of us will scout the pass. That's our archers, our skirmishers, Ichika, and myself," Hanhau said. "The rest will tend a camp by the lake."

"You've got to be joking," Rad said.

"Ysalane has given me and Ichika command of this mission. We've judged our best course of action, and it will be carried out as an order."

Attalos cursed to his companions. "Might as well send us back to the city to sit on our hands."

Dam's gaze slunk to the ground. The warriors didn't trust him and his friends. They treated them like children. And Hanhau wasn't standing up for them. What had happened to being "comrades" on their mission? That was what Hanhau had told Dam after he had apologized for not standing up for Dam when they had first talked about organizing a squad to go after Calyiches.

But Dam didn't say a word. He looked to his friends while holding Hanhau in the corner of his vision. "Rad said it right. We're wasting time standing around talking about it. Let's get a move on."

❖

The hike through the grotto was as easy as Hanhau said it would be. The floor declined at a gentle grade. The walls echoed peacefully with the stream's chime and flow. It reminded Dam of childhood excursions to the countryside where his cousin's family had a villa with terraced gardens, lily pools, horse stables and riding trails, and acres upon acres of wooded land. He and Aerander enjoyed exploring a creek burrowed in the bay leaf forest. They used to catch newts and crayfish there.

Those memories were nice, but they didn't dispel how sore Dam was at Hanhau. He could feel the same resentment bottled up in his companions who trudged along in sharp silence. Dam wondered if they resented him as well. He was their representative. Attalos knew about Dam's special relationship with Hanhau. Hanhau had visited his home a lot. Likely that news had traveled around his group of friends, and now they would all be wondering why Dam couldn't have had a word with Hanhau about treating them like tag-alongs while the warriors handled the real business of their expedition.

But what was Dam supposed to do? Hanhau was in charge, and the captain of the company needed to be respected. Dam couldn't go strutting up to him to demand that his team be given more responsibility. That would embarrass both of them.

They passed by a campsite with quenched coals encircled by rocks. Bloodied rags had been tossed around the bank. One or more of the thieves had been injured badly in the Fire Canyon. Dam remembered the warriors whose faces and bodies had been scorched in the eruption of the Oomphalos Tower. Burning was the worst kind of injury. Little could be done to encourage healing, and cleaning and re-bandaging the wound was excruciating for the patient. Any one of Calyiches' party deserved that misery. Dam wished that it was Calyiches himself. With their leader encumbered, their party might have fractured while they bickered over who should lead them forward.

Later, the grotto opened up to a gulf of water. A strange cloud of light hovered over that glassy expanse like the milky aura of a crisp night sky. A fresh breeze as strong and boundless as the seaborne wind swept against Dam's face. Hanhau had mentioned a lake. Its proportions faded into the obscurity of the horizon.

Blix explained that the patches of light were from underground mayflies. Like many creatures of their country, the mayflies could conjure fire. This was the season when they mated and laid eggs on the water. The company wound along a ledge to the lake's lapping beach. Light like burnished silver reflected onto the shore. The coastline was a barren rock steppe as far as Dam could see.

A buzzing, blinding curtain of light whooshed toward the group from offshore. Dam ducked and shielded his eyes as the mob of mayflies rattled over his head and out to the water.

Hanhau and Ichika led the group onward. A short jaunt along the shore, they spotted another outpost of the traitors. Calyiches' party hadn't covered much ground after their previous harbor, leaving more bloody rags. It felt like icy wraiths of death hung over the spot, but no body was to be seen. Dam overheard Rad and Blix.

"I thought the Oomphalos could heal wounds," Rad said.

"It takes a conjurer to focus the stone's energies," Blix said. "Otherwise, its magic is diffuse. A wee dose of medicine for a mortal wound."

Dam understood. It had taken many fortnights for the stone to rejuvenate Hephad's tongue. Whoever had been burnt in the Fire Canyon didn't have time for a gradual recovery.

"That's a fool's justice," Rad said. "The idiots stole the most powerful thing in the underworld, and they have no idea how to use it." He was silent for a stretch, and then he turned to Blix again. "What are the chances they could figure out how to master its magic?"

"Our people have spent one hundred lifetimes studying the stone and only unlocked a few of its mysteries. That knowledge goes back to ancient times when the ones who forged the stone used its power to make a grand kingdom that would be eternally protected. Then came Ouroborus. She led a faction of men to steal the stone and slaughter every one of its original masters."

Dam pushed into the conversation. "But Ysalane knows how to use the stone, doesn't she?"

Blix took account of Dam and nodded. "Ysalane was chosen as a keeper of the stone's mysteries. She'll choose but one successor from the new generation to pass along the knowledge. It is an awesome power and a responsibility. You have seen the horrors that were unleashed from the stone when Ouroborus possessed it."

Dam's mind's eye flashed with images of the serpent-people, the New Ones. Their black-scaled bodies crested three times the height of a normal man, and they had knife-sized fangs that wept deadly venom. Bringing one down took three warriors and a battery of bolts and spears.

"So the stone can also be used as a weapon," Rad said.

"That's a sorcery that has only been commanded by very few," Blix said. He glanced at Dam. "Ouroborus. And Aerander."

Dam had seen Aerander wield the stone and seen a bolt of light flare from it like Poseidon's spear cast from the heavens. That otherworldly missile had transmuted the three-headed serpent queen Ouroborus to brittle cinders.

"How did Aerander learn to use the stone?" Rad asked Dam.

"He didn't," Dam said. "I mean, he just did." His cousin was somehow connected to the stone through his heritage, the line of Atlas. But that was a story that Dam didn't understand so well. The whole conversation was making him uneasy, as though traces of their voices might be heard by the Oomphalos. The stone was neither man nor creature, but it had a sentience about it. It could pull at men's hearts as it did with Ouroborus. Dam had felt that hypnotic enticement. He wondered if Rad had as well.

Blix gestured back to the traitor's camp. "This is not good. The stench of blood will bring out scavengers."

"What sort of scavengers?" Rad said.

Blix shrugged. "Carrion-beetles. Gulley-grouts."

"That doesn't sound so bad."

"A carrion-beetle has a jaw span big enough to swallow your head and a set of horns that can dig through rock."

That squelched the conversation. They marched forward in a uniform line of pairs. Walking beside Attalos on the steppe-side of their trail, Dam kept an eye on the veil of shadow offshore.

❖

After a hike that left Dam's legs leaden and clumsy, they reached the shoals of a mountain range. Its colossal textures were scarcely silhouetted in the darkness that lay ahead, especially as he tried to trace its heights. But Dam could feel its presence, a still, impenetrable wall. The voices of the men ahead of him were tinny and diminutive beneath the gravity of the mountains.

Hanhau called out to the group to make camp. The middle warriors who ferried the bulk of their provisions laid down their loads. Others came over to rustle through the boxed freight for the fire coals, the food, and the drinking vessels. In other circumstances, Dam would have welcomed the chance to rest, but he pushed into the cluster of activity. Picking up his cue, Attalos, Callios, Heron, and Rad followed him.

"We'll help," Dam announced.

He grasped two flagons to fill in the lake, and the others started unpacking the boxes. The warriors halted their work, thrown off by the change in their routine, but no one spoke up to stop the boys. Dam and Attalos went down to the lake with pairs of flagons while the others scoured the shore for rocks to bank a fire.

They made their campsite on a granite bed above the shore. The warriors stoked a thick, smoky fire from the coals. Everyone gathered around to eat and drink. Conversation was brusque while they swigged down water and filled their mouths with fish to replenish themselves. Afterward, they sat around looking out at the mysterious play of light on the water.

The haloed swarms of mayflies had diminished. Just like aboveground, the tiny creatures mated and laid their eggs and died. Dam tried to imagine what it would be like when those eggs hatched on the lake, all together, a phoenix rising from the darkness.

Hanhau and Ichika stood to discuss their plan.

"At our next rising, our lead group enters the mountain pass," Hanhau said. "The rest will keep watch here." He held up a conch horn on a chain. "This will be our signal. One bellow will say that we have made it across, and the passage is safe. Two will be a call for reinforcements."

Dam stared into the obscurity of the mountains. If the fault shifted while Hanhau and the others were in there, they could be swallowed by that chasm and never seen again. He searched for the sound or the feel of motion on the floor beneath his legs but felt nothing. The party split to bathe down at the lake and roll out pallets. Dam remained in place. He hoped that Hanhau would as well. Dam ventured a glance up at him. Hanhau stepped over and sat down on the floor.

"How are you faring?" Hanhau said.

"You should let us come with you."

Hanhau inhaled a sharp breath.

"It makes sense," Dam said. "We're the weakest unit. Better us than the strongest ones if something goes wrong. You'd have a good group left to keep pursuing Calyiches."

"Nothing will go wrong."

They were silent. The space between their hands, resting at their sides, was miniscule, and it would have been entirely natural for Dam to take Hanhau's hand in his to say they were together in the mission and more than just two mates talking about it. But what if that made Hanhau angry? They could be seen by the other warriors.

Hanhau patted Dam's hand and stood. "You should wash up and get some rest."

"*You* need rest. Let my group keep watch overnight. You've got to let us do something."

Hanhau's brow wrinkled. His posture was weighed down, and the light drawn up in his face was faint. "I suppose you can take the first watch with Blix."

Dam shot up to his feet. He gazed at Hanhau gratefully. That was all that he could do to express his feelings. He clambered down to the lake to tell the others about the first watch.

Chapter Six

While the warriors bedded themselves at camp, Dam, Attalos, Rad, and Blix took up a post on a bluff of rock looking out to the steppe. Callios and Heron posted themselves near the beach, looking back the way their party had come. Their camp was hemmed in on two sides by the mountains and the lake. Hanhau said any danger would likely come from the rock plain, which stretched outward from the lake to a sightless distance.

Dam had brought an oil lantern, and he and his companions had put their shifts and chain aprons back on and holstered their scabbards on their backs. Blix had brought an iron crook and worn the conch horn around his neck. They all gazed out at the cloaked horizon. The lantern shone only a few yards into that vast void. A breath of wind whispered across the plain, but nothing more was to be heard.

"How long do we keep watch?" Attalos asked Blix.

"Until Kish and Puchan come to relieve us," Blix said.

After a while, Attalos piped up again. "How will they know it's time to wake up?"

"They will," Blix told him.

"I spent a night keeping watch on a maneuver through the jungle," Rad said. "My father had rounded up his best legionnaires to clear a path for a new route between the capital and our trade cities farther inland. That cursed backcountry was teeming with cannibals and saber-toothed tigers."

Dam and Attalos exchanged a look that was not precisely an eye-roll but close to it.

"How many cannibals did you kill?" Attalos said.

"Didn't have to kill any if you played it smart. If you ever saw a cannibal, you'd understand. Better to stay out of their detection rather than to take them head on."

"What about saber-toothed tigers?" Dam said.

"Same principle," Rad said. He glanced at Attalos and Dam, appearing to be adding up that they were making fun of him. He shook his head. "Bet neither one of you has ever even used a blade."

Dam hadn't, but he remembered using the blunt handle of Aerander's *xiphos* to batter the High Priest Zazamoukh in the back of the head when he had held Aerander and Lys prisoner and was going to feed them to the New Ones. He told Rad that story.

Rad snorted. "That took balls, but not much skill."

"It brought the priest down to the floor and knocked him out for the rest of the day," Dam said. "If I hadn't done it, none of us would be here right now. Aerander and Lys would be dead." He looked to the sightless ceiling above them. "You'd be fish fodder up there in the sea."

"You should learn to use the other end of a *xiphos*," Rad said. He stepped away, reached over his shoulder to unsheathe his blade, and brandished it in front of him in a fighting stance. He waved his free hand at Dam and Attalos. "C'mon."

Dam and Attalos looked at one another. Rad was full of himself and bossy, but both boys could use pointers on using their blades. Dam asked Blix if it would be all right.

"Go ahead," Blix said. "I'll keep lookout."

The two boys came over in front of Rad. He gestured for them to unsheathe their swords, and he went from one to the other to correct their grips.

"A *xiphos* is a one-handed weapon. Leaves your other hand free to box." Once he had molded their hands on the hilt of their swords, Rad stepped back into an open space and deftly made some cross-strokes in the air while throwing out his fist at different angles. That left Dam confounded. It was like trying to follow the movements of a pair of scissors on wheels. Attalos gave it a try and dropped his *xiphos*, which landed on the ground with a clang.

"That's more advanced technique," Rad said. He came around Attalos and mantled the boy's body with his taller frame. "The foundation of everything is balance." He pivoted Attalos' hips with his hands so that the boy stood sidelong, and he nudged apart the boy's ankles so that his legs were spread with one foot anchored behind the other. Rad positioned Attalos' upper body so that his fighting arm was thrown forward with his blade standing vertical. He bent Attalos' other arm at his side.

Rad patted that arm. "That's your counterbalance. Don't worry about using it for fighting yet. Just remember to keep it tucked and loose. That helps when you need to swivel to the side or dart away."

Dam gazed at Attalos with admiration. He really looked like a fighter.

Rad stepped over to Dam and went through the same motions with him. Dam tried to bury a blush from the contact of the young soldier's warm, martially trained body against his. He felt small and shy, but Dam pushed those thoughts out of his brain. He had to maintain a serious attitude. He didn't want Rad thinking he was girlish.

After that lesson on stances, Rad told them to try maneuvering their blades. The motion came from the wrist and the forearm. After trying to skirmish with his blade, Dam understood why Rad's forearms were so impressively developed. His were sore and drained. He felt like a weakling.

"It takes work to build endurance," Rad said. "There's exercises to get those forearms stronger. But the best way to get you into shape is to practice sparring." He clipped Dam on the arm to draw him over to a spot where they faced one another. Rad assumed a fighting stance. Dam did his best to imitate him.

"Besides your blade, your most important weapon is your eyes," Rad said. He came at Dam with shallow swings, staring at him like a wolf locked in on a kill. "Never take them off your opponent," Rad said. "Home in on the spot to plant your blade. Keep your eyes fixed there and follow through with your attack."

Dam raised his sword to block Rad's advance. Rad came at him slowly and deliberately, and even though Rad held back for the demonstration, Dam struggled to parry the boy's swings and lunges. He sidled backward, lost traction with his sword, and Rad's weapon poked into the mesh of his apron covering his heart.

Rad turned away and drew Attalos into a practice skirmish. Attalos managed better than Dam had at first. He parried Rad's attack, pivoting around defensively, but Rad wore him down to a point where Rad trapped his blade helplessly in front of his chest. Rad cuffed Attalos' throat with his free hand.

Rad pushed off Attalos with the ghost of a smile on his face. "You learn best fighting a more experienced opponent," he said. "I had to do daily rounds with the veterans in my father's company. We don't have time for that kind of training out here. You ought to practice with each other."

Dam locked eyes with Attalos grimly.

"Go on," Rad said. "You're not aiming to open an artery. Just get used to protecting yourselves. Keeping that blade raised."

The two boys squared off. Even though it was play, Dam's heartbeat pulsed at his temples, and his head was damp with sweat. He had to show his best in front of Rad and his friend, but on the other hand, they each had weapons that could gouge a serious flesh wound if they weren't handled right.

Dam held his *xiphos* in front of him. Attalos swiped at him tentatively. Dam parried back, and the boys tried out each other's strength, clashing and scraping their weapons. Hanhau was an expert warrior, Dam remembered. He ought to learn something that would impress Hanhau. Dam went at it more forcefully. He caught the side of Attalos' blade, bending it away from him. It felt like he was gaining an advantage. Attalos twisted his weapon out of that and clobbered Dam's blade, the vibration shuddering up his arm like a hammer on a bell. Dam's sword fell feebly from his grip.

"That's the idea, city boy," Rad said to Attalos.

Dam looked down to his weapon on the ground. It was a painfully humiliating moment that was quickly cut short. Just then, Blix shouted back to the boys.

"I need you all up here now."

❖

Dam grabbed his *xiphos* and hurried over with the others to the lip of the bluff where Blix stood. The warrior stared out at the pitch black field. His hand was tensed on his iron crook, but Dam couldn't see anything out there. He listened keenly, finally hearing a scurry of feet that made Dam think of an infestation.

"What is it?"

Blix pointed his crook at the field. "There."

A shadow emerged from the darkness into the lantern's glow. It was a gargantuan insect with a shell as big as a rowboat, barbed forelegs, and a scissoring mandible, alerted to the opportunity to shred flesh. The creature halted in the light, seeming to take notice that it had been discovered.

"Carrion beetles," Blix said. "They must have been drawn out to this region from the smell of blood that Calyiches' party left behind."

Beetles? Dam thought. *Meaning more than one?*

The creature charged at them. Beyond, the silhouettes of more domed monsters scurried after it in a swarm. Blix bellowed out an alarm from the conch horn to call the men to arms back at the camp. He gestured for the boys to spread out along the ridge of their lookout. In proportion to the beetles, the bluff where they stood was not much of a barrier.

The first beetle charged up toward Blix, who batted its barbed forelegs with his crook to stop its advance, and then he drove the sharpened hook of his weapon inside the creature's spiny jaws and ripped it out with a spatter of black blood. The monster foundered down the slope onto its back with a hair-raising squeal. It was quickly buried by a pack of its kind who sprung from the shadows to feast on its blood.

"We need archers," Rad called out.

Blix shook his head. "That won't help much. Iron bolts can't penetrate their shells. You've got to get in close range to stab inside their mouths and gore their brains. Or if you can get them on their backs, strike between their plates into their guts."

A line of beetles clambered over the feeding frenzy to advance to the shelf. Blix and Rad held their ground at the top, swinging their weapons for any legs they could reach. Sensible instincts told Dam to run, but their outpost was the only barrier between the monster beetles and the camp. He gripped his sword in front of him as Rad had shown him and surveyed the space below. Whether he was ready or not, the time had come for him to be a soldier.

A giant beetle scuttled up the rock shelf toward him. They were blind creatures, but as Blix had said, they had no problem sniffing out a meal. Dam swung his sword at one of the beetle's forelegs, but the beetle had five other legs powering it. Dam swung at its other foreleg. The creature climbed higher. Its bristly antennae licked the air at Dam's feet, and its spiked jaws—big enough to swallow his arm—gnashed.

Dam pounded his sword into the cap of its head. That barely dazed the creature. One of its forelegs grasped the top of the ledge. Dam jumped from that spot, searching wildly for a place to strike the impenetrable creature. He lunged for the spot between its snapping jaws, leaving his hand far too close to the creature's mouth. He didn't make a clean strike, but he heard a pop of soft tissue. The beetle's head reeled. Dam cried out ferociously and struck inside its jaws again, carving his blade upward. The husk of the beetle collapsed while its legs writhed feebly. Dam swallowed back bile from his throat.

His victory was miraculous, but before Dam could take much account of it or glance to see how his companions were doing, two more beetles climbed over the one he had maimed. Dam swung for the one closest to him and tripped it. The other beetle gained up. Dam had barely handled one. How was he going to survive two?

He thrashed his *xiphos* and hacked off one of the creature's antennae. He turned to the other, exploding with a roar, and struck out wildly for its jaws. That pushed the monster down the ledge a bit. From the corner of Dam's eye, he saw its partner crawling up to the top. Its last pair of legs were crowning the lip.

Dam swiped cold sweat from his brow and faced the creature. Its barbed jaws were at the height of his belly. If it stampeded, it could easily knock him over and rip him apart with its knife-sharp legs. Dam slashed his sword in front of him. He had to try to intimidate the thing until he figured out some way to kill it.

The creature drew toward him warily. His strategy wasn't working. He glanced back at the ledge where he had held off the other beetle. Its antennae and jaws had crested the hill. Dam backed away, caught his heel on uneven ground, and fell on his bottom. He did not drop his *xiphos*, however. That weapon was welded to his hand.

The monster lurched toward him. Dam sat up and guarded himself with his blade and his outstretched hand, praying to the gods for the best. He clashed against the creature's pincer jaws. It pushed forward, pressing Dam's back against the ground while he grasped his *xiphos* with both hands to brace the creature's gnashing shears.

It felt like the end. Dam's blade was caught at the back of the beetle's jaws, and those pincers reached one hand's width from his face. The rank stench of its insides curdled in his throat. Even if he had the strength to maneuver his blade to puncture the beetle's mouth, its jaws would rip into his face when he did so. Dam remembered something Blix had said. It was a desperate tactic, but what choice did he have?

He relaxed his blade from the creature's forward momentum for an instant so that its jaws hovered over his head and his sword was bent back parallel to the ground. With his knees bent and his feet dug into the ground, he used the traction of his sword to slide beneath the beetle. As the creature lurched forward, Dam stabbed upward wildly. He met thick walls of shell that wouldn't give. Darkness closed in from the corners of his eyes. His strength was slipping away in a swoon. Dam screamed out hoarsely to will away his panic.

He jabbed his sword into a fleshy crevice of the beetle's belly, and then he wrenched the blade out and stabbed even more viciously a second time. Thick, black blood poured down his arms. The creature wailed in distress. Dam forced his blade upward again and again, breaking open a gash that no monster, however big and powerful, could withstand. The beetle shuddered. Its lifeless body collapsed on top of Dam.

Now the danger was suffocation. The animal was mainly husk and weighed no more than a large man, but it spread over Dam like a tarp and was saturating him with its blood and guts. He tried to push it up and away from his body. That didn't achieve much, so he tried to twist and crawl his way out from under it.

Scurrying movements surrounded him. A herd of beetles? Sharp legs scraped against the shell of Dam's kill. Weight pressed down from its carcass. The horrible things were on top of him. They were probably on all sides of him. They had come to scavenge the dead beetle and when they discovered him, he would be a succulent surprise for their dinner.

Dam fumbled to get a grip on his *xiphos*. When the creatures turned over the shell to feast, it would be his last stand. By the gods, he would take as many of them along with him to his death as he could. Jaws scraped and dug beneath the shell. Adrenaline flooded Dam in a second wave of anticipation. The creature's carcass lifted from his body.

There was a hail of metal arrows, and the carcass fell back on top of Dam. War cries ripped through the night. Beetles gnashed and squealed. Blades shrieked against the armored creatures. Warriors gutted their opponents with juicy pops. Gradually, silence settled over everything. Men's voices drew up frantically around Dam.

The shell heaved over, exposing Dam to the night. He tried to wipe the blood from his eyes and face with his bare hands, but they were shaky and coated with the foul stuff as well. He searched through a stinging blur to make out the men who had rescued him.

A hand gripped his and pulled him up very forcefully from the ground. Dam wobbled a bit on his legs. The world seemed to be careening like a ship on the open sea. The man who had helped him up supported his weight against his shoulder. Someone brought over a cloth, and the man cleaned off the blood from Dam's face.

An opalescent glow brightened before his eyes. Dam recognized Hanhau. His boyfriend looked stricken by the sight of him. Dam couldn't imagine how gory he must have looked. He had been smothered by a gutted beetle the size of an ox. Hanhau gripped Dam hard against his armored chest.

CHAPTER SEVEN

They didn't have a moment to rest or even to speak about the victory over the carrion beetles. Ichika called the other warriors to action, hauling the carcasses into piles so they could be set ablaze. Every bloody part of them had to be incinerated so they would not draw more scavengers to the camp. In the stingy underworld, creatures scoured stone for any sort of flesh. The greatest worry was fire scorpions.

Miraculously, not one of Ysalane's sixteen had been lost during the invasion. Blix had taken a gouge to his arm, Heron was bandaged from a hard fall on his head, but otherwise the battle wounds were routine scrapes and bruises. The warriors had mobilized quickly to back up the boys at their outposts.

Dam followed Hanhau to wash up down at the lake. He spotted Rad and Attalos helping the warriors clean up the camp site. They stopped their work for a moment and glanced at him with quiet respect.

Dam threw off his metal mesh apron and peeled his tunic over his head at the shore. The tunic would have to be burned, and he was happy to be rid of the bloodied thing that reeked of the beetle's entrails. In the wake of goring the beetle and nearly being smothered by it, everything around him felt distant and unreal. He stripped bare in front of Hanhau without any modesty.

Then he looked down at his sandals. Anguish welled up from his heart. His sandals were the only thing he truly owned. He had cut out the soles himself by tracing his feet and cobbled together the laces at the leatherworks in the priests' precinct. Now they were blackened with the creatures' blood. They would have to be burned.

Hanhau bent down and gently removed the sandals from his feet. "They can be washed," he told Dam. Hanhau stripped down to his under-skirting and carried the sandals and an armful of washcloths into the shallows of the lake.

Dam waded into the water. His arms, his legs, and his hair were slathered with greasy black blood. It had congealed in places into a putrid crust. He squatted into the water to submerge himself completely, and he scoured and wrung his hands through his thick hair. The water did its work, but still Dam wondered if he would ever rid himself of the awful beetle stench. No soaps could remedy that stink.

When he resurfaced, Hanhau guided him near and took up a washrag to scrub Dam's face. He rinsed the rag and wrung it out and ran it clean over Dam's neck and shoulders, down one arm then another. Dam hadn't been bathed by someone else since he was a child. Having Hanhau wash him was many times more luxurious. He crouched down on the floor of the lake so he was covered below the waist.

Hanhau slid the cloth across his chest, and it tangled on something. Dam remembered he was still wearing Aerander's amulet. Beneath his tunic and his apron, it had been easily forgotten. Dam hadn't liked thinking about wearing the amulet anyway. He had plenty of strange things to think about on the expedition without wondering if the voice of a goddess was going to enter his head out of the blue. Hanhau's face was pained.

"You could have been killed."

Dam guided his boyfriend's hand to wash beneath his arm. "I wasn't."

Hanhau's hand stayed suspended in the air. He spoke in a strained mutter. "I thought I was prepared for this. I thought I could keep you safe."

"You don't have to stop washing."

Hanhau looked at him crossly. "I'm serious, Dam. This expedition is incredibly dangerous."

"I've caught on," Dam said. "You might have noticed that I got covered in beetle guts."

"It's not funny."

"Truly? I look like I've been birthed from a beetle's bowels."

Hanhau hid his face in shadow. Dam stood up in the water. He was getting an uneasy feeling from Hanhau again.

"You're not going to tell me that I'm going back to the city."

Hanhau said nothing.

"I could have been killed. *You* could have been killed. Any of us could have been killed. But we weren't," Dam said. "You said that we're comrades out here. That means that you have to treat me as an equal."

"We're not just comrades. You're more than that to me." Hanhau hesitated for a moment. "Your people call us 'the banished race,' and the elders teach us that we were forsaken by the Creator God. But when we met, I knew that wasn't true. He sent you to me, from the surface world, and gave me someone to love."

Warmth spread across Dam's chest. He clasped Hanhau's bare shoulder and massaged the tension in that spot. Pushing up on the tips of his feet, he pressed his lips against Hanhau's. It was just a peck, and no one was around to see it. They were all back at the camp. But Dam could feel Hanhau's body compacting warily.

"You're more than a comrade to me too," Dam said, "but if we can't do a little thing like *that*, we might as well just be comrades."

Hanhau slid his hand into Dam's. He squeezed, and all his pent up tension nearly crushed Dam's bones. "You have to be careful," he told Dam.

Dam removed his aching hand and shook it with a scowl. "I'm doing my best. I took on two of those carrion beetles."

"You fought honorably. The other warriors are impressed."

Dam grabbed a washcloth drifting nearby and scrubbed at his belly. "Blix and Rad did most of the work. Rad taught me and Attalos how to use our swords. We did all right, I guess."

Hanhau grinned. They sat together in the gentle waves of the lake looking back to the camp while Dam finished his washing. Bonfires sparked and raised up fiery columns on the shore. A commotion broke out about the horrid stench. Everywhere, burning embers floated in the air like a snowfall of shiny gold.

Hanhau held Dam's hand below the water. "We can't clean up everything," he said. "There's blood splatter all around the camp. The beetles will come back."

"What can we do?"

Hanhau stared toward the shrouded mountains. "We'll have one last rest and take that passage through the mountains where Calyiches led his party. All of us will go. It's not safe for anyone to stay back at the camp."

❖

Later, when everyone was gathered around a fire for food and drink, Hanhau proposed the change in plans. Rad, Attalos, Callios, and Heron shot up to their feet and hollered. The warriors joined in thumping their armor-scaled chests. They were one company, and they would stay that way through their expedition.

Blix cried out, "The iron belly of the caterpillar drums forward. Let our enemies cower from the rumble of our march or die from the hail of our blades."

CHAPTER EIGHT

The trail into the mountain headlands was narrow, with steep climbs and far-spread footholds. They took things in stages to conserve their energy and to allow Hanhau and Ichika to scout above for the possibility of falling rocks. Naturally, without sun or sky, Dam found it impossible to perceive the extent or height of the barrier they scaled, and the terrain was too troublesome to manage torches. When the warriors' light was near, he could make out the mountain's marbled textures. In spots, it was as white as ivory; and as black and grainy as silt elsewhere. It was an ancient range of mountains, cropped up from the steppe like the colossal teeth of a titan.

Should its jaws tremble and clench, his group had geared up with harnesses strapped across their chests and around the high flanks of their legs. They had linked to one another with a climbing line. Blix was the lead, and he looked after Rad. Rad spotted Dam for their climbs, Dam spotted Attalos, and so on to Callios and Heron and the flail bearers.

After they had achieved some height, Hanhau called for them to stop at a ledge where they could take swigs from the water flagons. Dam looked out the way they had come. Beyond a few yards, all he could see was an eternal hollow of shadow. The mating of the fireflies on the lake had ended. Somewhere down there, they had left mounds of ashes from the bonfires of the beetles. Everyone said the beetles would come back to scour the land clean of any trace of blood and flesh. Wind shrieked from the heights above Dam. As hospitable as their anchorage was, it seemed like a harbor between one wicked zone and another.

For the next leg, they rounded the treacherous rim of an escarpment, and then they came to a steep hike that traversed the face of a higher shelf. Dam kept pace with Rad and looked back to Attalos to see he was keeping up as well. The danger of being chained together was that it took just one of them falling out of step to drag their whole line back and downward.

To preserve the breath in their lungs, they climbed without talking. Dam's thoughts wandered to his cousin, bedded in the city infirmary, hopefully gaining strength or at least holding down food and water until they returned with the Oomphalos. Wryly, it occurred to Dam that if Aerander had been well, he would have embraced their journey with unflappable optimism. Faced with an army of ox-size beetles, Aerander would have led the charge, armored by his belief that honor always prevailed. Without a doubt, he would have prevailed. He had faced the giant, three-headed serpent queen Ouroborus and brought her down. As Dam had often said, Aerander had been dipped in gold at his birth.

But now Aerander was blind and crippled. That situation ached deeper in Dam's bones the farther he traveled from his cousin. Dam had turned from Aerander at times because he felt his cousin didn't need him, but he realized now that the Fates had given Aerander labors that would crush an ordinary man. Worst of all, Aerander had watched the sea wash away the Citadel and drown his family. He was haunted in his dreams by his father, whom he had not been able to rescue from death.

And since the evacuation, the one thing Aerander had wanted above all else was for the two of them to be brothers again.

Dam hadn't done right by Aerander. He had pushed him away at a time when Aerander needed him the most. Dam wished like mad he could speak to Aerander at that moment, to say that he had been a stubborn fool and to ask for his forgiveness. He hated being stuck with those feelings so many miles away from his cousin. All Dam could do was to hope to get through their mission quickly and to pledge on his heart that he would make it up to Aerander as soon as he returned to the city.

Voices called down the line, scattering those thoughts from Dam's head.

"They reached the mountain pass," Rad told him. "It's level ground, and a good spot to rest."

❖

At the height of their climb, two horns of stone towered into the darkness, and there was a scrabbly descent into a slim gorge in between.

That was the mountain pass. It was only wide enough for two men to walk abreast. The cloak of a starless night obscured its depth, and Dam couldn't tell if its colossal escarpments had caved in some places or verged together to pinch the route closed. It was going to be like blindly excavating a cave.

They detached their lines and harnesses and stowed their equipment in their cargo crates. Dam hadn't noticed the change in temperature during their grueling scale into the headlands, but when his company sat down for a spell, he was quickly cold and damp in his sweat-soaked shift. He had no more clothes to change into or to layer over what he was wearing. The boys had dressed in their spare pairs of garments after they had stripped off their bloodied tunics to burn in the beetle bonfire.

The warriors set up a brazier and pitched a kettle of soup above the flames to warm the meal. Dam and his friends sat near to the fire, flexing their grip-sore hands against the heat of the coals. Rad's red-bristled, fire-cast face twisted up in a scowl. "You have to credit the bastards. They sorted out a way through the mountains."

Attalos and the others nodded along with him. But Dam wasn't so sure about the pass that Calyiches' party had found. He had an awful feeling about it, and just then, the bone amulet trembled against his chest. Had that been the shiver of his own body? Dam stared into the ravine ahead of them, listening and trying to sense movement in the ground. There was nothing.

Attalos nudged his ribs. "What do you think they put in that kettle? A wee dram of beetle guts for some extra flavor?"

The other boys groaned and grimaced.

"Least it's warm," Callios said. "I'm tired of cold, salted fish."

"What's the difference?" Heron said. "It'll be *warm*, salted fish. Tastes the bloody same."

Attalos leaned back with his hands interlaced behind his head. "I dream of meat."

Callios and Heron exchanged a bawdy grin. "What's that?" Callios said. He cupped his hands between his legs. "A plump and juicy sausage?"

"Or Hephad's meat-balls," Heron said.

They cackled like fools. Dam glanced at Attalos. He was chuckling and taking it in stride. The boys heckled each other back and forth. Dam tried to loosen up and join the conversation, but that ominous sensation he had felt in his chest bothered him. They ladled their soup into bowls and wolfed it down like starved dogs. When all the soup had been drank, Hanhau stood to address the group.

"We hike forward for another stretch. There's no time to waste if we want to make up ground on our quarry. There's signs of their camp faltering farther in. With a good push, we can gain up on them in another portage."

"Will there be more beetles?" Rad said.

"Not likely. They nest in deeper parts. The principal danger is millworms. They can drill clear through rock. That's mainly what they eat, but they won't turn away from grinding whatever's in their path into pulp."

"Big?" Rad said.

Hanhau encircled his long arms in front of him. "You'll see for yourself. There's a bore hole up ahead. It's noisy work drilling, so you'll hear them coming. We haven't noticed any sign of them, which is another good reason for us to get a move on."

Rad's face relaxed. He looked over his companions. "We'll be ready for them."

Ichika joined in. "No millworms is a good thing on one hand, but a possible danger on the other. The creatures can sense the fault in these mountains. They burrow to safer ground when they feel it seizing up."

Dam flattened his hand on the ravine floor. It was still. No sign of man-sized, drilling worms. No trembling from faults shuddering open, either. Let it stay that way, he prayed.

Ichika told the boys, "If there's a tremor while we're in there, there's a few things you can do. Find cover under the escarpment or a fallen boulder. If you can't do that, stay in place, get down to the floor and protect your head."

Dam exchanged a dubious look with Attalos. That didn't sound like much help if they faced a barrage of falling rock.

❖

For their trek into the passage, the warriors kept their raised hands aglow like torches. That provided a trail of signals for the route ahead. Fallen boulders had spilled into the gorge in places, and the floor was fractured badly enough to trip on. Some of those splintered spots looked deep to Dam. It was too dim to say for sure.

They stopped for a moment to marvel at the wormhole that Hanhau had mentioned. It was a smooth socket, perfectly rounded, on the side of the ravine and at the level of their shoulders. Blix, the boldest, stuck his head into it. The hole was three times big enough. Blix turned to the others with a grin.

"An old trick—you might be able to hear what's going on at the other side of the mountain."

He ducked his head back in and bellowed, "Hello." Then he leaned in with his ear. He came back with a shrug. "Guess there's nobody there."

Rad passed by the hole, leaned his head into it for a breath, and went on his way.

Dam looked into it. The walls were ribbed in even bands, which brought to mind a helical motion of a creature's body, like the bit of a carpenter's drill. The burrow was still and obscure. Dam backed off from it to let Attalos take a look. He wasn't going to holler his name into it and rouse something in there.

Continuing, he walked shoulder to shoulder with Attalos for some stretches and in front of him where they had to go single file. Besides the rustle of their movements and the occasional echo of quiet conversations among the pairs, the ravine felt very quiet and peaceful. Initially, Dam had been wary of the narrow walls that stretched a sightless distance above him. He imagined them crushing in from both sides, having nowhere to run, being suffocated by rock. The easy hike pulled him out of those worries. Besides, Attalos liked to talk when he was nervous, and that kept Dam distracted.

After a short, silent spell, Attalos turned to Dam and said, "This might be a funny time to ask. But did you and Hanhau ever…"

Dam grinned. "Looking for pointers for when you get back to Hephad?"

"Just curious is all. You don't have to tell me if you don't want to."

Dam told him bluntly, "We can't."

Attalos' breath quashed. Though their faces were shadowed, with the light from Blix' hand a good five strides ahead of them, Dam could picture the contortions of confusion on Attalos' face. It made him grin.

Attalos stuttered, "You mean, he doesn't…"

"He has everything that you and I have," Dam said. Just because the warriors washed up separately and didn't walk around camp fresh from their baths didn't mean a person couldn't detect certain things.

Attalos sounded entirely earnest. Dam decided to explain things less flippantly.

"For one thing, we can't do it at camp. If one of us is lying down to bed, the other is keeping watch. It wouldn't be right anyway since we have to keep our focus." Dam hesitated, trying to find the right words for the rest of the story. "For another, the big reason, it's that they change when they're with someone that way."

Attalos' voice sprang back at him. "Change how?"

"They molt. The scales around their chests fall off. They grow back, but he can't very well lead an expedition unprotected like that."

A nervous laugh hiccupped from Attalos. "That's kind of gross, don't you think?"

"I think it's kind of gross that you like Hephad."

"It looks the same underneath the scales?"

"Just like you and me."

"How do you know?"

"They open up a bit, and if you look real close you can see underneath."

"That's bonkers, Dam. But…everything else is the same?"

Dam smiled. "So far. I guess I won't know exactly until we get back to the city."

Attalos guffawed. "I guess he is sort of handsome. Putting aside the scales and the fueling-on-and-off like a lantern bit. You really like him?"

"I do."

"Makes it hard, having to wait?"

"Hard like a brick."

They both laughed at the pun.

"Hephad wants to wait too. At first, I guess he was self-conscious about his tongue. Then the big disaster happened, and we had all that work to do and me leaving on this trip. I think he was afraid that if we did it, I'd come back not wanting to be with him anymore. You know he's a bit jealous. Especially of you."

"What does he have to be jealous of?"

"I told him that. He's a bit insecure."

"A bit."

Attalos drew a breath. "This isn't meant to offend you. But people talk, and, you know, they say you've been with a lot of boys."

Heat rose up Dam's collar. "*A lot of boys*. How many do they say I've been with? How many have you seen me with? We practically live in the same house."

Attalos spoke in a hush. "I'm just telling you what other people say."

"People. Like Hephad?"

He didn't reply. Dam breathed in deeply. He felt ready to explode. Why couldn't people just ask him instead of talking behind his back about what he did or didn't do? Normally that pushed him to make up stories even wilder than what people were saying just in spite, but he realized Attalos genuinely wanted to know.

"Hephad and I have known each other a long time. He knows I've been with a few boys in the past. If you're wondering about Leo and Koz, the answer is yes. Biggest blunder of my life. And you can bet that ninety-nine out of a hundred stories they told about me aren't true."

"I didn't think..." Attalos started to say. "I mean, Hephad is very careful is all."

Dam sighed dramatically. "He thought I wouldn't be able to resist perverting you?" He reached to pat Attalos on his bottom.

Attalos laughed. "Some men are like that, you know. They'll do it with anyone."

"Three-quarters," Dam said.

"What's that?"

"It's fractions. It's something I do in my head when I can't sleep at night. I figure out how many boys or men I ran into that day, and I think about how many of them I would do it with. Usually comes out to three-quarters."

"That's a lot!"

"Try it yourself. You'll be surprised." He faced Attalos. "There's a difference between wanting to do it with someone and actually doing it with them. We're men. It's the same with the ones who like women. Remember what Rad said? Think about how many boys are dreaming about getting one of those seven women to bed because they're so mad for sex."

"Some of the women are old, and not even pretty." Attalos' voice rose up incredulously. "They'll have the pick of the litter."

"Right."

Each of them minded his thoughts for a moment. Traveling

shoulder to shoulder in the murky ravine, it was a lot like the nights when Dam and Aerander had stayed up late talking in bed after the lamps in the men's side of the estate had been turned down.

"Do you talk to Hanhau about fancying other men?" Attalos said.

"No. He's kind of…virtuous about those things."

"I could never say anything like that to Hephad. Fun talking about it, though, isn't it?"

"It is."

Attalos was quiet for a stretch. That piqued Dam's curiosity.

"You're counting, aren't you?"

"Quiet now. You made me lose track."

"It's just the people you met today. There's only sixteen of us."

"I was trying to decide if I should count the warriors."

Dam told him flatly, "They're men." Dam waited while they took a dozen or so more strides. "What did you come up with?"

"I think it's two-thirds. But I was never good with numbers."

"Your father was a pawnbroker."

"He didn't have me counting purses on the deeds."

"How were you supposed to learn the business?"

"I kept up the shop. Put items in the vault and hauled them out for customers. Kept things polished and dusted off so they would sell. I don't think my father intended for me to learn the business. My older sister Eugenia was always better with coin. He put her in charge of customers when he was out."

Dam laughed. "Never mind. What number did you come up with?"

"It's twelve."

"That's not two-thirds. That's three-quarters."

"Can't be so!"

"Well, you don't count yourself, so it's twelve by fifteen. But it works out close enough."

"Think it's the same fraction for every man?"

"Probably." Dam's eyes gleamed mischievously as he bumped his shoulder against his friend. "Bet Rad's in that twelve."

Attalos snickered. "Almost left him out because he's such a know-it-all. Suppose it doesn't matter, though, if his mouth is closed."

"Or occupied."

They giggled.

"Twelve minus four of us boys means there's at least eight warriors on your list."

"I thought things through a bit broadly."

"I bet I can name them."

"Quiet now. Don't be an idiot."

"Blix."

"Dam!"

"Hold on a moment. There's eleven warriors, and three of them are women. You'd screw all eight of the men."

Attalos wrangled Dam's arm behind his back. "Stop it. It's not funny."

Dam couldn't help his laughter, Attalos caught it, and they both burst into hysterics.

"Are you serious?" Rad hollered back at them. "What the hell are you two cutting up about?"

"Sorry," Attalos called out.

Dam straightened out, too. But was there really anything wrong about joking around a bit?

"You two are stumbling along like sailors on a bender, and there could be giant worms bursting out of the ravine," Rad said. "We're all on lookout, and we're counting on every man to keep his wits together and have a quick hand on his blade."

Dam told him, "It won't happen again."

"Really nice show for the House of Atlas."

Dam almost responded sharply to that comment, but a cry rose up ahead, startling everybody.

"Company, halt."

CHAPTER NINE

They idled in the ravine waiting for the call to proceed. Dam fretted over what the matter could be. A tight underpass in the trail ahead? A dead end? Something worse? So many things could be worse. Dam's body was steeped in dread and anticipation, but he was ready to take on whatever danger awaited him.

After the scolding from Rad, he and Attalos didn't dare to talk while everyone stood around, glancing from time to time at the hazy aura of light from Blix's upraised hand. There must have been a bend in the trail in front of him. Dam couldn't see any farther than the lead man of their team.

Finally, Blix waved their unit forward. They traveled around the bend. The beacons of the unit, the freight bearers, appeared ahead. After another bow in the trail, they came to a broader hollow. Everyone in the company had halted there. From the combined light of the warriors, the socket was as well-lit as a room with fully fueled gas lamps, but they were pressed together pretty tightly. Dam perched on the tips of his sandals and craned above and around the backs of the front line warriors. Hanhau was standing farther ahead beneath a notch in one side of the ravine, and Ichika and the archers were drawn up beside him.

Hanhau motioned to his countrymen. "Let them through."

Blix led Dam's group through the parting of the warriors, nudging against shoulders, taking it sidewise, until they came to the place where Hanhau was standing. Hanhau looked at Dam gravely. He stepped away from a shallow notch in the ravine wall. He and Ichika summoned a white glow into their hands and reflected it against the wall.

A body, pale blue with death, lay curled on the floor. Dam trapped his mouth with his hand and glanced away a moment. Then he looked back at the corpse again. One leg was charred black with an angry gash where the skin had shriveled. The body had wasted and set like plaster into a cringing, skeletal pose—spine bowed, knees drawn into the belly, elbows bent, and a rigid, bony hand covering its face. Dam recognized the shaggy hair crowning the head, though it had dulled and yellowed like a dried jasmine flower. He recognized the high cheekbones and the snub nose that the hand had been too weak to shield.

It was Leo.

"A miracle he made it so far," Rad said. He looked to Hanhau. "You've got to figure they carried him as far as they could. There's no way that leg could have withstood any weight."

"He's not long dead," Ichika said. "His body hasn't loosened from the grip of death. Even here in the mountains, scavengers like crone midges find their way to rotting flesh in short time."

Dam had seen crone midges before. They had spectral wings, as big as the palm of his hand, and a needle-like proboscis for penetrating any sort of rubbish. Mostly, they buzzed outside the sculleries before the rubbish bins had been sealed up.

Rad meanwhile carried on a conversation with Hanhau speculating on how long ago Leo's injury had occurred and how it had progressed to his morbid state. Though Ichika clearly was as knowledgeable as Hanhau, Rad acted like she wasn't there.

Blix spoke out. "We should push on. The rest of his party should be a short stretch from here."

Dam stared at Leo's body. It was justice, but seeing the boy so profaned clutched at a tender spot in Dam's heart. Maybe the gods were truly paying attention to what was happening in the underworld. They had served Leo a fatal dose of the misery he had caused.

"He should have his rites before we move on," Dam said.

Chain mail skirting clinked as the warriors shifted their weight around him, sighing in exasperation.

"His own traitorous friends couldn't see fit to honor his death," Blix said. "Why should we waste our time with it? Every moment we delay gives them a lead on us."

Dam locked eyes with Rad. The older boy nodded. "Traitor or not, every soldier deserves his send-off."

The warriors bristled.

"He's a thief, not a soldier."

"He's earned his fate. He ought to be left to the scavengers."

A swell of courage rose up in Dam. He faced the warriors. "He's our countryman. He needs to be sent off to the afterworld in honor of the gods, not in honor of the person that he was. If you can't abide by that, consider this. We can overtake the others, but there's no route back except coming through here. By that time, there could be a horde of scavengers to deal with."

A pulse of light throbbed from Hanhau's face, and like a general, he passed a look over his warriors to show that he would brook no argument about dealing properly with the body.

Dam and Rad carried Leo's body to a broader spot where they could build a pyre of coals, place stone markers around his body, and let the sacred flames carry his soul to the afterworld. The boy was disturbingly bony and light. Of all the unbelievable things Dam had done on the expedition, this deed counted as the most surreal.

How had he been fated to lead the funeral of a boy who had hurt him more than anyone in his life? Yet the fragile corpse in his arms was no longer that person. Dam could think about him as a stranger who deserved the respect of any man. When he had been a novice priest, he had attended the last rites of many dozens of people who had lived their lives far removed from his.

He could think about a time, it seemed so long ago, when Leo had made him feel like he was part of an elite clique much too clever to be impressed by contests and ceremonies that supposedly made boys men. He could think about things in a philosophical way. Getting mixed up with Leo had been part of a chain of events that led Dam to discover the underground world and, with Aerander and Lys, to save people from the flood. It was a journey that had led him to Hanhau. That felt better, reckoning what he was doing for Leo on those terms.

They came to a juncture where the warrior's fuzzy globes of light were aligned straight in front of him, and the gravity of the ravine seemed to fall away as though they had ventured out in the open. It was a chasm in the trail. Dam couldn't tell how extensive it was. He and Rad halted. It had to be a good place for Leo's funeral pyre. Rad called out ahead that they were setting Leo down on the floor. No one answered back. The globes of light dispersed slowly and carefully outward to the perimeter of their surroundings.

"Oil lamps. Weapons at the ready," Hanhau cried out.

Jumpily, Dam gripped the handle of his *xiphos* on his shoulder. Rad retrieved a lamp from the provision pack on Blix's back. Attalos, Callios, and Heron gathered close behind Dam. Rad scratched at a flint and lit the lamp. That light faintly illuminated a few yards of the gorge. The floor was flat and scattered with what appeared to be minor debris from above.

Warriors passed back lamps and flints for each of the boys. Dam struck a spark to light his lamp. His hands were cold and quivering. He didn't like what he was hearing. The warriors had spread out all over the place, calling out in their language, "Look here" or "Look there." Dam couldn't see what they were discovering, but he recognized the foul scent from the infirmary.

More lamps flamed on, laying bare a greater portion of the gorge. Dam spotted a body tossed to one side of the ravine. The black coals of a fire had been flung around as though a typhoon had passed through and camp provisions were scattered far and wide.

Blix guided the boys to place their lamps at positions to improve their view of the gorge. When it was done, they stood together in the center. Dam pivoted around in a stupor. Calyiches' party had made camp in the place for sure. Abandoned weapons, cloaks, drinking vessels, and fish rations were dispersed helter-skelter. Streaks of blood stained the floor. In shadowy places along the sides of the gorge, Dam spotted the worst of it. Bodies, blistered and bloated, languished in their own vomit and feces. Callios retched behind Dam.

"What could do this?" Rad said.

Dam knew. They had fangs more poisonous than any creature above the ground. They had scales that withstood a battery of iron blades. They were perversions of men with shriveled arms and legs hanging from their more powerful serpentine bodies. But their queen was dead, and they had been slaughtered. No more than a few dozen could have slunk away when the Old Ones reclaimed their city. Without the Oomphalos to protect them, they were supposed to have shriveled and died.

Ichika answered Rad. "The New Ones." She looked around to the warriors who were sorting through the debris. One by one, they shook their heads. Ichika sighed bitterly. "Calyiches brought the Oomphalos right to them."

❖

They spread out to gather the bodies, silent from the horror of the task, never mind its implications for their mission. Everyone was jittery and stumbling a bit, even the hardened warriors. They all knew it had to be done, and the quicker the better.

Ichika and one of the archers laid out the coals for a giant pyre. Dam and the others dragged the putrid bodies to a spot in the center of the gorge. Dam tried not to mind their faces, which were blue and distorted from the serpents' deadly strikes. They accounted for ten of Calyiches' party. Leo made it eleven. That was every one of the traitors. With that work done, Hanhau stepped to the middle of the group to speak.

"Our journey ends here. We gained on the traitors in a fraction of the time that they fled the city, but we were too late."

The warriors bowed their heads. Dam and the other boys did the same.

"Our objective now is to return to the city in due haste. With the Oomphalos in their possession, the New Ones have a powerful advantage. We will reinforce our fortifications. We will prepare for battle. We fought this scourge before, we will do it again."

"How many of our enemy are there?" Rad asked. Hanhau did not answer. It was impertinent for Rad to question Hanhau, especially in front of his countrymen. "I mean no disrespect, sir," Rad said. "But these...*things* that ambushed Calyiches can't have made off far. If we go back to the city, we'll lose our chance to track them. We could catch them with the Oomphalos before they gather more of their kind to launch an attack."

Dam shot a look at Rad to quiet him. He was trying to be helpful, but he had never seen what they were up against.

Ichika answered Rad fiercely. "We're not tracking beetles. It could take all sixteen of us to bring down one of the New Ones."

"I asked how many?" Rad said. "We ought to take account of what we're up against." He scanned the warriors. "You've scarred your arms to commemorate your conquests of the beasts. It can be done, can't it?"

A grudge had been brewing between Rad and Ichika since Rad only addressed Hanhau and the male warriors.

Hanhau stepped in. "We cannot risk losing a single warrior. The city guard is already compromised from its losses when the tower was demolished. They're unprepared for an attack." He gazed sternly at Rad. "We return at once."

Rad backed off. Some of the warriors helped set up the pyre coals. Dam had a slender opportunity to catch Hanhau unoccupied. "How did the New Ones do this?" Dam said. "They were defeated."

Hanhau grimaced. "So we thought. We drove them from the mori-mori mines by the city, but there are other lodes in the backcountry. They must have found one and renewed their strength."

Seeing Hanhau wrought with so much worry hurt Dam.

"Their desire for the Oomphalos is unyielding," Hanhau said. "There was a report from one of the watchtowers. Someone or something lurking in the canyon beyond the city bridge. It was never confirmed, and Ysalane never thought much of it."

Dam shivered, remembering that story. He also remembered his uncanny feeling about being watched while traveling home from the bathing lake where Calyiches and his friends had stripped out of their niter-smudged clothes to wash up.

"Could they have helped Calyiches with his plan to steal the Oomphalos?"

"It's possible. They could have promised Calyiches safe passage to the surface if he brought them the stone."

It suddenly made perfect sense. They had never truly reckoned how Calyiches—a soldier, not an engineer—had figured out how to use explosives to demolish the tower. Further, the New Ones had corrupted Zazamoukh in a similar fashion many centuries ago when he brought them the stone from the surface. They had promised him immortality, but it had come at the cost of being their slave trader.

Hanhau gripped Dam's shoulder firmly. "We cannot linger here. The New Ones planned the exchange here in this passage. They very well could have anticipated our mission to stop the thieves. This could be a trap for us too."

Dam nodded. He was antsier than ever to move out of the confining ravine. Glancing back at the progress with the pyre, he could see that it was laid and people were searching the grounds for a flint.

"I left a flint by my lamp. I'll go get it." He put his hand over Hanhau's, gave him a tight smile, and ran off to retrieve the flint.

Dam had set his lamp down by the neck of the gorge. He jogged around the pyre and came up on the spot. Squatting, he searched the ground. He had been in a jumpy haze since they had entered the gorge. Once he had placed his lamp, he had set down his flint without any thought about needing to find it again. It was nowhere to be seen. He reached his hand around the blind side of the lamp, and he felt the flat, grainy bar of stone.

Dam called back to the others. "I found it."

The floor trembled. The walls of the ravine wobbled like giant loose teeth. Dam's lamp spun and tipped over, extinguishing itself. Shouts broke out. More of the lamps jostled, and they went out in quick succession, plunging the space into darkness. The seizure rumbled on.

Dam ducked against the side of the ravine and gripped the flint as though it was his only safety. He stole a glimpse of the far side of the gorge where Hanhau had been standing, where everyone else had been. There was a blur of warrior light. Then the horrifying thunder of an avalanche rained down, blotting out everything in a suffocating cloud of dust.

Dam cried out for some confirmation that people still lived. It had seemed liked the group was farther down the gorge than where the curtain of rocks had fallen. Now Dam was entirely cut off from the others.

An arm's reach away, a boulder pounded into the floor with a force that rattled Dam's bones. Ichika said to stay in place if a seizure came, but panic pulled Dam up to his feet. He had to get out, or he would be buried beneath tons of falling rock.

He staggered out from the side of the gorge and toward the trail where they'd found Leo. The seizure threw him hard against the ravine wall, jamming his arm. The floor cratered, and he fell into it on all fours as he cried out.

The surface shifted beneath him, shattering apart like the thin ice of a mountain lake. He made a shallow leap to get out of the crater. The floor of the gorge zigzagged open with an angry crack.

Dam held on to the lip of the crater. The ground crumbled away from his feet. He hung by his arms while he listened to the seizure rip apart a gash in the floor of the ravine. Dam scrabbled to pull himself up and out with every ounce of his strength, but the seizure was too much. One of his hands slipped, then the other, and he plunged feet first into the cleft of the ravine.

PART THREE

CHAPTER ONE

A short depth into the cleft in the ravine, a ledge of rock broke Dam's fall. His legs were temporarily palsied from the impact. Everything was a sightless void, but shaking. Dam felt like the world had broken free from the very stanchions that kept it in place.

Foul, warm air rose up from beneath him. He could sense that the tremor had opened up a deeper pit, from which he had been spared. Then his ledge foundered. Dam grasped for a spur of rock to cling to, but his muscles were rattled and unreliable. He slipped into a free fall again.

His arms swung wildly as though to climb the thin air. He tried to remember prayers for divine protection to almighty Atlas, to the Mother of Mercy Pleione, to the Great Poseidon, who might take pity on His acolyte, as lapsed as he was. He was certain that an excruciating death awaited him when he met the bottom of the pit.

Dam plummeted into a warm and brackish pool.

His first thought was of the merciful gods who had spared him from being crippled. Rapidly, a new danger became apparent. He had plunged into an untold depth of water. It was thick and scalding hot in places, thwarting his effort to push to the surface for air. Dam freed himself from his chain mail apron. He considered relinquishing his blade and scabbard, but he quickly decided that he couldn't let go of his only weapon, and he tucked it in its holster beneath his arm. He kicked out stubbornly with his legs and grasped to crest the water. He came up to the surface gasping for precious air. Hot bubbles gurgled and spat out a poisonous steam. A putrid grease clung to his arms and his face. He had landed in a tar pit.

Dam treaded the water and shifted around, searching for a

direction. It was so dark, he couldn't tell if the pit was a vast ocean or a minor pond. He crawled through the water to one side. It was as good a direction as any other. Along the way, thick pockets of bubbling tar bit at his skin.

One of his hands touched a stone wall. That was good. He could grasp around the perimeter of the pool to find a foothold where he could climb out.

Dam foraged along the wall, shrinking from the pool's boiling currents and dragging himself through patches of tar. It was cooler but denser at the water's edges. He discovered a shelf. Dam beached his sword on it and grasped the shelf to beach himself.

When he pulled his legs out of the mire and onto solid ground, Dam lay down on his belly, retching salt water steeped in poisonous tar. His lungs clenched for fresh air. In defiance of his panic to get back to the others, an eddy of dizziness swallowed him into dark slumber.

❖

Dam awoke thirsting for buckets of water. He sensed vaguely he had washed ashore from some briny body of water. His skin had dried tacky and tight. Raising a hand to touch his face, Dam discovered he was smeared with a greasy substance. What had happened? He was lying flat on his belly on the hard ground as though it was his bed, and his surroundings were pitch black.

A noxious smell and a faint bubbling sound brought back dismal memories. He was trapped in a tar pit cavern. The mountain pass had been demolished. Dam balled his fists and wept hot tears. Only a miracle could have spared Hanhau and Attalos and the rest of their party.

Even if they, or some of them, had survived, the pass had crushed in right in front of Dam. No one would be able to decipher what had happened to him. They wouldn't even be able to search the way he had come. They would have to travel around the other side of the mountains to rescue him, and Hanhau had said that was an incredibly long distance.

Dam sat up and bit down on the side of his hand to control the panic threatening to overwhelm him. He had to orient himself. He had to think of some plan. Water was a concern. Food would soon be another. To the heavens, he wished he had kept hold of his flint and oil lamp. How was he going to find his way to a water source when he couldn't see his hand in front of his face? He could as easily fumble his way into a den of carrion beetles as a fresh water spring.

He sat dazed by his predicament for a spell. Then he shuddered. Something had fluttered against his skin. He captured it in the fabric of his tunic with his fist, and he clenched hard to squash whatever deadly creature had crawled inside his wet clothes. It was hard-shelled, uncrushable, and its sharp edges smarted against his skin. Dam remembered he was wearing Aerander's necklace. It was the bone amulet that he had captured like an oversized tick. That realization made his situation slide back and forth in his head from less to more terrifying. What could make a fork carved from bone quiver like a dragonfly's wings? He brought the amulet out from the collar of his shirt.

His eyes nearly burst from their sockets.

The amulet glimmered, and a glow as strong as a fully fueled lamp radiated from it. The light scorched Dam's eyes, and he glanced away for a painful moment while his vision readjusted. A blessing from the heavens was in his hand. Aerander had never mentioned such a thing. Dam wondered if his cousin had even beheld such magic coursing from the amulet. Wouldn't Aerander have told him about it?

Dam recalled Aerander saying that Calaeno would help him if he needed it. Dam had doubted that. Truly, the idea of the amulet possessing a magical connection to some centuries-old princess had seemed crazy at best and sinister at worst. Here he was in the most desperate situation he could imagine, and somehow the amulet had sensed that. Dam had light. There really was a goddess looking out for him.

He held the amulet out in front of him and looked upon his surroundings for the first time. It was a cobbled bank of rock around the tar pit. The ceiling was beyond his sight, and he could make out the depths of the bank only a few yards from his position. But he could explore down that way. He could root through the caverns of the mountain and find fresh water now that he had a beacon to guide his way.

First, it seemed proper to thank the spirit that inhabited the amulet for giving him the gift of light. Dam squinted at the glowing bone trident. Aerander had said to clear his head and let Calaeno's voice come to him. That would count as the most bizarre thing Dam had ever done. Even when he had made prayers to the gods, he had never expected to receive an answer back.

He shut his eyes and opened his mind to the possibility. The amulet's vibrations seemed to spread out from his chest and up into his head, a ticklish sensation at first. Dam supposed that the best thing to do was to call out to Aerander's heavenly guardian. How was he to address her? She was Atlas' daughter, a Pleiade, patroness of virtue and justice.

"Princess? Your Grace?"

❖

A woman's voice called back. *"Prince Damianos. I was afraid we might never meet."*

She sounded so ordinary and so clear and so close by, Dam broke from his concentration and glanced around him. He wondered for a moment if he wasn't alone in the tar pit cavern and someone was playing a very elaborate trick.

"Have I lost you?" She muttered to herself. *"Aerander was to explain to him how to use the amulet."*

The glowing amulet wagged like the clapper of a bell. Dam struggled with the impossibility of that for a moment. Then he concentrated on answering her.

"No, your Grace. I'm still here. And Aerander—he did explain how to use the amulet." Another wave of disbelief passed through him. Had he lost his marbles, imagining voices in his head? No one was around to take stock of what he was doing and to point out just how batty it was. So he allowed himself to explore it further. He spoke words in his head: *"I'm sorry. This is a bit strange to me."*

"Strange," the voice repeated, as though it was a word with which she was unacquainted. She came back to Dam cheerily. *"That's precisely how I would put it if someone asked me to describe it. But I haven't had anyone to talk to except Aerander, and now you."*

Dam sat back, not knowing what to say or what to do. Was it truly a goddess of the heavens he was speaking to? On the other hand, who else could it be? Dam remembered the strange sensation he had felt against his chest while approaching the mountain pass.

"I'm sorry if you were trying to get my attention before," he said. *"I didn't understand."*

"You're very polite. Like your cousin. Are all men in Atlantis well-mannered now?"

"I think they would be in such circumstances." Dam felt himself veering warmly toward her. *"I thank you for the light."*

"Most unnecessary. I only hoped to draw your attention. I'm pleased that it did. I was worried that something dreadful had happened to you. And if the amulet was lost, I might never be able to speak to a soul again."

Dam's mind fidgeted about. *"May I ask you, Princess, how is this possible?"*

"If I may call you Damianos, you may call me Calaeno. Or would you prefer just Dam? That's what Aerander calls you, and we're family, after all."

That struck Dam as very generous. They were family if you considered House Atlas to be a tree that grew as large as a giant poplar. She was a deep, vigorous root. He was at the very top, a tiny leaf on the shoot of a many-forked limb.

"I'm sorry, Dam. You were asking me a question," she said.

"Yes. I wondered if you could tell me how is it possible that we can speak to each other like this?"

"Through the amulet, you mean? Hasn't Aerander told you the story?"

"He has, but I'm afraid I'm still a bit confused."

"Then I shall be delighted to tell you all the way from the beginning. The amulet was given to me by my father. There was nothing special about it back then. I used to think it was a bit gruesome, actually."

Dam grinned at that.

"It is a special heirloom, though, handed down to my father from my grandfather. I gave it to Eudoros. He's the one who made it magical. He summoned power from the New Ones' stone so that our thoughts could travel to one another. So that we would always be together when he was wearing my amulet, even when we were worlds apart."

"Who's Eudoros?"

"I forget. You know him as Zazamoukh. He never liked that ugly name that had been given to him at his birth. So he took a new one. He was my suitor." She paused. *"Surely Aerander told you that story?"*

Aerander hadn't mentioned Zazamoukh being her suitor. Dam would have remembered that. It had never occurred to him that Calaeno and Zazamoukh had even known each other, though he remembered that the foul priest had lived through centuries and kidnapped men as old as the prisoner Silenos, who had lived when Atlas and his daughters had made the Citadel their home.

A chill crept up Dam's spine. The amulet in his palm had been worn by Zazamoukh. It had been enchanted by the crooked hand of the man who had threatened Dam's life and smuggled hundreds of his countrymen into slavery. What sort of person would want to marry him? Calaeno must have heard from Aerander about the evil things he had done, yet she brought him up so casually and fondly?

Dam shied away from saying any of these things to her. Respect was owed to a goddess, though he felt quite a bit uncomfortable all of a sudden being linked to her so intimately. It was like they were speaking to one another through a supremely thin wall even though he could not see her.

"I didn't know. You'll pardon me, Your Grace, but I haven't much time to talk. I need to get back to my expedition. I left the others above in the mountain pass when the seizure struck. Can you tell me what happened?"

"I'm sorry, Dam. I cannot tell you that. The amulet is my only way to look into the underworld. And that of course is only when the person wearing it tells me what they see."

Dam bit down on the side of his hand again.

Calaeno spoke out encouragingly. *"But I can help you find your way to safety. Eudoros showed me all around Agartha. Through the centuries of my exile, I had little else to do but put to memory every acre of that kingdom. I thought it would be helpful if I was to return one day. It's a beautiful place, isn't it?"*

"I need to find water and food."

"All right. Describe to me where you've been and what you see."

"We started at a mountain range on the side of a lake. A swarm of fireflies was mating there. We were traveling a narrow pass through the mountains. The earth shook, and it cleaved open. I fell into the mountain's belly and landed in a tar pit."

Calaeno was quiet for a moment, but he could hear her faint breaths as she took it in. How could she possibly guide him? She was two realms above where he had gotten himself trapped.

"Is the rock around you blue-gray or gray-black?" she asked.

Dam shone the amulet on the wall of the cavern. *"It's blue-gray."*

"That's good, Dam. You see, those are water crystals in the

mountains. That's what the blue marbling is. You'd have to do a lot of chiseling to get them out, but you can find a deeper passage where those crystals have been squeezed out by the weight of the mountains. That tremor that you spoke of may be a boon. It might have pressed open an aquifer."

Dam thirsted as he envisioned it. He thanked Calaeno, strapped his *xiphos* on his back, and went to search the walls of the bank for a cleft that might lead downward.

CHAPTER TWO

A short hike ashore from the tar pit, Dam found a rent in the cavern that looked big enough for him to climb through. He crouched down to the floor and shone the amulet inside. That didn't help much, other than ruling out that he was headed into some snapping creature's lair, at least not for the few yards he could see. But he wasn't going to find drinkable water inside the tar pit cavern. He had to search it out. Dam crawled into the burrow and followed a bumpy passage on his hands and knees.

He had never minded traveling alone, even at night, but now he was fumbling his way through unfamiliar parts of the backcountry, many leagues from the city. It might have been nice to hear Calaeno's voice, like someone was traveling with him, but Dam had decided to close off his thoughts to her for a while.

Prior to meeting Calaeno—if one could call it that—he would have considered speaking to a goddess to be a feat of grace. Only the aged priests of the oracle were said to have been gifted with the ability to hear the voices of the divine. Strange. His wonder had fallen away, and an uneasy feeling had settled into his gut. She had sounded so ordinary, a lonely girl who desperately wanted him to like her.

Dam supposed he should reserve his judgment. He didn't understand much about her nature, like how did a person come to be exiled to the heavens and freed by the answer to a riddle? Somehow, Dam had expected her to sound more noble and self-assured, like the ladies of the palace court, like Aerander's stepmother Thessala. Calaeno had shared so easily that she and Zazamoukh had been lovers.

That made Dam's palms dampen with cold sweat.

Why wouldn't Aerander have told him that? The priest had

nearly killed them both. It was hardly incidental that Calaeno had been associated with him, even if it had happened centuries ago. She had spoken of Zazamoukh as a loving suitor. Did she still hold an allegiance to him? Dam couldn't understand why his cousin trusted her given their history. And Aerander expected Dam to trust her as well? Calaeno had also said she had put a map of the underworld to memory in case she was to return some day. What had she meant by that?

The passage declined and emptied into a broader vault of rock. The air was damp and cool. Dam sighted a way ahead that was high enough to walk through. He breathed in fresher air, and the cool density of moisture surrounded him. That was encouraging. Dam quickened his pace. Some strides ahead, he heard streaming water. His legs carried him toward that sound. Icy water pooled at his feet. He launched his amulet in front of him to see where he had arrived.

He stood on the edge of a cistern cavern. It was filling from a spout of water some yards in and some yards above the floor. Dam stepped farther into the water and shone the amulet on that water flow. It was coming from what looked like fractured ice crystals, but they were deep blue like a lode of precious gems.

Dam waded into the cistern and cupped his hands to drink from it. Water in heavenly abundance! By the gods' mercy—Calaeno's mercy—he had a drink and a washing. Dam doused his head and pulled out clumps of tar from his hair. He scrubbed his face, his arms, his legs, his sandals, and his feet.

When he had rid himself of the tar as best as he could, he trudged over to the cistern bank and lay down on his back for a spell while the chiming waterfall resounded in the cavern. He would make his way back to the others. Finding water was a good start. He just needed to take things step by step.

The amulet flapped against his wet tunic like a beached minnow. Dam stared at it for a good while before deciding on what to do.

He emptied his thoughts.

"Hello."

"Hello, Dam! I was beginning to worry that I had lost you again. How goes your search for water?"

Dam sat up. *"I found it. Thank you."*

"I'm glad. You must be really happy to have something to drink."

Dam said nothing. A long silence stretched between them.

"Is everything all right, Dam?"

"It's fine."

"I know using the amulet is strange to you. But we were talking so easily before. I wonder, was there something I said that bothered you?"

Dam scratched at his chin. An itchy beard had grown in over many nights without shaving. *"I have a lot on my mind."*

"Naturally, you do. When I have a lot on my mind, I find it helps to share those things with another person. Would you do that, Dam?"

Her voice seemed to grope inside his head, searching for what he was holding back from saying. Dam lightly fingered the amulet. His first impression had been that it was haunted by a sinister spirit. Unquestionably, the goddess who was bound to it had helped him, though he truly knew little about her character. She sounded eager and friendly, but the gods played tricks on mortals. Dam was suddenly afraid to say anything to her.

"I did say something to upset you, didn't I? Won't you tell me what it was? I only want us to be friends."

Dam hesitated. He wished that he could see Calaeno. The tone and cadence of her speech could disguise her intentions. If he could see how she held herself and could look her into her eyes, he would be better able to judge her motives. In the end, he blurted out what he thought.

"Do you still love Zazamoukh?"

She was silent at first. *"Is that what's bothering you?"*

"You know what Zazamoukh did to Aerander? What he did to our country? What he did to me?"

"I knew him when he was a young man. He was different then. But yes, I know about his crimes."

"I was his attendant. I know the kind of man he became."

"I've watched Eudoros from afar for many centuries. I've watched him change. It makes me very sad."

"Sad?"

Calaeno trailed off again. When she came back to Dam, her voice had a spark of challenge. *"It does make me sad. I thought that you would understand."*

"Understand? Why?"

"Aerander told me you shared your heart with a boy named Leonitos. A boy who became a traitor to his country."

Dam's heart skipped a beat. *"Aerander told you that?"*

"He did. We used to talk about everything."

Embarrassment sawed through Dam, and then the Furies lashed at him. That was a private matter. Aerander had no business sharing it with Calaeno like it was everyday news.

"I'm sorry, but I don't see what one thing has to do with the other."

"Love transcends the deeds of men. It transcends reason, but it is no less honorable for it."

"I don't know what Aerander told you, but I fell out of love with Leo a long time ago. I don't feel sad about the traitor he was or the even bigger traitor he became. He's paid his price now, so there's no point holding a grudge either. If you think I'm still mooning over him, you're mistaken."

"I'm sorry if I presumed, Dam. Listening to Aerander talking about you all this while, it felt as though we already knew each other. I've been separated from the world for so long, Aerander's stories are all I had. Can you imagine what that's like, being nothing but a pair of eyes that cannot look away from a world you can no longer touch or even hear? Without a soul to speak to? Perhaps my imagination got the better of me, thinking about Aerander's life and your life and thinking what it would be like to be part of that, like we were friends."

Dam thoughts stumbled around in his head. He had never heard of gods who were lonely for the company of men. He knew of loneliness, however.

"How can you still love Zazamoukh after everything he's done?" Shielded to himself, Dam thought, *Zazamoukh was a master of deception. She was a child. He must have tricked her into loving him and bound her loyalty with lies.*

"Do you think that's foolish of me?"

Dam didn't answer. She was still a goddess.

"Would you like to hear a story about the two of us from a time long ago? I think it might help you understand."

Dam nodded. *"Yes. I'd like to hear it."*

And so, Calaeno told her story.

CHAPTER THREE

The first thing you must understand is that I was not always a girl. Surely, that sounds strange to you. Impossibly strange, it must be. But by the larnax of my mother's ashes, I swear that it's true. I was born into the world swaddled in the cerulean lambswool of a prince.

From the time I can remember the kind face of my mother and the violets pinned in her hair, she dressed me in a boy's square-collared shifts and goatskin shoes. My playthings were wooden soldiers and exotic finds from my father's adventures around the world. He brought me war masks, blowpipes for shooting darts, and lacquered arrowheads from the barbaric people he had conquered.

They called me Atlas. They told me I was my father's pride. I was a miracle. After six daughters, at last the Emperor had made an heir. I had no reason to question anything anyone told me, being so little. When I was old enough to wonder why I could not play games and braid my hair with my sisters in the women's harem, my mother explained it was improper for a boy. I was joined with my sisters at suppers, and of course at the fancy feasts to hail my father's return from this or that campaign from across the seas. On those occasions, my eldest sister, Alcyone, always insisted I sit on her lap. After suppers, she would recount to me stories about the faraway places my father had been. But mainly I was kept to the parlors and the gardens of my father's side of the palace. It was a world apart from the girls.

I didn't have nursemaids like my sisters, but my mother doted on me. I knew I was her favorite. In my alone times, I would stare at the door of my bedroom chamber, listening for the sound of her arrival. When I heard the trail of her footsteps, my heartbeat would quicken like the wings of a tiny bird. Each morning, she would look upon me with an enormous smile, and she would lift me into her arms and press warm kisses against my face. She was my first love. For a time, I believed I was hers, as devoted to me as she was. It was a blessed childhood.

As I grew older, that little, cozy world expanded in frightening ways. Older boys were introduced to me as my tutors. I'm embarrassed to say I tried to hide from them at first, crawling behind the divans of the parlors or slipping behind the bunting that decorated the walls. I had only known my mother and my sisters. My father had been like a god, swooping into my life on the gilded wings of fortune. I loved and admired him, but his nature had been ungraspable to me. Besides, a new adventure always called him away. He never stayed with us for more than a season.

Those tutors seemed like a strange breed of creatures with their squared and rangy bodies and hairy arms and legs. But my mother insisted that I needed to have my lessons in letters, and I needed to train in the arts of war if I was to become my father's rightful legacy.

I overcame my shyness around those earnest young men and even enjoyed their company, particularly the ones whose faces I had begun to recognize as handsome and those who rewarded a good recital of my lessons with a fond grin. But during that time, the household changed. I came to understand that I was the cause of that, though I did not know why. One by one, each tutor disappeared from my life, replaced by strangers whom I was loath to trust. By the time I had gotten used to this or that new teacher, he would disappear just as the one before him had.

I cried to my mother over the cruelty of it. What had I done to be forsaken without even the thought of saying good-bye? My mother had stories about each of the men who had left me. He had an ailing parent to care for or been betrothed to a wife with whom he would start a family, or he had a sudden errand to attend to abroad. Even as a child, I perceived a hollow timbre in her explanations. I could only reason that I was a very stupid and untrainable boy. Barring that, I had to be an intolerable companion.

My desolation deepened as I realized I had made my mother a liar. She offered me those stories like bouquets of pruned and budded lilies. It was because my mother knew I was inferior, and she feared I could not withstand the truth. My heart veered away from her. She saw me as a moppet, crafted in my father's image but never destined to be the man he was. In my young mind, I blamed my mother for my inadequacy.

Her coddling felt like a mockery of me, and I wondered if she had ever really wanted to bear a boy.

I began to recognize my mother's other habits. My uncle Gadir turned up as a frequent visitor to our home. Though he bore my father's likeness, my uncle was a prim pheasant to the strutting peacock of my father. He would stay after suppers when I was put to bed. Curious, I would listen from my room while the servants cleared the platters and trenchers. The noise from the grand atrium, between the men's and women's side of the palace, would fall away to quiet chatter and little bursts of laughter. I could not hold the words that passed between my mother and my uncle long enough in my head to understand what they were saying, but I recognized them as much gentler and more familiar than any conversation I had ever heard between my mother and my father.

Those nights, a tight pit formed in my stomach. I knew nothing of love between a woman and a man, but as the simplest of creatures is born with instincts, I knew those visits were improper. My thoughts wound back to my faults again. Had the shame of me turned my mother away from my father? Was she planning on making a better son with my uncle?

When my father next returned, my parents had an awful row that put the whole house on edge. I was certain my father had confronted my mother about my uncle, and I worried over whose side I should take. I felt it would be right if my mother was exposed and punished, but I was frightened of what would happen to me. My mother could be turned out of the house with her children so my father could take another wife. I had heard such stories in my morals lessons. I could have pled for my father to take me with him, but I was afraid of that as well. He was Atlas the Golden. He traveled with an entourage of gruff and hardy military companions and a strange assortment of foreigners whom he had won over on his adventures. The only ones with whom I felt a kinship were the pretty slave boys whom I resembled with my slight build and timid inclination. The notion of me proving myself as a second to my father was unthinkable.

A few days later, a clamor of activity burst from the women's harem. I had been told not to leave my father's compound, so I could not spy upon the noise. When I looked out from the terrace of my bedchamber, I saw a line of horse-drawn carriages that had been brought into the yard inside the palace gates.

My mother came to me at midday and told me the news. My father had ordered my sisters confined to an apple orchard in the northern countryside. I had never set foot beyond the palace walls. My sisters might as well have been ferried across the sea. My mother and I wept together like widows. For a while, I scarcely wondered about the cause. Having my sisters taken away from the palace was like carving out a lobe of my heart.

Later, I wondered about many things. Had it been my mother's punishment? I had made many hateful, silent oaths against her, and I thought it was possible the gods had heard them and brought my spite to life. Part of her was broken after that day. Forever after, she was surrounded by a pale aura of grieving. It shames me to remember I despised her more for that. I was a heartless youth. I wanted her to stand up to my father and refuse his cruel commandment. If he could banish my sisters, what was to say he would not banish me?

You are wondering now how this all relates to my meeting Eudoros. Perhaps I have been long-winded in getting to that part. But as a planter must understand what conditions will favor this or that crop to grow from the earth, so must you understand the climate in which our love affair took bud.

A season of winter and summer had passed since my sisters had been taken away when I first met Eudoros. I had outgrown the height of my mother, and my martial training had begun to shed the fat from my boyish body and strengthen my limbs. My father decreed that the kingdom would hold a spectacle of games and feasts to celebrate my passage to manhood. You know such ceremonies now as a Panegyris. I was the first prince to be feted in such a lavish manner.

It was a new terror for me. My training in formalities and athletics was to be handled privately as it always had, but I would hold the reins of my father's chariot at a grand procession to the splendid temple that had been built to preserve the memory of my grandfather. A priest was hired to train me in the oaths and oblations of the temple ceremony.

He was a stalky and awkward young man, and not at all appealing to me at first. I pray it does not offend you, but the sight of his stark, bare scalp made me worry that he was cursed or diseased. I had never met a priest before. I did not know about your rites of grooming and certainly had no understanding of what purpose those habits served. We were both cautious around each other.

In those days, since I had grown too old to be looked after by my mother, a bodyguard had been assigned to chaperone my lessons. He was a bullish man named Kanos whose face was nearly entirely concealed by a coarse, sable beard. I think his presence made Eudoros nervous. After our third or fourth meeting, Kanos would leave the two of us alone for stretches of time. It might have been because he took pity on Eudoros. Kanos may have been bored of his lessons. Maybe he just sensed that my welfare was hardly at risk in the company of such a slight and unremarkable young man.

In our privacy, I took account of the priest more freely. His features and his mannerisms, which I had found so feeble, became more intriguing to me. Mischievous, I asked Eudoros questions about his life beyond the palace just to draw out a pained, uncertain look from his face. He had been indoctrinated in the private manner of your kind, but he could not refuse to answer a prince. Did you know he had been orphaned like yourself? Everything about him fascinated me. My other tutors, bookish as they were or handsome as they were, seemed very ordinary in comparison. It was as though Eudoros had been plucked into this world from another realm. I saw that sadness in his eyes. From that sympathy grew affection.

I challenged his teachings about the spirit realm, from whence burst out such outlandish things as winged tigers and gorgon women who froze men to stone. I was a skeptical and moody child who had seen practically nothing of the world. As the son of the Great Poseidon, my father was said to be a demi-god, but my sight had begun to penetrate the glamour that surrounded him. Mostly, I simply enjoyed teasing my new companion and drawing out the mornings we spent together. I said before instincts were born in me that needed no cultivation to bloom. They needed only time and the occasion to present themselves. During my lessons with Eudoros, the coy arts of courtship came to me as naturally as putting one foot in front of the other.

It perplexed me mildly that a man should evoke such tendencies in me. My mother had spoken to me about one day taking a wife. My father had never dallied on his visits to discuss such things with me. I had grown to believe that happiness and marriage were notions far removed from one another in any case. Eudoros made me happy. That was all.

I noticed Eudoros leaning toward courtship in his own shy way. He had always been dour and careful around me. Allowing himself to break a grin seemed to be a tremendously reckless thing for him to do, but he did grin in my company. He allowed me to draw nearer to him as we sat together on the fleece of my father's salon room, or beneath a shade tree in the gardens when my protests to feel the breath of springtide wore him down.

We were to have a dozen lessons at the extreme. As you well know, the vows and offerings of a boy's Panegyris are fairly rote. I could have sworn them to memory in a day. Beyond appearances, there was no need for Eudoros to be profuse. I was the grandson of Poseidon, after all!

Still, I pretended to forget my oaths and begged Eudoros that I needed more time. With nearly as fine a dressing, Eudoros threatened he would have to report to my father I refused to take instruction and let my mind wander too freely. By the grace of the Fates, my father's return from abroad was delayed by the squall of the sea. Naturally, a spectacle in my honor could not take place without him. Eudoros and I were free to meet until the day when my father's sails would be sighted cresting the horizon beyond the city harbor. My mother made no effort to interfere with the time we spent together. It could not have gone unnoticed. As much as she was lost in her unhappiness, I do believe she was complicit in our deceit. She had her own reasons to tempt my father's ire.

One day when Eudoros and I took our visit in the salon while rain pattered down on the gardens, a delicious aching clutched my heart. I clasped Eudoros' hand and brushed my cheek against his. I told him that I loved him.

Delicately, he guided me beyond his reach. I was stricken, and I asked him, "Do you not love me?"

He did not answer. Scalded by the thought that I had presumed too much, I asked him: "Do you not love me because I am a boy?"

I did not know what to make of the gaze that fell upon me. It made me feel more childish than I had ever felt in my life, yet it was moist with fearful tears. Then he spoke words that exhumed a buried horror. He brought me to a fancy looking-glass that had been fashioned for my father and installed on the wall of the salon. There, he told me to undress. He turned his back to me for the sake of my modesty.

A season before, my mother had taught me to bind my breasts. She had said that it would stop them from blossoming so that the rest of my body could catch up while I was growing into the body of a man. Before that, when I had bled and cried out for her, she had taken me by the hand very firmly and dragged me to my bedchamber. There, she had shushed me and helped me clean myself. She had told me that I must have broken the flesh from my exercises. She had brought me a special tea steeped with very potent and unsavory herbs and instructed me to drink daily to heal the wound.

Some years earlier, I had stolen into my mother's dressing room and discovered on the sill a pretty silver locket encircled in burnt sage and cast in the dawning light of the sun. It was identical to the trinkets that each of my sisters wore. My mother had commissioned those keepsakes from our jewelry-maker to bless each of the girls on the days of their births. The locket I had found looked as though it had been set aside in remembrance, and it was inscribed with the name Calaeno. I had stumbled away from the discovery at the time, thinking I had uncovered a private tragedy my mother had kept from me.

I had studied likenesses of men and women on the painted walls of our home, particularly the unclad warriors my father favored. I had wondered when that male part of me would grow. Still, I was a boy. That was what I had always been told. Everything I had believed peeled away as I stood before the looking-glass. Glaring back at me was a girl I had never known.

A shriek rose up in me, but for the sake of Eudoros, I willed myself to calm and merely covered myself. I shrank from him and prayed the sky would fall and forever shroud me from the eyes of men. Eudoros left me to myself. I took to my bed and did not speak to anyone for many days, feigning fever and fatigue.

Meanwhile, my mind was adrift like my father's storm-tossed galley. My life had been a lie. In a distant way, I understood my parents' scheme. They wanted a son so that the bloodline of my father wouldn't end with him. Nearer to my heart, however, was the question of how they could hate me so much to have raised me to show off like one of my father's silver steeds. They could have just as well chosen one of my other sisters. Alcyone, Merope, and Electra all had fair hair like my father. But I was the one who had been dressed up as his replica like an actor in a play.

In peaks of that private storm, I felt unleashed. I finally realized the reason I had always felt unable to be my father's heir. It was nature.

But I was still bound to my father. A frightening future splayed out before my eyes. The truth of me would have to forever be a secret. I would be sealed off from the world and never know the intimacy of companionship and certainly never love. I realized that my sisters had been taken away from the palace not for any misdeed on their part or on my mother's part. It was to keep them from perceiving they had another sister rather than a brother. For the same reason, my tutors had been dismissed, if not hanged, so they would not come to understand my nature too well. I could not guess how my parents planned to continue the charade as I grew to womanhood. But at my Panegyris, I would be announced to the world as Atlas' son. Thereafter I would be imprisoned in the lie, someday even to succeed my father as a king.

I realized I could only talk to one person about these things. I emerged from the mire of my bedchamber and called for my mother. I told her that I was fit to resume my lessons with Eudoros.

A delicate part of me feared he would not return after having exposed my parents' conspiracy. It had been immensely dangerous for him to do so, and I had seen men who were much stronger and more audacious than he dance delicately around my father for fear of suffering his wrath. I prayed the world was not so cruel. I had desperate plans on my mind if Eudoros abandoned me.

He arrived the next day, and we repaired to the quiet of the men's salon. As soon as Kanos left us, I could not help the tears from returning to my eyes. I told him everything I had reckoned about my parents' deceit, and I begged him to believe I had not been part of it. I spoke of my terror about going through with my father's festival, a ceremony to seal my fate. I told Eudoros that I could not do it, especially since it would mean forsaking our companionship.

Eudoros sheltered me in his arms. He said he loved me as well, and he knew a way to rescue me from my fate. He told me about a place where we could go and never be discovered. He pressed into my hands a drawing of a path through the woods beyond the palace. I was to meet him there at full dark.

Of course, you know the rest of the story. He had shown me the way to the magic gates to the underworld. There, I shed my life as my father's son and started anew as Calaeno, which was the name my mother had promised me but set upon a sill in ashes. Eudoros was my savior. He had shown me what I was and still he loved me.

CHAPTER FOUR

The story held Dam in a spell for some time after Calaeno stopped speaking. He had never been coerced to pretend to be anyone other than himself, but her troubles fitting into the world of men aroused a sense of kinship. He had also known the falseness and cruelty of palace society. He had turned away from it himself, though he had been a boy of no consequence.

Calaeno had refused her father, the mighty Atlas, and jeopardized his line of kings. Dam wasn't sure if that made her love affair more or less honorable. In any case, he kept his thoughts to himself.

Many interesting tales must have followed Calaeno's flight to the underworld, but Dam was anxious to know the finish to the story. *"Why did it end between you and Zazamoukh?"*

"I could blame the Oomphalos. As it corrupted the New Ones, so it poisoned Eudoros with greed. Our joyful time together ended when I learned how he had discovered the underworld. As a novice priest, I daresay about your age, he had tripped upon a portal and been ensnared in a pact with the serpent-men. They promised him immortality if he would bring them the stone, which the Old Ones had banished to the above-world so that it would not be misused. Eudoros did that, but he was never paid for the deed. Instead, they tempted him to be their slave trader. For each man Eudoros brought them, they allowed him to bask in the stone's life-giving energies for a short while.

"I begged Eudoros to disavow that bargain and free the prisoners. Just as desperately, Eudoros told me he could not live without the stone. He had another plan. He would steal the stone from the New Ones, and the two of us would live together for eternity.

"I could not do that. My eyes peered deeper into the vision that beguiled Eudoros. I did not see happiness. I saw fear and suffering.

"I took back the amulet that kept us bonded, and I left him to make my way on my own. By the grace of fate, I found refuge with the Old Ones. From them, I learned about the terror the New Ones had imposed over their kingdom. I swore to help them win their freedom.

"Eudoros did steal the stone, and he found me. When I refused to join him, he summoned a powerful spell that imprisoned me in the heavens, where I would live forever but never be able to reveal his treachery. Of course, he didn't succeed in keeping the stone for himself. His mastery of its power failed him, and the New Ones retook it and kept him bound as their slave trader."

"You still say you love him after all that?"

"I see that's strange to you. He was the only person to have the courage to show me who I really was. That goodness was always inside him. His thirst for the stone consumed it, but it was never destroyed completely, only buried.

"Even when he banished me, I knew he loved me still. His curse left a provision for my release. When the lie that had erased me from history was revealed, I would be freed. Maybe Eudoros thought of it as a secret oath that would reunite us when one of us had a change of heart about his bargain with the New Ones. Maybe he devised it as a mystery for some wise man to unlock and bring that bargain to an end. In either case, he sealed his reckoning in the curse that sent me away."

So it had been when Aerander spotted Calaeno in the sky and spoke her secret on the night when the sea rushed toward the Citadel to bury Atlantis in its entirety. That had allowed the heavenly princess to shine light on a portal to the underground so that Aerander and Lys could evacuate the highborn boys. That had allowed Aerander to tell everyone that the High Priest had been plotting against the kingdom.

"Aren't you angry that he banished you? He took away your life."

"At times it's been horrid. I saw all, but I could do nothing.

"I saw my father blacken his face with char from my funeral dais where they burned my chiton and my lariat as my only remains.

"I saw my mother stare at illusions of her mind from the single slat window of her resting chamber. She had been confined to a locked vault beneath a watchtower because she had shredded her fancy clothes and needed to be helped to wash herself and eat.

"I saw my eldest sister Alcyone torn from her true love to marry

a 'proper' man. She became not much more than a brood mare to birth grandsons to continue the line of my father. I saw sickness and age claim every one of my family, some of them alone, without anyone to comfort them. I saw the deaths of every generation after them.

"Have I been angry at Eudoros? Surely, I have. But it's been my fate to watch over the world from the heavens. It's been my fate to help our country at a time when people most needed me. Perhaps that was what my grandfather required from me in penitence for abandoning Atlantis so many years ago. I didn't understand that all at once, but I feel no anger now, nor regret."

That seemed like a very steep punishment to Dam. He couldn't figure how Calaeno had come to terms with it. Was it possible for anyone to be so forgiving? *"When you were down here in Agartha, were you tempted by the stone's power?"*

"I felt its magic, but I was born with a protection from its temptation. The same protection that you possess. As does Aerander."

Dam had no idea what she meant.

"It is like the child who falls ill with the pox and lives through it to never suffer that sickness again, even when he is bedded with his stricken brothers and sisters."

"I don't understand."

"It's the bloodline, Dam. Long ago, my father was enchanted by a bit of the stone's power, and so we are bonded to the stone's mysteries, every generation down to you and Aerander. The few who know that story no longer speak to me, so I can only suppose how it happened. My grandmother Cleito had possession of the stone at one time. My father was her favorite, and it would stand to reason she summoned powers that would place him above all other men. Perhaps she did not know the stone minds its own mysteries. It can bless its beholder on one hand and curse him on the other. My father was invincible in battle, but he could not sire a son as even the simplest of men can do. That turned him to madness, and we come full circle to the beginning of my story."

Dam followed gradually. Though he did not feel bonded to the stone as she had said in any way that he could perceive, Aerander had once described it like a magnet buried in his gut that pulled him toward the stone. Dam had never felt that. He had something else to ask her.

"Maybe that's what happened when Zazamoukh used the stone to banish you? It backfired."

Calaeno chuckled mildly. *"If you can call ten centuries of exile a backfire, I suppose. It was a strong curse, but you are right. Some airy tentacle of the stone might have reached into Eudoros' heart, making true a longing that we would be reunited one day. It allowed me to return with the magic of the gods. I only wish I was powerful enough to breach the underworld. The snake queen Ouroborus sealed those portals to me."*

Dam fell back on his present troubles. How much time had passed during their conversation? Hanhau and the others had been trapped in the mountain pass. The New Ones had reclaimed the stone. They would attack the city, where Aerander lay blind and crippled.

"You know what you must do, Dam?" Calaeno said.

Dam gazed heavenward. He wanted very much to know what she was thinking.

"You must claim the stone and return it to the Old Ones."

He gaped absurdly. *"How am I supposed to do that?"*

"It is a dangerous quest. But it was done by your cousin. Before that, it was done by Eudoros."

"Aerander had that special bond to guide him. I don't feel anything like that." Dam shook his head. *"No. I've got to get up to the mountain pass. If I can find anyone who survived, we'll make our way back to the city to warn people. Maybe we can organize a campaign to get the Oomphalos back. It'll take more than one man. The snakes are powerful."*

"I know the snakes as well as you. Better, I daresay. With their advantage, they will rush to avenge the murder of their queen. If you do not stop them, I fear there will be no city for you and your friends to return to."

"I can't leave the others in the mountain pass while I go searching for the stone. They could be dying up there."

"You'll be very little help to them without it."

Dam felt cuffed at his wrists. *"I can't steal the stone from the New Ones by myself. It's impossible. Sure, you say two people have done it before. One of them is blind and nights away. The other is dead."*

"The other is not dead."

Calaeno's words hung in the air for a moment. But Zazamoukh had been swept up in the flood back on that tragic night, hadn't he? No one had seen the priest since they had come underground. Dam did not want to believe the evil man could still be alive.

"On the night Aerander returned to the Citadel, I shone a beacon to the portal to the underworld. There was time for a few score of your cousin's friends to escape. And Zazamoukh."

Dam winced. He supposed that it was possible. Calaeno had said she could see everything from the heavens, though she couldn't see into the underworld.

"How could he still be living down here? He can't live without the Oomphalos."

"I do not know. But it is certain he still lives. I was bound to the amulet by the magic he cast. If he were dead, the two of us would no longer be able to speak."

That took a moment for Dam to follow, and then it seeped in like a foul smell.

"You must go to him to find out how you can retake the stone."

❖

Dam felt broken and very hungry. He needed to find food, and he told Calaeno so. She suggested a route through the cistern cavern toward balmy, stillwater pools in the underground where seaweed and mushrooms were hedged around the water. At the far end of the cistern, the cavern narrowed to knobby passageway with crystallized walls of stone. Dam tramped that way for a stretch. Then he found a climb down to a lower bank of rock.

He felt warmth and smelled a smoky current as from a shaft above burning lava. He followed those markers. Above him, water dripped from upside-down spires of rock, hanging like icicles. The water collected in little pools in the scarred floor of the cavern. Dam shone the light from his amulet around. Up ahead, he spotted a harvest of colorless mushroom buds. In a little pool nearby, he found slimy stalks of seaweed.

Dam filled his mouth with the treasures. Only starved and at the end of his wits could he think of those underground dregs as delicacies, but they made a meal to fill his belly. That settled him a bit. Dam found a spot in the floor where the ground was dry, and he sat down to think.

He could ignore what Calaeno had said and go looking for Hanhau. That was what his heart was telling him to do. Dam closed his hand around the iron wristband Hanhau had given him. Calaeno didn't understand. His loyalty was to the men from his expedition and most especially to Hanhau.

Dam's thoughts rushed back on themselves. He could manage ignoring Calaeno's advice, but what would Hanhau want him to do? Dam had a chance to take the stone and save the city from the New Ones' assault. He had to try.

Asking for Zazamoukh's help was a hateful irony. Zazamoukh was to blame for the New Ones laying siege to Agartha the first time around. What made Calaeno think Zazamoukh would help Dam get the stone? Did she think she could persuade him herself?

That was one heck of a reckless strategy. Zazamoukh could take the amulet for keeps, and Dam would have nothing to guide him through the backcountry. His countrymen would have no link to the above-world. They would never know how or when they could return to the surface.

Whatever it was he had to do, he had to get going with it. The New Ones could be readying their attack. Dam emptied his thoughts and called out to Calaeno.

"I'm ready. How do I find Zazamoukh?"

"I am proud of you, Dam. This must be very hard for you."

Dam sighed. She had no idea how hard it was.

"There is a lair in the depths of the backcountry, unknown even to the New Ones. Eudoros told me it was the place we were to hide after he had taken the stone. I pray he sought out that hideaway in his exile."

CHAPTER FIVE

Calaeno's instructions were to find a passage to a volcanic shelf below the cavern. Guided by a warm draft farther in, Dam traveled beyond the mushroom furrow and came upon a cleft in the floor where the stench of scalded rock was strong.

His descent was nearly blind. He needed both hands to grip notches of rock while groping for footholds with his feet to make his way below. The amulet hung from his neck, not improving his view of the gulley much. Meanwhile, the air grew thick with heat. Faintly, Dam heard rumblings below like the sound of the Fire Canyon.

Some yards down, he arrived at a landing and stopped to get his bearings. He had farther to go down that narrow gulley. Dam wished he had the rappelling cable they had used on their expedition. Even better, he wished he had his troupe to go with him. He gathered his breath as best as he could. The air was foul from the molten rock that burned below. How hot and choking would it be when he reached the bottom? Dam reminded himself that he had crawled from a tar pit, slain beetles as large as bulls, and kept pace with warriors driving up mountain cliffs. He sorted out another vertical descent.

After a steep maneuver downward for a while, the gulley gradually rounded and opened up like a horn. Dam slid down with his legs in front of him. He arrived above a smoky bed of craters.

Dam shone his amulet over that crater field. He could not see far, but it felt vast. He heard distant rumbles and hisses of steam. The floor was shattered with fine crevices. He wondered how stable it was. Dam called out to Calaeno for advice.

"Can you see the molehills of lava?" she asked.

Dam stared across the murky distance. Along the horizon, tiny, red caps sparked through the darkness. He reported that to Calaeno.

"Make your way there. Beyond those hills, there will be an aerie. That's where you will find Eudoros."

Dam felt pulled from two ends again. He had undertaken this mission to retrieve the stone, but he had also abandoned Hanhau, now many leagues above him.

He had come this far. He had to forge ahead and hope to be speedy about it. Dam leapt down to the field, trying to make a gingerly landing. The floor didn't give way from his weight. Dam trudged toward the tiny, fiery beacons in the distance.

The fire-caps of the hills grew brighter on the horizon as he traveled, though they seemed to be always farther ahead. Meanwhile, sweat poured from Dam's brow. He had never been so deep underground. The heat wrung the strength from his body. Dam soldiered on. It would make good sense for Zazamoukh to hole up in the smoking bowels of Agartha. Not even the snakes would have relished looking for him there.

Dam arrived at his destination nearly before he had reckoned it properly. He understood then why Calaeno had called them molehills. The fire-caps came from mere cones of rock that had sprouted from the ground. He saw a cropping of them a few dozen wide and a few dozen long. None were more than twice his height. They were miniature volcanoes. Dam was relieved he wouldn't have to climb them, though he would have to trek around them to avoid their spatter of lava.

Dam skirted to one side and tried to make out his surroundings. A rocky bulwark some yards beyond the lava molehills looked like it completely hedged in the crater field. Training his amulet in another direction, he doubled back on an odd sight. It was a wall of fog, or steam. That was curious enough for Dam to explore. Steam meant a source of water.

He ventured farther toward it, and he noticed rivulets racing by his feet in the grooves of the scorched floor. That water disappeared in the pores of the ground, certain to be boiled below. Dam followed the crisscrossing rivulets, anxious to find their source. He headed into a dense zone of fog like the cool breath of the sea at morning.

The moisture coated his heated skin, which brought some relief, but he couldn't get his bearings. The clapping of a vigorous rainfall tantalized Dam's ears. He closed in on that sound. Mist pecked at his face. Dam shone his amulet in front of him, desperate to behold what all his other senses were telling him. Water must have found its way down from the crystallized mountain beds through a fracture in the ceiling.

Dam didn't see it, but he stepped beneath it. That fracture had created a minor cataract where the water spilled and rose from the ground in folds of steam. Dam craned his head back and stretched open his mouth to catch a drink. It was warm from the heat but still mercifully quenching.

He passed through the cataract and arrived at the mouth of a cave. His amulet illuminated a steep passage inward. Surrounded by mist from the cataract, Dam took account of the exterior as well as he could. It was a tall shaft of rock. The cave led up to its height. That certainly could figure as an aerie.

Dam called up a psychic bridge to Calaeno. He described what he had found.

"Yes," she said. *"You must climb to its pinnacle. There's a berth inside that was to be our hideaway."*

Dam's heartbeat quickened.

"What am I supposed to say to him?"

"Whatever you can to win his help."

The last time he had seen Zazamoukh, Dam had bashed him on the head with the butt of a *xiphos*. That didn't put him in a very favorable bargaining position. He told that to Calaeno. Didn't it make more sense for her to try talking to the priest?

"Better to use the amulet as a bargain when you absolutely must. He will want to talk to me, and that could slow you down from your task. Remember, he has reason to hate the New Ones as much as anyone. They kept him as their pawn for centuries, and he was never paid with the prize he craved. Without the stone, he's a dying man."

Dam drew a breath. Best to get on with it rather than being plucked to shreds by his nerves. He told Calaeno he was going in.

"Dam, you mustn't hurt him. No matter what he says. Promise me."

He gave her his promise, and then he climbed into the cave.

CHAPTER SIX

It was a twisted, rock-strewn climb up through the cave—a cruel stairway to a cruel man's home. In spots, the walls of the passage had crumbled and piled high to the ceiling. Dam had to scale forward on his hands and knees, scraping his legs along the way. There was no light and no trace of habitation until he neared the top. A loathsome fug of urine, the stink of unwashed men, and the cloying odor of rot assaulted him. A pale aura of light bled into the passageway like the cast of the setting sun.

Dam climbed to the lip of a hardscrabble slope and arrived at a hollow. The space was still and dank. Dam shone the amulet around. It was a pocket that looked to be the size of an antechamber.

The source of the room's strange illumination was a glowing tin bucket on the floor. Dry fish bones and soiled cloths were scattered around. Dam searched the space beside the bucket.

Reptilian eyes stared back at him.

Dam kept the amulet trained on the priest and reached over his shoulder to withdraw his sword from its sheath. He had subdued the priest before, and he was not afraid to do it again if the situation required it. By the man's position, he appeared to be laid out or hunched low to the floor. Dam climbed into the den.

Zazamoukh's thirsting voice halted Dam's steps. "Is that death come for me? I thought my prayers had warded you away. Are there no gods left to hear the living?"

Dam stepped closer and took account of the priest. His face was shrunken from starvation, and a wiry gray beard had grown in during his exile. In all respects, he had become decrepit. His priestly braids had withered to spindly shoots of colorless hair.

He had managed to raise himself to his elbows on the matted fleece that was his bed, but his wasted limbs lay enervated. Wheezing breaths rose up from his chest. His aged skin, the color of wash-water, clung to his bones. This was the man who had commanded an army of priestly followers and brought crowds of peasants to their knees when he decreed the commandments of Poseidon.

As diminished as the priest was, Dam kept his guard up. It was a miracle that Zazamoukh had survived so long in his remote den. Dam crept up to the foot of the man's bed, displaying his raised blade.

"What gods do *you* pray to?" Dam said.

The priest's reptilian eyes sparked. He looked over Dam's amulet with a delicate longing, then his gaze came back at Dam, returned to its haughty authority. "Not death, then, but a boy who wants to be a hero. Put down your weapon." He nudged one bony shoulder toward the glowing bucket. "Help me to a drink."

"I'm not a boy. And I'm not your caretaker."

The priest fell victim to a hacking cough that made Dam shield his face with his blade arm to avoid the spray of the man's foul breath. Zazamoukh spoke hoarsely. "What are you, then? That churlish tone plucks a familiar chord. My mind does not hold all that it used to."

Dam's disguise could have figured as an advantage, but his pride preceded any strategy. He had suffered as the priest's assistant for three years.

"Shall I joggle your memory with another bludgeon to the head?"

The priest's eyes widened. Then, horridly, his toothless mouth stretched open in a ghostly cackle. When he recovered from that fit, he looked Dam over. "By the gods' grace, Damianos lives. Fashioned so gallantly. A soldier are we now? The survivors must be in dire straits. The only trade I recall you being good at was getting buggered by noblemen's sons."

Dam crouched beside the priest and pressed the tip of his *xiphos* into the man's brittle throat. "Shut your wretched face. I've business with you."

Zazamoukh looked up at him. "I suppose the Fates have woven together a comedy at the expense of both of us. The kingdom's least sent to bring justice to the kingdom's greatest traitor. Be done with it, then. I've no defense. As easy to finish off as a fish flushed ashore by the tide."

Dam hesitated. He hated his predicament. No shred of sympathy held him back from murdering the priest. He could avenge the many beatings he had received at Zazamoukh's hand. More importantly, he could avenge what Zazamoukh had done to Hephad and Attalos and every person he had kidnapped, including the dying prisoners. But Dam needed the priest's knowledge of the stone. He had promised Calaeno he wouldn't hurt the man, and if he killed Zazamoukh, the spell that linked the amulet to her would break.

Zazamoukh's penetrating gaze beheld that dilemma. He gasped out a laugh. Dam noticed that the man's ugly gob was blackened and chafed from some sort of vile consumption. "You haven't come for my death," the priest said. "It's something else. Say it. There's barter I could use." He looked at the amulet hanging from Dam's neck.

Dam caught that look and hovered over Zazamoukh ferociously. "You're going to tell me how to claim the stone."

He bent his sword arm and braced himself to deliver a blunt, shattering blow to the priest's nose if a taunting word came out of him. Oddly, Zazamoukh fell silent. His face was washed of thoughts and emotions, but Dam knew him too well to trust that ploy.

"You've traveled far to find me and must have stories of your own," Zazamoukh said. "Let's trade one for the other. I've been apart from the world for longer than I can know. News is all that I require for currency." He glanced over to his bucket. "News, and a drink."

❖

Dam took up the bucket. It contained a red, glowing substance as thick and shiny as yolk. Mori-mori. The blood of the earth. Dam did not comprehend its nature, but he knew the prisoners had mined it for the New Ones, and it was all the giant serpents fed on to survive. The Oomphalos had been forged from the substance. Dam supposed that Zazamoukh had subsisted on the stuff while hiding, though it hardly looked like it was doing him much good. Without the life-giving energies of the Oomphalos, the priest's aged body had been claimed by the laws of nature just like the freed prisoners. Zazamoukh had to be about the same age as the prisoner Silenos, who had died.

He brought the bucket to Zazamoukh and tipped the rim to the man's lips. A fingerbreadth of liquid was left. Zazamoukh gulped greedily for it. He could not raise his hands to help himself. As the mori-mori seeped into his mouth, he winced and tears sprouted from his eyes. The light from the substance spread out from the priest's throat, illuminating every blue vein and capillary in his pale white flesh. That strange rush of magic was brief, and it faded away once it had reached his belly. Dam put the bucket back in its place.

Zazamoukh gasped and sputtered like a drowning man surfacing for air. He calmed after a while and spoke. "Must be amusing for you."

Dam said nothing.

"It is the way of the world that boys come to loathe their masters." Zazamoukh strained to slide his elbows out from under himself so he could lie down on his back. "You won't have long to wait to see my final breath. That should make your boyhood trials worthwhile."

"Won't the mori-mori sustain you?"

Zazamoukh cleared his raspy throat. "Only until my body refuses it completely. It is not meant to be taken by our kind." Dam wondered how much the mori-mori had corroded the priest's throat and stomach already, and whether it would be better to bring him more or to starve him of it.

"Shall we begin our bargain?" the priest said.

Dam sat down on the floor beyond the priest's reach. He posted his blade at his side.

Zazamoukh called to him. "Host's privilege. You go first. I want to know how the survivors fare."

"It's your turn. I fed you your meal."

Zazamoukh snickered. "The agreement was news for news."

Dam bristled over what to do. As helpless as the priest was, Dam had no way to coerce him to speak first and reveal how he had stolen the stone. Zazamoukh had the advantage, and everything Dam knew about the man told him he wouldn't honor the bargain he had concocted.

"I haven't long. Speak to me."

Dam frowned. He had to tell Zazamoukh something, and rather than try the priest's cunning, he decided on the truth, even though Zazamoukh didn't deserve it. Dam told him about the theft of the stone, the expedition to stop Calyiches' party, the ambush, and the tremor that wracked the mountain pass.

"Your turn," Dam said. "How do I get the stone from the New Ones?"

Zazamoukh lay feeble in the cast of the trident amulet's glow. Dam was certain he was silently exalting. That information created a pitiable position for him. Dam attuned to the weight of the sword in his hand, A thrust of the tip into the left side of the priest's chest would be the cleanest way to kill him. Then his delay in searching for Hanhau wouldn't be completely fruitless. Justice dangled before him. Could he really do it? Dam had never done anything so violent.

The priest spoke. "The New Ones will reclaim the city. How many did you say devised the ambush?"

"I didn't. I said, it's your turn." Dam leaned forward so he could see the priest's face. "How do I get the stone?"

Zazamoukh smacked his lips in an irritating manner. Maybe it was because his mouth was burned and dry, or maybe he was putting Dam off to get underneath his skin. At last, he spoke. "The New Ones have taken haven on the other side of that mountain pass. I traveled through those parts on my way down here. There's an abandoned mill-worm hole that leads to their nest. They must have found a mori-mori lode nearby to settle in that area."

Dam waited for more. The priest closed his eyes, and his mouth went still.

"You haven't finished," Dam said.

"I have. You asked how to get the stone, and I told you where to find it."

"You know that doesn't do me any good unless you tell me how to steal it from the snakes."

Zazamoukh coughed. "You must be more precise with your questions. The questioner's privilege returns to me. Tell me, how did you know where to find me?"

A furnace of indignity rose up in Dam. Zazamoukh was playing a child's game. The only thing that buffered Dam's anger was not wanting to give the priest the satisfaction of seeing him unsettled.

He gave a quick account of Calaeno's release from Zazamoukh's curse, her bestowing her amulet to Aerander and then to himself, and her instructions on where to find the priest. Zazamoukh had shown he recognized the amulet. If he hoped for more detail on what his former love had told him, Dam was happy to let him suffer with the scantest of facts. As it was, the story softened Zazamoukh's demeanor. He pushed himself up on his elbows and gazed at the amulet. For a strange moment, that sight recalled to Dam Calaeno's description of the young, pained man with whom she had fallen in love.

"Did she speak of me with contempt?"

"You're not playing by your own rules," Dam said. "I answered you. It's my turn again." Dam composed his question carefully. "How do I get the stone from the New Ones?"

Zazamoukh frowned, and then his eyes twinkled as though beholding a very amusing vision. "You cannot. It would take magic well beyond your knowledge to overpower the snakes. Even then, you would need to understand the stone's nature so you could use it to protect yourself in escaping from their den."

Dam bristled. Answers in bits and pieces. Meanwhile the snakes were preparing to storm the city in the shelf above them.

"Your turn," Zazamoukh said. "Tell me what defenses Ysalane holds in her city."

"Why do you want to know that?" Dam blurted out.

"You haven't answered. If that's your question, it will have to keep until you pay me with your reply."

Dam's mind stumbled a bit. "No. That's not my question." He had to be more careful to not fall into the priest's traps. He thought over the city plan. "It's moated and walled. There are archer outposts at the drawbridge, and the tunnel gates have a vaulted door a yard thick and solid iron."

Zazamoukh grinned. Dam did not know what mischief he was being drawn into, but he was anxious to be done with the priest's infernal game. He arrived at the most specific question he could think of.

"How did you steal the stone from the snakes?"

The expression on the priest's face soured. Dam stared at him keenly.

"Beyond the lava molehills, there is a black embankment of rock. Atop that shelf, there is a well that flows from the very pith of the earth. This was told to me by a pair of ancient warriors. They were twins, banished by their tribe."

An eerie hand clutched Dam's heart. Hanhau had spoken of such twins, abandoned to the backcountry, though he had said the story was a folktale.

"I ventured to the well on their advice," Zazamoukh went on. "If a man is willing to dive into its pool of blood and drown, he will be reborn with the power he most desires to master. That was how I was able to take the stone from the snakes. You see that even that sorcery would not allow me to claim the stone for long. The well's magic wears away with time, and it will only allow a man to take from it once."

Dam worked through that story quickly. He had seen the embankment. He knew what to do. He got up from the floor to go.

"Not yet," the priest said. "I've more questions."

"We're even now. It's a good place to end."

"But you have no idea what power to ask for from the well."

Dam ignored him. He had wasted enough time tugging answers out of the priest. He looked to the passage down to the waterfall and the crater field.

The amulet lifted itself from his neck and fluttered over his head. Dam grasped for it, but it had somehow sprung to life with motives of its own. He jumped to catch it, but it was like trying to clasp a bird in his hands. The amulet flew to the priest, hooped over his head, and nested itself on his chest.

Zazamoukh chortled. "I've life yet. I can still command the things that belong to me."

Dam dove to the floor beside the man and reached for the necklace's chain. Invisible sparks stung his hands as though he had been struck by frozen needles. Dam threw back his sword arm to plunge his weapon into the priest's heart. He stopped short.

The priest gazed up at him. "You know that if you kill me, you'll break the link to Calaeno. And if you break that link, you'll never know when it's safe to come aboveground. Your countrymen will be imprisoned in the underworld, unless they want to try their luck swimming from the bottom of the ocean."

Dam shoved himself off Zazamoukh's limp body. He didn't even want to look at the hateful man.

"Now we've got real barter to trade," the priest said. "Take that bucket to the well. You keep me alive, and I'll tell you how to get the Oomphalos from the New Ones. Mind yourself very carefully on your errand. That region around the well is a favorite spot for fire scorpions."

Chapter Seven

Dam crawled and stumbled his way down from Zazamoukh's den, silently cursing himself and Calaeno. Why hadn't she told him that the priest could command the amulet? Had it been her plan all along to deceive Dam into bringing it to Zazamoukh so she would be reunited with her lost love?

Dam could not reconcile it. When the princess had been set free from her exile, Calaeno had given the amulet to Aerander, not Zazamoukh, which seemed to show she was honorable. But unless she was dim-witted, which seemed unfitting for a goddess, she had deliberately sent Dam on a fool's mission to squander the one device that could bring her countrymen back to the above-world. Shouldn't she have told him to hide the amulet from Zazamoukh?

He pushed through the misty waterfall and out to the lava-baked field. He had no amulet for light and instead a bucket for the loathsome task of fetching mori-mori for the priest. The lava-capped molehills showed him the way back to the place where he had started. He remembered the direction to the bulkhead of black rock. Traveling around the crop of lava-spouts, Dam came up on that tall, impenetrable barrier. He decided to have words with Calaeno when his misadventure was over. Now, Dam needed to somehow hatch a plan to outwit the evil priest.

Dam shouted with a force to deafen the underworld with the injustice of his situation, and he batted his sword against the face of the high ledge of rock with a mighty clash. Using a path of footholds, he mounted the shelf. Farther above, he found a ledge trailing along the face of the escarpment, making the climb easier.

He reached the top of the mount and gathered his breath. It was a flat plateau that stretched onward for an undecipherable distance. The caps of the lava molehills below were miniscule, like stars on a hazy night. Some yards inward on the plateau, Dam sighted a cloudy source of light that seemed to breathe up from the floor. That had to be the mori-mori well which Zazamoukh had spoken of.

The priest had mentioned fire scorpions. Dam was too consumed by his anger to worry over such things. He strode toward the well with the bucket swinging in his hand and scraping against the ground. If the Fates decided to send fire scorpions as a finishing stroke to his disastrous detour, he would welcome it. His pent-up fury might just get him through an encounter with the deadly monsters.

Dam came up on the strange aura of the well. Its pit wasn't more than the length of a man across. Shiny mori-mori filled the reservoir up to a hand's reach from its lip. As he looked down upon it, a gentle reverberation passed through his body.

He thought at first it was merely hunger. But the thrumming energy passing through him like the perpetual rhythm of a tide was specific and familiar. Within the rising glow of the mori-mori, ethereal wisps swirled and drifted lazily toward the ceiling where they disappeared in the darkness. The well's mysterious radiance was not as strong as the Oomphalos, but they were unquestionably alike.

Dam set the bucket down and idled in the exquisite pain of anticipation. The magic in the well might be the solution to his predicament. Truly, what other option did he have? He could dive into the well and emerge with the ability to fight the snakes. He could claim any fantastical power that his mind could imagine.

But what if Zazamoukh lied? The glowing well looked poisonous and hot. Zazamoukh could have meant to tempt Dam into diving into the well in order to be rid of him. After all, if Dam truly could claim magic from the well, wouldn't the priest want to keep that secret to himself so Dam couldn't use magic against him?

Dam fell back on his original instinct. What else was he to do but try? If he didn't, he would be indentured to Zazamoukh again. He could not abide that. Death would be better than being beholden to the bastard.

Dam stared into the well. His thoughts traveled to the twins. Zazamoukh had mentioned them. Was that a clue? It stood to reason that being born of the underworld, the twins would have known which powers were best to master in order to navigate the backcountry's dangers. There were two possibilities: light or sound.

The shiny skim of the well held no answers, but its glow dandled warmly at his face. It was a beckoning, whether good or evil. Either way, he would drown in the well's thick marrow. Dam looked to the ceiling and prayed to the ancestral mother Pleione to look after Aerander, Hanhau, Hephad, Attalos, and all the others.

Before panic or reason could hold him back, Dam dove into the well.

❖

He could not change his mind once he sank beneath the surface. The well engulfed him. He tried to reach one side to climb out, but he kept sinking deeper. Terror set in. Dam would feel every agonizing moment of his death as the mori-mori filled his lungs, choking him from the inside out.

The valorous thing to do was end it quickly. He would show whatever god or spirit inhabiting the well that he was unafraid. Dam opened his mouth and gulped for his death. Venom, thick as plaster, clogged his throat. His body, which was bound to other interests besides valor, retched to expel the mori-mori, but its defenses had been brutally broken. The molten death claimed his insides as though he had swallowed a titan's fist. If the well had powers to bestow to the brave, it knew no kindness.

It held him suspended without breath or the pumping of his heart. A deathly shroud pressed in on the corners of his mind's eye. Just before he thought he could not withstand the pain, a distant sound like thunder echoed in Dam's ears. Then there was nothing.

CHAPTER EIGHT

A hand thrust through the membrane of the well and grasped its scalloped rim. Dam froze in on that sight as though he was disembodied. He was a ghost hovering above his final resting place. Whoever that stranger was, he possessed the strength of a god to forge his way up from the depths of the mori-mori well. Either that or the fickle well had granted him mercy and relaxed its leaden grip.

A second arm and a head emerged. The stranger found a mooring on the side of the well. He gulped and heaved for air. He strained to raise himself from the pool. Scrabbling a knee up to the edge, he threw himself over to the side and collapsed on his back like a corpse dredged from a mucky grave.

It was a young man in a tunic lacquered to his slight body. A sword and a tin bucket stood nearby. He must have left those implements behind before his audacious plunge. A fool or a daring champion?

That image faded. He opened his eyes to a shuddering blanket of night. He reckoned groggily that the shudders came from within him. He lay flat on his back on the bank of the well, drenched in its gilded batter, bleating with breaths and throbbing from the rapid drumming of his heart. The aura from the well lapped at one side of him. Dam had died and been reborn.

Lost in the impossibility of it, Dam worried for a moment if he could trust his memory. Could he have slipped into the well and pulled himself up from its shallows in a panic? He was enervated, not charged with magic power.

As he gradually regained breath and strength, Dam sat up and wiped the mori-mori from his face and his head where it dripped into his eyes and stung. He collected his sword and used it like a strigil to scrape the well's batter from his body. The substance rolled from his blade in fat, phosphorescent sheets. Dam remembered the waterfall. He could wash up there after completing his errand. The bucket was a short distance away. He crawled to the bucket and carefully reached it into the well, filling it halfway for the priest.

When he stood, aware of his surroundings, he noticed for the first time something had changed. Though the darkness blunted his sight, he could sense the contours of the smoking crater field below. Sounds from the depths of its shadows filled his ears. A rumble of shifting rock. An eternal gust whistling across its barren floor. The patter of anthropoid legs in the shelf above the ceiling.

Dam knew instinctively those sounds were far away even though they were sharp and distinct in his ears, as though he could reach them with an outstretched hand. A hidden world had been unveiled. Every kind of matter had its own distinctive sound. The floor of the bank where he stood hummed from some underground current of energy. The well echoed like a conch shell. Deeper within, he could hear the bubbling pinpoints of air rising up its molten shaft and breaking at the surface with tiny pops.

Dam's own body was a wonder of grotesque noises, from the pumping of his blood to the gurgle of gases through his intestines. He could hear the creak of his bones when he walked. He could hear the scrunch of his muscles when he flexed his biceps. Dam took up his sword to behold the tinny song from the strange vibrations of its metal. Every miniscule thing was in his ken, and when he looked around him, he could see those sounds drifting and swirling, suspended in the air like traces of the wind.

He spoke his name and watched it fog out from his mouth and drift away on a boundless journey. He spoke it louder to make it denser and send it on a faster path. Then he spoke his name a third time. Imagining balling it in his fist, he crushed it into a higher pitch and hurled it, screaming across the crater field below.

These things he understood now. He was the Master of Sound. Dam would have tried out more of the astounding possibilities, but a troubling noise approached. An army of spiny legs scratched across the well plateau. They were near, advancing on Dam's location.

The well's aura illuminated a shallow perimeter around Dam. He stared beyond into the shadows. Maybe his vision ought to have been a secondary consideration, but it was still the habit he was used to.

Flashes of flames blinked through the darkness. They had to be fire scorpions, as Zazamoukh had mentioned, and they had come out to devour him.

Dam zoned in on the monsters' strange chatter. They had a language, though that thought never would have occurred to Dam before. It sounded like rabbeting, rusted shears, but he knew that if he studied it, he could decipher patterns, cadences and tones. He could then mimic it to blend in as one of their kind or send them searching for a better meal elsewhere. Before Dam grasped that plan, the herd emerged from the darkness.

They stood the height of stallions and had fore-pincers as big as giant cudgels. Their towering tails were wreathed with stingers long and sharp enough to hack through a man's gut and come out on the other side. Blue flames breathed from the spiracles under their bellies. Each one was a furnace that could launch a flaring jet from its serrated gob. They numbered at least one dozen.

Dam threw up his hands as though brokering a truce. Rad's lessons in swordsmanship had barely saved him from the carrion beetles. They were of no use against an army of monsters that could kill men through impaling or venom or flame. The monsters spared him a brief moment while they cocked their antennae-crowned nub heads, flooding vibrations at him to lay bare every contour of his body. Then they pressed in on Dam from three sides.

Dam searched for the trace-like currents of sound he had seen before. As many as he could spot, he imagined gathering them with titan hands into a globe above his head. He pressed in on that globe to make it dense and wicked. The weight of it nearly foundered on top of him, and it pulsed and clamored like lightning from its capture.

The fire scorpion horde hissed plumes of flame and drew back from that ominous mystery. Dam cried out fiercely, drawing out his voice to the roar of a colossus. He hurled his globe of sound at the fire scorpions like a boulder from a sling.

It blasted with a force that shook Dam's legs out from under him. The sound shattered against the distant borders of the crater field and echoed back. Dam stumbled to his feet to get his bearings. The well plateau was deserted. The fire scorpions had scattered. Their footfall skittered to far-off hiding places. They were not likely to venture back for quite a while.

Dam shouted out a taunt to keep them cowering for days. He felt tall enough to reach the shelf above him. He had been imbued with the powers of an immortal.

That gave him plenty to think about, but he remembered he had tasks to do before his powers were lost to him as Zazamoukh had mentioned. He needed to take care of the priest first, and then the snakes.

CHAPTER NINE

After scrubbing the mori-mori thoroughly from his clothes and his body, Dam reentered Zazamoukh's cave. The priest had not budged from his position on the floor. His silent face was aglow in the light of the amulet. He either slept or he had closed his eyes while concentrating on a conversation with Calaeno. Dam needed no trick of sound to steal up on him and drop the bucket a breath away from one of the priest's ears.

Zazamoukh shook awake and made a fearful survey of his surroundings. He looked at the bucket and then Dam, who stood in a far corner of his vision. Without a doubt, he wanted to swat Dam, but all he could manage was a reptilian scowl.

The priest hissed, "What was that for? You ought to mind your manners."

"Sorry," Dam said. "I wanted to bring the bucket close. The handle slipped." He massaged his hand.

"Stand closer." He tried to take a better account of Dam. "What was all that commotion out there?"

Dam stepped forward a bit. The priest must have been referring to the giant blast Dam had created to scare off the fire scorpions. It had been loud enough to travel miles. "There was a tremor," Dam said. He looked at Zazamoukh's face with concern. "Are you not feeling well?"

The priest winced. "I feel as horrible as ever." His face darkened and trembled as he struggled to raise himself on one bony elbow. It took the breath out of him, and when he had recovered from that, he trained his gaze on Dam. "Feed me. You dallied too long on a simple errand. I can see there's mischief brewing in that marble brain."

Dam came nearer, but halted with a curious look at the amulet. "What's that?" He clutched the necklace with his mind and surrounded its chiming energy with an invisible sheath. He trapped those sounds and pinched them together to make them sharp and loud. Releasing them from his grip, an explosion of noise like a sack of bells tumbling down a hill surrounded Zazamoukh.

Zazamoukh threw back his head.

Dam pointed at the necklace. "I saw it move."

The priest glanced from the amulet to Dam and back again.

"You didn't see it?" Dam said. He called up an eerie sound from the dark side of his imagination: a woman's tortured screams. Slyly concentrating, Dam pulled the sound from his head and sent it spiraling into the amulet, where it broke free with an anguished wail.

Zazamoukh collapsed to the floor, gasping.

"Something's wrong," Dam told him. He summoned into his palms the cries of children torn from their mothers, the howl of widows, the clanging of cuffed chains on prisoners' ankles. Anger fueling his psychic energy, Dam rolled those noises into nut-sized balls and bowled them through the air to break against the amulet around Zazamoukh's neck. They burst open into a horrible lament that besieged the priest. It was so loud that it filled the cavern with its resounding chorus of misery.

"Take it off me," Zazamoukh cried out.

Dam stooped down and rustled the amulet over the priest's head. Zazamoukh lay back stunned and pale. Just in case he recovered quickly and launched some nasty complaint, Dam grabbed a fist-sized void in an invisible hand and stuffed it in the priest's mouth like a gag.

He swaggered over the prostrate priest. "Someone must have cursed it while it was out of your possession," he said. "It seems you can't command it as well as you used to." Dam looked to the bucket. "Here's your meal."

Dam dumped the bucket over Zazamoukh's head. It wasn't enough to drown him. It was just enough to humiliate him, and it would give him the chance to lick off a few more rations to stay alive. Then Dam ran off with the amulet, cloaking his steps as though he walked on air all the way to the bottom of the cave.

❖

Now Dam faced a far more ambitious task. He had to enter the serpent's den, grab the Oomphalos, and make it out alive. He needed to work out a strategy, but first, Dam had to reconnect with Calaeno to settle some things.

Her voice returned, strained with worry.

"Dam—that's really you? I feared something had happened. Eudoros sounded so weak and desperate."

Dam raised his voice in disbelief. *"You didn't know that he can command the amulet?"*

"Of course. I knew that he could use it the same way as any of its wearers."

"I meant, summoning it away from me and trapping it around his neck?"

There was a sharp intake of breath. *"He told me you had given it to him. I didn't believe him. But he promised he hadn't harmed you."*

"He didn't mention that he had taken the amulet hostage so I'd be bound to him as his servant?"

"You must believe me, Dam. I knew that he had forged its mind portal, but I had no idea he could take the necklace away from you."

Dam wasn't sure she was speaking the truth. And if she wasn't speaking the truth, a terrible thought occurred to him. Maybe she couldn't be trusted to say whether or not it was safe for the survivors to come aboveground. Maybe all she had wanted was to find her way to Zazamoukh. Zazamoukh ought to have drowned in the flood. Had he made it to the portal by chance or had Calaeno aided him?

"Dam, how did you get the amulet back? Was there a fight? Was Eudoros hurt?"

"He's fine. We're speaking, so you ought to have known the answer to that." Having said it, he even wondered if the story about the amulet's power depending on the priest's life was a lie.

"He's dying," Calaeno said. *"I knew it before he spoke the words. I could tell by his brittle voice. The last thing that I heard was an awful scream."*

Dam bristled. *"If you're so worried, should I take you back to him?"*

Calaeno muttered, *"You don't understand. How could you understand?"* Her voice gained courage. *"He's lost his way. Maybe it was wrong for me to lead you to him. I should have foreseen that he would do anything to cling to life."*

"I got what I needed," Dam said. *"I suppose that's the only thing that matters in the end."*

"I feel like I've gone mad," Calaeno said. *"You don't trust me. Tell me what I can do to repair that?"*

The question stumped Dam. Speaking to her through the amulet's mind portal felt so unreliable. Dam had no idea what she was hiding. She could have been smiling while her voice portrayed worry and remorse.

"Why did you give the amulet to Aerander?"

Calaeno hesitated. *"I told you. So I could tell him when it was safe to bridge the portals to the surface."*

Dam rubbed his scratchy chin. He made a decision then. She called out for him, and he shuttered his mind and opened his eyes to the crater field. He would work out a plan to get the Oomphalos by himself. If that all went right, he would return the amulet to Aerander. Until then, Calaeno could keep to herself without spying on the underworld. Aerander could work out whether or not she was honorable.

PART FOUR

Chapter One

Zazamoukh had told Dam the location of the snakes. If the Fates' grace was in abundance, they hadn't moved out yet to attack the city. Dam's first dilemma was how to get up to their lair with speed. He had fallen and climbed down two tiers below the mountain pass, and it had to be a good hike to the other side of the mountains even from there.

He scaled up the platform of rock by the well. Aboveground, he could have hastened his journey with a horse. In the below-world, he would have to improvise, and he had learned a bit about that from Hanhau and the slug-sledges. Dam prayed the underground's more ferocious creatures could be tamed in the same manner.

He called up from his mind a memory of a shrieking carrion beetle gored in battle, and he sent it spraying into the shadows. That could have brought out any number of freakish scavengers from their hiding places. The response was quick, and the ones to respond to Dam's ploy were the most treacherous of all. The fire scorpions skated out from a crusty burrow on spiny legs, venturing through the crater field and toward the well bank.

Dam captured in his head every sound of their approach. He sensed some rudimentary communication between them unrelated to the shearing noise they had flailed at Dam to threaten him. Beneath that noise, he heard a scraping of tiny limbs, some device below their fire-venting gobs that sent out the direction for their route from the captain to his anthropoid vanguard as well as his admonition to be wary based on the memory of what had happened at the well before.

An infantry of towering fire scorpions came up on Dam, shrugging their stinging tails. Dam let the distress signal slip from his mental grasp. He was unveiled as a mere boy on the well bank, but the hulking monsters shirked back from him. They remembered his clamorous display of might. Whatever reverberation they detected from his tiny body, they took for a superior enemy. One scorpion rasped its twiggy whiskers, and they took flight into the shadows.

Dam hadn't thought out how he would bridle one of them, but he had somehow imagined he would have more time. How was he to use them if they burrowed away at the slightest notice of his approach? He grasped out quickly to capture one of the fleeing creatures with his mind. Then he mimicked the bristly vibrations he had heard from their leader.

The creature halted from its flight while the rest of the swarm scattered. Concentrating sharply, Dam menaced the fire scorpion with a tyranny of vibrations. As sure as Zazamoukh had commanded the amulet, he brought the creature back to him with the power of his mind. Dam buried his quarry in a cloud of forbidding sound. It bowed its head and pincers and relaxed its tail. Dam held the fire scorpion like a leashed dog.

He came up on the animal for the final and most precarious step in his plan. He gripped a horn in its shell above its gob, anchored his foot in its side, and mounted the animal. A bridle and harness would have been helpful, but Dam had to make do.

He roused his awesome steed by sending vibrations to its antennae It lurched forward. Dam held on tight to the lip of its shell and braced his legs. He commanded the fire scorpion into a trot and then an eight-legged gallop. It was just a matter of conjuring faster and louder vibrations to control the animal's speed.

They were off at a brisk clip, a boy mounted on a titan fire scorpion, skittering across the crater field toward the passage back to the mountain pass.

❖

They scampered up the gulley and through the passage where Dam had found water, and farther to the tar pit cavern where Dam had fallen during the tremor. Dam was psychically fused to his fire scorpion steed by a language he had not known he commanded. The thought of a direction or a precaution manifested itself as a rhythm of vibrations in his head, and that signal radiated out to his eight-legged carriage as pulses of sound.

It was as though Dam had possessed that otherworldly power his entire life. If he pondered on that too much, he would have been lost in its impossibility. As it was, he didn't have time to think about such things. He didn't want to break his concentration. They were making good speed, but he was impatient to reach the serpents' den.

At the tar pit cavern, they needed to find a way up the cleft where the mountain pass had split open. It had been a sightless vertical drop, and Dam had no idea if he could find footholds along the walls of that cleft or hidden passages in the cavern that would lead up to the mountains. Those concerns thrummed down to his charge as easily as they had occurred to him. The fire scorpion skirred around the tar pit, stopping here and there to twitch its whiskers beneath its gob and tap its forelegs on the bank. It was sorting out a route.

It scampered to a side that Dam had not explored and found a narrow ledge. It climbed up and onward, winding around the pit, eking out an upward path Dam would never have been able to manage. Dam was jostled forward, backward, and side to side while his carriage scaled the steep and wicked route. The foul breath of the pit surrounded him. Dam held on tight to the creature's shell. He did not care to take a plunge into the scalding pool again.

The cleft narrowed and became more workable. The air turned cool and fresh. Dam reached out with his acoustic senses. A breeze washed through the ravine above. As it gusted through hollows and swirled back from the edges of the ravine, an image of the mountain pass formed crisply in his mind's eye. His steed crawled out of the cleft and into the blank night of the ravine.

Dam commanded the scorpion to halt. He needed to sort out one direction from another. More than that, the sensation of ice-cold dread had clutched his gut. The last time he had been in that spot, the ravine had shuddered and rained down boulders on him and every member of his party.

Dam sent out a flood of vibrations to plot the faces of the gorge. Toward one end was a narrow hollow, which was the way Dam's team had come up from the lake. Toward the other, a tall mount of rubble dammed the ravine.

Dam thought of Hanhau, Attalos, Callios, Heron, Blix, and Rad. He grasped each name from his mind and sent them searching through the wall of rubble like ethereal tentacles. A chorus of names bled through the gorge in Dam's voice and echoed back to him bleakly. He commanded his steed to climb the hill of fallout so he could survey the site more closely.

His hearing roamed through the wreckage searching for the faintest breath or the drumming of a heartbeat. Dam visualized Hanhau's leaves of body armor and wondered if he could pick out the particular sound of his voice rippling back from him. Vibrations could lay bare everything. They bounced back swift and sharp from hard matter and slower and fainter from softer things, like flesh. His fire scorpion possessed that kind of perception, and Dam was mastering it quickly.

He fanned out his voice and sorted out its reverberations. Buried in the rubble, he found metal tools and weapons and pieces of earthen things—all remnants of the expedition party, but nothing corpse-like or gory. That was a hopeful relief, yet still a puzzle. He had crested the dam of fallout, and it filled the entire rotunda where they had discovered the remains of Calyiches' party.

A cold bolt of fear struck Dam's heart. A pattern of sound had traveled back to him and formed a vivid image. Bodies were piled on top of each other in the wreckage. His survey of sound revealed the texture of flesh and bone, but no breaths or living sounds came from the buried bodies.

Dam remembered they had laid out the dead for a pyre before the tremor struck the ravine. That death pile had to be what he had located. It was too deep beneath the fallout to confirm with his eyes, but he had no other answer. He compelled the fire scorpion farther into the ravine, still searching for traces of human life. The wreckage declined to the surface of the ravine where a buckled trail snaked through the mountains.

Could scavengers have cleaned out other bodies? A swirl of echoes caught his attention. He zoned in on that sound and pulled his steed in that direction. Faintly, he made out a depth of darkness on one side of the ravine.

Coming up on that spot, Dam saw it was a mill-worm hole like the one Blix had pointed out farther back in the mountain pass. The tunnel was approximately at shoulder height and wide enough for men to climb into. He halted there and listened.

A channel of inert vibrations stretched to the extremity of Dam's hearing. It would have made for a solid shelter from the tremor. Far away, the winding burrow opened up to a broader place, but many tunneled branches led to dead ends in the mountain as well as berths filled with spiny, chattering things.

Following the tunnel would lead Dam far aloft from his destination, and it wasn't big enough for the fire scorpion to get through. Dam cursed himself that he hadn't thought about the power to be in two places at once. His heart was pulling him to climb into the tunnel, but he leashed it brutally and pressed his carriage onward. He had to get the Oomphalos first. All he could do was pray that Hanhau and the others had escaped into the mill-worm hole.

The mountain pass emptied into a valley shored in by furrows of hills. Dam called his fire scorpion to step slowly and lightly as though traversing a spider's web and to pay attention to the mountainside. Unless Zazamoukh's story had led him on a fruitless mission, the serpents' den was near.

Dam scanned the faces of the mountain with a supremely delicate auditory touch, finding many nooks and spurs until the entrance to the lair revealed itself as a translucent spout of arcane energy. Dam hardly needed to plumb the mountainside for its location. The round hole that Zazamoukh had described was a portal to the Oomphalos. The snakes must have cached their prize deep inside to hide its brilliance, but its magic was too powerful to be smothered completely. It radiated vibrations, and its energies pervaded as far and wide as the sun itself.

Those vibrations reached the skin of Dam's face and pulsed gently through him. How many serpents guarded the jewel that would enable them to conquer Agartha again? As fast as Dam had sped toward the place, fear held him captive for a vulnerable moment.

The errand had to be done alone. Even if the fire scorpion could fit inside the lair, it was too large a target for the serpents. Besides, keeping the scorpion in step with his commands would take too much of his mental focus.

Dam would need to concentrate every filament of his power on stealth. The serpents couldn't see well, but they had a keen sense of motion. Dam recalled the speed with which their queen had sorted out their route when he, Aerander, and Lys had snuck into her nest to retrieve the Oomphalos. The only way they had managed to give

Aerander a chance to claim it was to split off and create scattered targets for her to chase. The serpents also had the intelligence of men. A surprise commotion, like the one Dam had conjured to frighten the fire scorpions, wouldn't work on them. They would fall back to protect their precious stone.

Dam dismounted the scorpion. He wished that he had the means to tether it to a spur in the mountain pass. The creature would no doubt be useful if he had to make a quick escape.

Turning to the nearest border of the valley, Dam sent waves of sound into the sightless hills. Slow vibrations echoed back to him, unveiling lodes of thick and bubbling mori-mori in that ridge, just as Zazamoukh had described. With a quick, little rasp, Dam prodded the fire scorpion in that direction. Hopefully the creature would find a fractured trough of mori-mori where it could graze, and it would remain nearby when he emerged from the den.

Dam hid his sword and sheath behind a crag in the mountain shoal. He didn't want to leave them, but the iron-forged weapon rang out with vibrations he couldn't afford to cloak on his mission.

Dam looked back to the mountainside and was almost on his way when he remembered one last task. The glow from Calaeno's amulet needed to be extinguished. He couldn't slip into the serpent's stronghold with that lighted target on his chest no matter how stealthy he was.

It would be the greatest test of his mettle, relying entirely on his mastery of sound. He called out to Calaeno. Dam wished he had thought about that earlier. He wanted to be done with the princess.

"Where are you, Dam?"

"I found the den. But I can't go in with this light around my neck."

"Oh—I thought—well, never mind. That's easily enough done."
The amulet faded and disappeared in the darkness.

"You can't light it up again. Not until I say so."

"Of course I wouldn't."

"Right. Well, I'm off then."

"Dam, be careful. You'd let me know if you're in danger, wouldn't you?"

She sounded sincere, but Dam didn't know whether it was because she genuinely cared about him or because he was her only link back to Zazamoukh.

"Sure," he said, and then he shut her out of his mind.

CHAPTER TWO

A pproaching the mountain socket, Dam cloaked his body to absorb his movements. It occurred to him, however, that the trick was not enough. The snakes' forked tongues were like the antennae of the fire scorpions. They lapped the air to taste displacements in their surroundings, and the vibrations of their tongues would reach that sheath around him and echo back, revealing an intruder. Besides, the energy of the Oomphalos would halt and ripple like a stream parting from a rock that jutted through the surface.

He needed to imagine himself as spectral as a dead man's soul drifting through a crypt. It required an extraordinary amount of concentration. The air was filled with hundreds of currents of sound. Dam had to anticipate each one of their trajectories and to visualize them passing through his body unbroken, as though he wasn't there.

Meanwhile, he had to scope out the way ahead. Dam climbed into the tunnel, shifting from one priority to another. It had to be worse than heading into a swarm of arrows. Even a battalion of archers let up from time to time to reload their bows. Sound and vibration was eternal and infinite. Dam ventured forward, modulating the vibrations that traveled in and out of the tunnel so that it seemed like they were passing through him. When he found a bunker in the cave to hide behind, he quickly fanned out a faint wash of vibrations to paint the next stretch of his path.

His other senses picked up the danger farther ahead. The foul odor of overcrowded reptiles crept into his nostrils.

Dam came to a junction of tunneled passages. He shrank against the wall and focused on acting as a porous veil. Movement echoed from one of the tunnels. It rose up in a rumble, and then a giant serpent trundled through the junction. Its flickering tongue nearly skimmed Dam's face. Dam grasped his breaths in an invisible fist while its enormous trunk skirred past him.

The creature headed down a tunnel that led to the Oomphalos' cascading energy. Dam followed, gaining courage from the success of his disguise. He had been a thief before. The stakes then had been miniscule in comparison, but he knew the feeling of skating the edge of danger. It was a delicious thrill.

Down that tunnel, a torrent of vibrations swirled at him. He had no cover and no time to piece through the commotion to visualize its sources. He needed all of his focus on maneuvering around the beams of sound, and when he couldn't duck or bend away from their projection, he had to imagine his body as the sheerest of membranes and mimic the sounds passing through him.

For a moment, he was marooned and panicked. The dilemma was overwhelming, like trying to capture every current of a typhoon and recreate its path beyond him. Dam wondered if he had overestimated his powers or misjudged his strategy. He would be trapped in the tunnel hiding soundlessly for eternity, and he didn't have eternity. His powers would fade. Sooner than that, the snakes would move on to attack the city.

Courage swelled up in Dam. He was the Master of Sound. He only needed to slow down the passage of its currents in his mind, like freezing time. He crept ahead with a newfound acuity and fearlessness. His mind was a whirring machinery, capturing every vibration and guiding it on its way. Soon that flurry of commands came together as second nature, just as easy as skulking through the tunnel. He was a walking void. Every gust and ripple of noise passed through him. He arrived at the end of the tunnel. Dam visualized a sea of movement in a wide pit below.

Coiled and writhing monsters undulated in that pitch black expanse. It was the serpents' habit to nest together as one gory horde. When they held the city, they had numbered in the thousands. They had been cut down to dozens when the prisoners revolted and the Old Ones came to reclaim their city. Dam was stunned by how many snakes inhabited their den. Several hundred? They must have bred, and no doubt the Oomphalos had catalyzed that effort.

Across the pit, the magic of the Oomphalos radiated out like an invisible beacon from atop a tall platform of rock. The relic was buried beneath a mound of man-sized spheres. Even under all that, the stone had to be covered by a solid cage to muffle its energy even more. Perhaps they were wary since the Oomphalos had been stolen from them before, or maybe it had been hid in that mound for another reason.

As Dam zoned in, he noticed that each of the mounded spheres gave off a drumming, squirming energy. Cold dread poured over him. The spheres were serpent eggs being nurtured by the stone's strange power, a new generation of monsters to terrorize the underworld. Three serpents guarded that hatchery.

Dam traveled around the narrow ridge of the pit. Rustles, squirms and hisses clamored up from the serpent nest below. Edging around the pit, Dam bounced those noises back as though he had melded into the walls of the den. As he neared the platform of the Oomphalos, he realized his impossible predicament. He could cloak himself to slip past the serpents guarding the eggs and the Oomphalos. If he did it very quickly, he could avoid their dull and cloudy vision. But he would have to dig the Oomphalos out of the egg mound. As soon as he did that, its full, brilliant energy would flood the den, and the entire horde of snakes would launch at him to defend it.

As he fretted, a method struck Dam. He could use his magic to squelch the stone's vibrations like muffling a buzzing bee with his hand. That would panic the guards to sift through the eggs to investigate. Dam wouldn't be able to do anything about the stone's throbbing glow, but if he hid near, he could take advantage of the moment of confusion to grab the Oomphalos and tuck it in a pocket of his tunic. The stone would be plunder, not a weapon. Despite what Calaeno said about the line of Atlas, Dam couldn't fathom commanding the Oomphalos as Aerander had done. He was just its thief. He would have to work by decoy and stealth to accomplish his job.

The gamble was perilous. For one thing, Dam did not know if his power could quench the stone's vibrations even temporarily. For another, he would have to be as quick as lightning to run off with it before the serpent guards took notice of him. Afterward, he would have to seal up both his vibrations and the stone's to escape from the den while every serpent in the lair leapt up from the pit to catch him. His odds weren't very good, but Dam had surrendered himself to fate from the moment he had entered the den. Besides, fearlessness was his nature as it had been with his father.

He came up on the platform of rock overlooking the pit, and he stole into position behind the trio of serpents watching the hatchery. Beneath the mounded eggs, he perceived a horned shell caging the Oomphalos. It might have been the husk of a carrion beetle. The serpents' weakness was that they lacked the industry of the Old Ones. Having shed their limbs through their monstrous transformation ages ago, they depended on human slaves for any type of craft. Maybe that was why they were biding their time to attack the city. It took greater numbers to enslave an enemy than to annihilate it.

Penetrating into the depths of the hollow, farther inward on the cliff where he stood, Dam perceived pens walled with boulders hobbled together by the serpents' snouts and constricting trunks.

The Oomphalos throbbed beneath its shell. It generated thrumming halos of energy that seemed strong enough to travel out to an infinite circumference. Hazily, Dam could visualize its silhouette, but it was hard to capture exactly in his mind's eye. A great welter of vibrations fought to get out of that shell. The stone's energy was distorted, and it seemed at times multiple entities were beneath its cover.

Dam drew up near. He had to camouflage himself precisely. Two of the serpents were bunkered around the egg mound. The third looked out over the pit, reared to its full height and lashing its tongue, performing some foul accounting of its tribe. Dam called up orbs of smothering silence into his palms. He had one chance to perform his trick. If he only accomplished a hiccup in the stone's energy, he would be easily discovered when the serpents locked in on the egg mound to sort out the irregularity.

The orbs of silence grew in Dam's hands, drawn from every void of sound in his ken. When they felt strong enough to cloak an erupting volcano, he flushed them deep into the egg mound to grasp the shell around the Oomphalos. They made their mark, spreading around the husk, and billowed back from the stone's tremendous energy. Dam bore down on them. He was fighting magic with magic. He needed to channel more silence from his surroundings and bear down on the stone with greater strength. Dam managed a solid grip on the shell and muted the Oomphalos completely.

The two serpent guards snapped to attention, and their lookout curled back to the egg mound with a reptilian gasp. Two of them nudged through the eggs. The third made a keen appraisal of the perimeter with its flicking tongue. Dam prayed that they unearthed the Oomphalos quickly. He was starkly in their midst with only a sound barrier for cover.

The eggs tumbled away from the shell. Angry hisses scraped through the air. The serpents had to be panicked, thinking that the source of their power had been stolen right from under them or worse, that its ancient energy had died.

Dam inched closer to the shell. As soon as the Oomphalos was unveiled, in that blink of confusion when the serpents found it shining but as inert as an ordinary gem, Dam would have to grab it. He kept his aura of smothering energy trained on the shell, ready to shrink it around the skull-shaped stone and lunge for the prize. One of the serpents moved the shell with its snout.

The shell flipped over on its side, and an inferno of light flared out to the cavern. Dam clenched his eyes shut from the shock of it. He struggled to narrow his beam of silence around the stone. Luckily, the shock of light surprised the three serpents as well. They recoiled from it, and that gave Dam time to act.

Grasping the stone with silence, he opened his eyes in a squint so he could find it. If a trace of the Great Atlas' blood bonded him to the stone, its only manifestation was an ability to adjust quickly to the stone's remarkable brilliance.

Just as Dam perceived its form, another sight beneath the shell halted him. He saw a miniature monster with three serpent heads clinging to the Oomphalos and writhing with silent squeals. The hatchling was a tiny replica of queen Ouroborus. They must have been keeping it cocooned with the stone so it would grow to be the dread beast that she was.

Dam reached for the stone and shook the gory little menace from it. But in the time he had been suspended by the discovery of the hatchling, he had lost hold of the silent shroud he had spread over the Oomphalos and the magic that had kept him cloaked. The hideous baby shrieked at him. One serpent locked in on him, then another, and then the third.

Dam shoved the Oomphalos in the pocket of his apron. In a heartbeat, any of the three creatures would lunge and capture him. They shriveled back their snouts, their knife-sized fangs dripping with deadly venom. Dam used the only weapon he had. He called up a mighty sound memory in his head, and pitched its roiling, sparking energy at the ceiling of the lair. It burst like a barrel of niterbats thrown from a catapult.

That sent the serpents flinching to the ground. Dam hurled a second and a third blast at the ceiling for good measure. He sheathed the stone and ran for the lip of the pit, circumnavigating the ricochet of vibrations he had stirred up. It wouldn't take long for the serpents to figure out that the explosive attack on their den had been a trick. Dam had to make it to the burrow that led out of the mountainside.

A legion of fanged demons skirred up the sides of the pit.

At the entrance to the burrow, Dam turned back, captured as many echoes as he could in his mind's hand, and whirled them into a cyclone of deafening chaos. Some of the serpents bounded down the walls of the pit. Others clung on and fought through the confusion. Dam raced into the burrow. That had been the best trick he possessed. Now he had to focus on speed. Serpents would be on his heels in no time.

CHAPTER THREE

Dam made it to the outlet to the mountains and stumbled down the steep escarpment. He reached out mentally for the ring of his *xiphos*. Its tinny signal led him to the rocky bunker where he had left his weapon, and he holstered his sword and scabbard. The whistling pass through the mountains was a short distance away. Could he make it through and across the great distance to the city before the snakes tracked him down?

A frenzy of lumbering vibrations erupted from the mountain socket above him. Many dozens of serpents were skating through that tunnel and fighting over one another to catch up with Dam.

A rivulet of sweat ran down the side of his face. His powers would be practically useless now. He could put all his energy into creating phantasms of sound to distract the snakes or put it all into outpacing them, but he couldn't do both of those things at once, and neither strategy held much hope against the legion of fanged demons closing in on him.

Somewhere in the scalloped ridges of the sightless valley beyond him, he knew of a possibility for expediting his flight. Dam threw scraping vibrations out to the hills. By the grace of the gods, an answer came back to him, and spiny legs galloped through the darkness. Above him, loose pebbles sprayed down the escarpment, and serpent snouts shot out of the mountain socket.

The fire scorpion bounded up from the valley. Dam clambered on its back, grasped a reasonably secure hold, and bore down psychically to send it fleeing into the mountain pass for its life.

Like riding a bucking bull, the scorpion's momentum threw him back. Dam clung on desperately. Serpent bodies drummed to the ground behind him.

Dam had no idea how a fire scorpion's speed measured up to the serpents. He had seen the creatures darting on their bellies, and they were longer than his scorpion at a full stretch. His steed careened through the ravine at a breakneck pace, surely as aware of the peril as Dam himself. The serpents plowed after them like a rumbling tide carving through the pass.

The serpents accelerated behind Dam. The skirring of their scaled bodies was practically in reaching distance, and then Dam heard a rush of noise from the sides of the ravine. A fanged snout lunged out from the shadows at the level of his carriage. Some of the serpents had sorted out a higher trail. Dam cringed away from one of them and swung back from the snapping jaws of another on the opposite side.

If the snakes overtook his scorpion, he would find himself dodging strikes from all directions. Dam hung on to the rim of armor above the scorpion's gob, spread out flat over its back, and called up his trick of melding soundlessly into matter.

A snout bucked into the scorpion, throwing one side of its legs into the air while Dam clung on to its armor for dear life. His steed raced forward and found its balance again. It lurched away from a strike on the other side.

Dam wasn't going to let himself or his steed get ripped apart by the serpents. He needed to use his powers to buffet them back, and he only knew one sound that could scare off a giant snake stampede. Dam drew it out of his head and imagined it thickening and growing into an orb as powerful as a hundred barrels of packed niterbats. He scoured the ravine with his mind to feed his phantom of sound every vapor of noise he could find. It had to be a perfect mimic to trick the snakes. Focusing fiercely, Dam imagined ripping the orb open to unleash its destruction.

The severing of that ghostly creation was so loud, the entire ravine seemed to shudder. Phantom rocks rained down from the height of its banks. A thunderous knocking rose up from the floor, and then he heard an ear-piercing crack as though the bed of stone was cleaving apart.

The scorpion scurried from one side of the ravine to the other until Dam got hold of a rhythm of vibrations to keep it focused on a straight path to safety. The rumble of the serpents' chase fell off in the wake of the angry tremor Dam had created. His trick had worked. Hopefully, it had sent the snakes racing back to the other side of the mountains. When its vibrations wore down, he would be able to tell for sure.

At least the trick had bought him some time. Dam climbed up to a better seat on the scorpion. He didn't waste a moment to gloat over his cleverness. He had a long way to go back to the city.

❖

Dam rode on to the far end of the mountain pass and descended to the bank of the lake. A drink of water would have been a divine ecstasy, but Dam decided to ride on. He had to make the journey home in a fraction of the time it had taken his expedition if he was to stay ahead of the snakes. It had been a long hike around the lake, and he still had the grotto, the Fire Canyon, and the dead lava fields to traverse.

He galloped along the shore of the vast, black lake. Dam kept attuned to sounds of pursuit from the mountains, but he heard nothing troubling for a long stretch. The mountains droned with a deep, ancient resonance, and gusts of wind shrieked over its peaks. Dam felt the Oomphalos in his pocket. It was a miracle that it had stayed secure through all the jostling in the mountain pass. Now he needed to bring it back to the city to heal his blind cousin and save the lives of the freed prisoners.

Far away, he noted a clap on the surface of the lake. Dam's ears homed in on that spot. Serpentine bodies splashed into the water from the shoals of the mountains. They zigzagged a vigorous tread to overtake Dam on the opposite bank. After Dam had scared them away with the illusion that the mountain fault had opened up, they must have found an alternative route through the range. No doubt, they were locked in on the vibrations of the Oomphalos, and they would fight to the death to retrieve it.

Dam urged his scorpion to a faster clip. The tinkling current of the grotto was near. Judging by the movement of the swimming snakes, he could make it to that passage before the horde reached the bank. It would be a terror of a race after that.

They scaled the ridge of the grotto and flew through its shallow waters. The scorpion sensed the danger again and needed no command to put as much distance as possible between itself and the snakes. They kept well ahead through the cavern and upward to the cleft tunnel that would lead to the Fire Canyon. Dam listened to the serpents beaching from the lake and trundling forward in pursuit.

When they arrived at the high bank of the Fire Canyon, the pursuing scourge was just yards behind them. The scorpion quickly sorted out a descent and a route from island to island across the scorching, incandescent flow of lava. Luckily, the creature had no aversion to heat or flame. It made fire from its own belly to power its limbs. Meanwhile, Dam sweated through the crossing, making himself small in the center of the scorpion's back, hoping to avoid the spatter of molten rock and the spray of steaming geysers.

The serpents skirred to the bank above them and delayed a bit with their strategy for fording the flame-spitting canyon. Dam swept up the sounds from the canyon floor and hurled a scorching blare at the snakes to menace them. The monsters reared back from it, but they quickly took up a direction for their pursuit.

When Dam reached the other side of the canyon, the snakes were halfway across. Now his scorpion had to make incredible speed across the dead lava field to the city. That would be even ground for the serpents. They would be able to torpedo across the rock floor and spread out to attack Dam from an array of vantages.

Dam thought of another problem. He would be approaching the city from its tunnel entrance. If the Old Ones had sealed up the city as a precaution, the tunnel gates would be closed. A watchtower was on that side, but it was a great height above the tunnel, mounted on the mighty shelf of the city plateau. Dam could send a signal to the men on watch, but even from a distance, no one would be able to make it down and draw open the gates for him before the snakes overtook him. The gates wouldn't be able to open and close quick enough to stop the snakes from breaching the city.

He would have to take a trail around the plateau to the canyon-side drawbridge over a broad trench of lava. He summoned his scorpion onward with a burst of speed. It would be a longer journey, giving the snakes more time to catch up with him. They had to travel like the racing wind.

Up the broad slope to the dead lava fields, Dam homed in on the distant sounds of the city. Its geared lifts cranked and churned with water. Its smelt-works clanged and surged, and Dam could even hear the sizzle of gas-lit flames. Dam's spirits soared. Those were the most joyous sounds he had heard in many nights. When he crested the slope, he feasted his eyes on the specks of light on the horizon that framed the magnificent, mounded city.

Dam directed his scorpion toward the rocky bank along the walled city shelf. That pathway rose up to cliffs of mori-mori mines, and beyond they would find the canyon that yawned at the foot of the city.

While the scorpion climbed the bank, Dam felt a rumble gaining up on them. A legion of snakes flooded across the lava field like a devouring wave. Dam goaded his scorpion to pick up its pace. For the first time, he noticed a strain in the creature's movements. The heavens knew it had covered an epic expanse of ground and mostly at a breakneck clip. Smoky breaths chuffed from its undercarriage. Its fuel was nearly spent.

Dam clenched down mentally with urgent vibrations and clopped his legs on the scorpion's sides like spurring a stallion. A tide of serpents was closing in on them. The scorpion lumbered up to the cliffs and staggered forward with its armored cage of ribs heaving.

Mori-mori flowed in the caverns of the cliffs where the scorpion could replenish itself, but they didn't have a spare moment for that. Dam felt bad for the beast. He would see that it was rewarded with a gluttonous drink and a good rest for its labor, but it needed to find a final charge within itself. Otherwise, they would both be buried by a sea of serpent trunks and fangs.

Dam's thoughts formed words in the quivering language that the scorpion understood. The animal sucked breaths through its vented undercarriage like a smithy stoking a brazier. Flames surged, not as vigorously as Dam had sensed before, but its crawl strengthened to a trot and then a gallop. Mercifully, the rest of the way was downhill. They hurtled to the foot of the cliffs and pressed onward toward the ridge of the canyon and the narrow trail to the city drawbridge.

The snakes avalanched down the cliffs to the canyon rim.

From hundreds of paces away, Dam locked in on the fiery beacon of the drawbridge watchtower, locating the vibrating energy of two warriors. Inside the city's encircling fortification, he could hear the dense current and chatter of its inhabitants. He could bullet his voice across the distance to the drawbridge guards and urge them to bring down its iron leaves, but the guards might be merely startled by that disembodied voice. He needed to warn the entire city about the encroaching army of snakes.

He visualized the mighty conch shell that called the warriors to arms. Dam held it hovering above the city walls and imagined a giant breath blowing through the conch with the fury of a titan. The blare was massive. It rang through the city with a paralyzing force. In its wake, a rapid footfall of soldiers hurried to the city's lookouts and archer towers.

Dam brought the Oomphalos out from his pocket and raised it above his head like a star grappled from the heavens. That would make him startlingly clear to the guards. A boy who had wrested the Oomphalos, saddled on a giant, fire-breathing scorpion, racing toward the drawbridge with a horde of serpents rushing after him.

The leaves of the drawbridge clamored down. The scorpion scurried to that passage, taking it with a leap while the platforms were still partially raised. The scorpion barreled through the narrow gap between the tall iron gates, knocking about both sides of the gateway.

Inside the city quay, it skidded and careened to a halt. Dam was thrown from its back and onto the stone floor in a tumble. The Oomphalos flew out of his hand. Sparks of pain blew up in his vision, and his hip throbbed brutally from his landing, but he couldn't begrudge the scorpion for bucking him loose. Through its Herculean effort, they had made it safely inside the city.

CHAPTER FOUR

As the blurry form of an underground warrior approached Dam to help him to his feet, he heard a terrible thud at the city gates. Cries hailed from the battlements of the city's stone wall curtain. A flurry of whooshing bolts sprung from crossbows.

Dam fought through his disorientation to take account of the situation. The serpents had been on Dam's heels, and now they were ramming the doors. Meanwhile, the Oomphalos blasted a blinding aura, and the scorpion rounded the quay like a loosed bull. It was sending archer reinforcements ducking and scrambling for cover. That had to be dealt with first.

Dam stood up and gathered calming vibrations for his steed. The scorpion bowed and answered with a gale of shearing complaints. It would hold for a little while. Dam went for the Oomphalos, which had been thrown a few yards away. Just as he picked it up and pocketed it, he was met by a familiar voice.

"How do you control that thing?"

It was Backlum. He was understandably bewildered by Dam's reining of the fire scorpion. Dam grinned, though the pain from his fall made him wince. He was happy to be in contact with people again and happy to see that the warrior was unencumbered by his neck brace.

"There's a lot to explain," Dam said.

Backlum clopped Dam's shoulder. "C'mon. We can pen it in a storehouse for now."

Dam cast a mental bridle on the scorpion and followed the warrior out of the quay and down a ramp to a district of vaults for the city's ore and raw masonry. They penned the animal in a brickhouse and rolled the metal shutters behind it securely.

Remembering his promise to the scorpion, Dam told Backlum, "It'll need to eat."

"There will be a feast for all of us if we make it through this night." The warrior took a peculiar account of Dam. "You found magic in the backcountry."

Dam nodded, wincing from the pain in his rattled head again.

"You took a hard fall. Can you help out with the front line?"

"Sure." The pain would wear off, and Dam wanted to do his part, although he wasn't really sure how he could help.

Backlum started back to the quay at a brisk pace. Dam jogged after him to keep up with the warrior's long-legged stride. He wanted to ask about the other members of his expedition party, especially Hanhau. Had he made it back to the city?

The sounds of battle drew Dam's attention away from that matter. The yard-thick city gates shuddered and rang from the assault of the hard-snouted snakes. Above, some two dozen archers fired and reloaded their crossbows to send back the enemy below the wall.

The battalion was scarcely enough to fight the snakes. Their ranks were sparse since many of the warriors had been injured from the explosion at the Oomphalos tower. Dam followed Backlum to a ladder leading up to the archer gallery.

Before Dam could climb up behind Backlum, he was halted by a voice.

"Dam."

It was Ysalane. Dam turned to the warrior queen. Her face glowed with a kind sheen.

"You have done what no one thought was possible," she said. "There aren't enough words in the world to thank you."

Dam didn't know what to say to that. It made him feel proud and humble at the same time. He noticed Ysalane glancing at his sagging pocket. Of course, she wanted the Oomphalos so it could be hidden and protected in a place where the New Ones wouldn't get it if they managed to break through the city's defenses. Or maybe, as Blix had said, the warrior queen had mastered some of its magic and could hold back the snakes.

Dam brought the stone out of his apron and handed it to Ysalane. They exchanged a quiet smile. Ysalane withdrew into the quay, carrying the brilliant stone beneath the folds of her cloak.

Dam climbed the iron ladder up to the battlements at the top of the wall. Backlum had taken up a position above the gates among a tightly packed fleet of archers. Dam glanced over the shoulder-high parapet and down the drop on the other side. Dizziness and nausea claimed him. It would be a fatal tumble from the archer's alley, which was no broader than one man across. Dam breathed in to buffer his dizziness. He swallowed hard.

He tried looking out again. Gradually the world stopped swaying, and it felt like his feet were on solid ground. The sounds and sights below were troubling. The snakes had managed to leap across the drawbridge before it had lifted upright, and their combined weight had crushed down its metal leaves. A shadowy mob of them rammed and wrenched at the gates. Light from the city bled out from a narrow gap between the iron doors. The snakes had made a deep dent in that spot.

They were easy targets for the archers, but even riddled with metal bolts, the snakes pounded the doors relentlessly. They were crazed in their pursuit of the Oomphalos. Dam noticed something even more worrisome. As the archers felled a few with tens of deep punctures, another line of snakes piled on top of the wounded, accomplishing a greater height. They were building a scaffold of bodies that would allow them to scale the battlements and pour into the city. The warriors had no chance of stopping the fanged monsters in close combat, even for those who were skilled with crooks and axes.

Dam called the shock waves from the battle into his grasp and crushed them together lengthwise like wrinkling together tight folds of fabric. He knew the snakes had a keen and delicate sense of sound. If he flooded them with a loud pitch of an exceedingly high register, it might deafen them and impair their assault. He hurled his menacing creation at the mob. It rang out with a harpy's squeal that could shatter glass. Dam had to cover his own ears, though none of the warriors could perceive it.

The snakes curled back from that phantom shriek. They were momentarily stricken, dumb and static targets for the quick fire of the archers. Backlum glanced at Dam. The warrior looked like he was adding up that Dam had performed some feat of magic. For a triumphant moment, the plan seemed to have worked.

Two-thirds of the gory horde were bolted down for good. But as Dam's stupefying shriek diffused out to the canyon, some of the snakes sprouted up from the mound of bolt-riddled trunks. They skated over the dead toward the height of the battlement. Dam realized he should have held the noise over them in a frozen grip. He reached out for more shock waves to launch a second assault.

The serpents spread out below to different approaches. They were clever to Dam's strategy. He would have to stun them one by one with his concentrated weapon of sound.

One of the serpents found a high perch on top of the felled bodies and reached to the height of the parapet. Archers hacked its snout and neck with their bolts, and it writhed and sloughed down the city curtain. Another serpent reared up to an undefended vantage. Dam honed his ammunition and aimed it at the creature, striking it with an ear-splitting blow. The serpent winced and tumbled over itself.

A third creature sprung up to the battlement and dragged itself past a pair of archers. It took skewers of bolts at close range and kept trundling over the wall. The beast skated down a ladder to the quay.

Backlum commanded the battalion to keep their aim on the enemy outside the wall. He looked at Dam. The warrior's sweat-slick face was grim with desperation. Dam understood. The archers were too few to split their attention between the inside and the outside of the city curtain. It was up to Dam to subdue the serpent that had breached the city.

Dam summoned sound as quickly as he could. The beast below beserked through the quay. It lunged for the warriors who buttressed the gates with their bodies and iron crooks, scattering them to the sides. It pummeled back a team of men with battle axes with its tail, and it turned and shrieked at a single archer who rifled bolts from one corner of the yard.

Dam zoned in on that brave warrior. He recognized something familiar in his bearing, or was it the distant, shadowy silhouette of his face? It was Hanhau, managing a crossbow with one wounded arm braced upright at his side. The serpent rose above him, preparing a strike at his head or his sides.

The sound blast that Dam had accumulated didn't have the density or throbbing power to deafen the beast, but there wasn't time. He slung it quickly at the serpent, praying for the best. It burst into a high-pitched wail. That was enough to startle the beast, but Hanhau was still cornered and fumbling to reload his weapon after that bizarre apparition of sound. Around the quay, every other warrior had retaken their places holding the gates.

A sole, slight figure entering the yard caught Dam's attention. He was no warrior. He was an unarmed, lanky boy in a kilt approaching the serpent as though he had some capacity to subdue it. Dam watched in disbelief. What did Hephad think he was doing?

Hephad swung his arm outward and upward and shouted. Three juvenile spotted tigers scrambled from the alley behind him and lunged for the serpent's neck. In the time Dam had been away, the kittens had tripled in size. That still left them at half the length of the serpent if they were all three lined up head to tail, but they each sprang onto the monster biting and ripping at its scaled skin with their claws.

The serpent thrashed and twisted to throw them off. One of the cats lost its grip and tumbled off, but its sisters hung on with feral mercilessness. The creature gasped and bowed to the floor of the yard. The cats bore down on it with their heft. The third one leapt back on the serpent's neck to help wrestle the kill. They dug their jaws into the collapsed beast until it lay lifeless.

That was a heartening sight, but sounds from the other side of the wall signaled an ongoing struggle. Three serpents had reared up to the battlement, with only pairs of archers to vie with each of them while the rest of the company fought to volley back the rising horde. At the gates, one of the serpents had wrenched its snout deep into the dent between the doors. Once the serpents broke open the gate, they would massacre the city. No power of archery, mastery of sound, or feline ferocity would stop them.

The crimson glow of the Oomphalos washed into the quay. The serpents shrieked greedily for it. For a moment, everything seemed to be stained in blood as though the world had hemorrhaged.

Dam perceived a figure in the quay who held the magical stone in front of him. A crowd gathered behind him, mostly boys who had come out to fight with short swords. Dam recognized Ysalane in the crowd as well as the warrior Ichika. They were following his cousin Aerander out to battle.

Aerander strode forward intrepidly toward the city gate. Either he was healed, or he was possessed by some otherworldly power that guided him, giving no hint of his injury. The men holding the gates parted.

The serpents high up by the battlements jettisoned down to join their brethren outside the gates. They must have sensed the opportunity to burst into the quay and claim the Oomphalos. Every atom in Dam's body winced at what was to come. He rushed to a ladder to descend to the yard.

The gatehouse in the quay rattled with its machinery. The warped, elephantine doors bellowed and grated open. By the time Dam had climbed down to the quay, the gears had separated the doors wide enough for two or three snakes to squeeze through.

For the space of a breath, there was a standoff between Aerander and the serpents piled on top of one another on the other side of the gates. They were a spellbound swarm of salivating snouts and beaded eyes in the rhythmic cast of the mysterious artifact.

The stone swelled and constricted rhythmically like a heart ripped out of a man's chest. Some current from within Aerander's body strengthened into a white-hot fire and pulsed down his arms, into his hands, and into the stone itself. In a blink, a bolt of light shot out of the stone and into the serpent horde. It held the monsters like a wall of frozen totems.

The bolt vanished. A profound silence, like the cloak of death, presided over everything. Then the swarm of gory snakes crumbled like crushed cinders.

Every last one of them had been incinerated by the Oomphalos.

Chapter Five

In the wake of the battle, Dam rooted through the crowded quay to try to reach his cousin. He could hardly hear for the teeming celebration of cries and fists launched high in the air. A group of boys lifted Aerander onto their shoulders to hail the serpent slayer.

Dam veered from one knot of bodies to the next. Even craning and perching on the tips of his feet, he couldn't see past the high-shouldered warriors in his way. He might just have to wait things out and find Aerander when the celebration had died down.

His ears detected someone calling his name. The distant voice was drowned beneath the cheers that filled the yard. Dam never would have perceived it before he had been magicked with the mastery of sound. That voice made his mouth curl into a smirk. Tracing it like a beacon, he shuffled through the crowd to the margins of the quay.

He came up on Hanhau before the warrior noticed him. Hanhau's black mop of hair was damp with sweat, and his face was strained from calling out for Dam, not to mention the stress of the battle. He looked at Dam, and his face flushed with light.

They stood together for a quiet moment. Hanhau reached out for Dam with his good arm, and Dam embraced him so hard he could feel Hanhau's heartbeat thrumming against his chest.

Hanhau brushed his lips against Dam's cheek. "I prayed, and the Creator God brought you back to me," Hanhau said.

Dam gripped harder for more of that embrace.

"You saved the city."

Dam glanced over to the center of the quay where boys and warriors jumped and hollered around his cousin.

"Aerander did it."

Hanhau narrowed his gaze reproachfully. "You brought back the stone. You fought the serpents to get it. If I hadn't listened to you and let you come on the expedition, the New Ones would have taken the city and sent us all hiding in the backcountry."

Dam agreed, but that was hardly worth dwelling on. Finding Hanhau after everything that had happened had been the greatest miracle. He remembered the mill-worm hole in the mountain pass that had been the only escape from the avalanche. Dam crushed his lips against Hanhau's and shut his eyes, savoring their embrace. For a wonderful moment, all of the commotion in the yard seemed to drift away.

Attalos' voice called out to him, trying to pry away his attention. As soon as Dam turned to his friend, more voices in the crowd piped up as people recognized him. Attalos goaded Dam to join him and his friends in the celebration in the quay. Callios, Heron, and Hephad called out to him. Farther off, sturdy Rad nudged his companions and howled out Dam's name.

Dam looked to Hanhau. Hanhau grinned. "Go on."

Dam ventured into the crowd. Rad fought through people, caught Dam by his legs, and hoisted him onto his shoulders.

Cheers of victory surrounded Dam. It was something he had never wished for and certainly never anticipated, but a hero's welcome was an insuppressible intoxication. He thrust his fist into the air.

Rad carried him alongside Aerander. A martial anthem broke out among the boys, and they clasped each other around the shoulders and sang a boisterous ballad of triumph from their homeland.

Dam visualized the strains and rhythms of that song, smoothing out its sharp parts, overlaying a harmony, and filling in a steady timbre like the drummers from a military parade. It came together as a symphony of sound that circulated through the quay. Pipes and flutes. Lyres and mandolins. Leather drums and clappers.

The crowd quieted for a moment, awed by that mysterious music. After everything they had seen that night, it didn't take long for people to shrug off that miracle and raise their voices to sing along. The underground city filled with the rowdy sounds of a festival from the old country.

PART FIVE

CHAPTER ONE

Ysalane proclaimed they would have three nights of feasts to celebrate the return of the Oomphalos and the defeat of the New Ones. Banquets were laid in the warrior queen's Great Hall of mirror-plated walls, and its surrounding yards were cleared for a tournament of games. The underground people had their traditions of archery challenges and hammer throws. The Atlantean boys organized wrestling bouts and foot races.

Everyone attended spectacles of music and dancing, some of which had been put on by the Old Ones with their drummers and their warriors' gymnastic jigs. Since everyone had witnessed the magic Dam could perform with sound, he was called upon again and again to entertain them with fantastical melodies conjured from some otherworldly realm. Dam would have preferred to enjoy the celebration quietly with Hanhau and his friends, but he supposed it would have made him quite a spoilsport if he didn't share his magic. While he wove melodies of phantom pipes and string players from vibrations suspended in the air, the Old Ones' engineers put on an awesome pyrotechnic display that dazzled the city.

That all made for the best party of Dam's life. Though it was the stolen hours in Hanhau's bed, when his warrior roommates had cleared out of the barracks, that Dam liked the best.

Hanhau's broken arm, which he had incurred from being thrown in the mountain pass, had been quickly healed by Ysalane. She had conjured magic from the Oomphalos to mend the bone as she had restored Aerander's sight when the New Ones had stormed the city.

After Dam and Hanhau lay together, Hanhau's body armor molted off in patches, stripping him down to fresh skin on his chest and back. In that private moment, they vowed that their hearts were twined in iron. They were promised to one another, two men living their lives side by side until the end of their days. Most of the other warriors strode about the city stripped of their body armor as well. The season of courtship had resumed.

When the feast was over, Hephad started a big fuss about recovering the bodies of Calyiches' party from the mountain pass. It wasn't a popular idea at first, but Hephad won the support of Aerander, who then asked Ysalane to endorse the cause. That situation stirred up the first lover's quarrel between Attalos and Hephad that Dam had witnessed.

Attalos thought it was sufficient justice to let the traitors rot beneath the avalanche. Hephad called him barbaric. Dam kept quiet, sitting safely on his pallet with Pleione bedded in his lap.

"If they don't get their funeral rites to send them off to the afterlife, their souls will roam the underworld for eternity," Hephad told Attalos sharply. "It's not for us to judge them now that they're dead. Their souls will have their reckoning in the heavens when Poseidon decides their fate."

Attalos stewed beneath a moody cloud. Since Hephad had recovered his speech, he had really come into his own, keeping the boys in line with their daily oblations and showing them how to cobble together household altars and fetishes. Everyone admired how he had trained the kittens to be fierce defenders of the city.

Attalos had good reason to heed Hephad's decrees. Attalos had given Hephad his family ring and proposed that they be bonded like a proper gentlemen's couple. A ceremony was planned. Hephad said that it could hold until after the funerals for Calyiches' party.

All of the members of Ysalane's sixteen volunteered for the second expedition. It was to take place in haste before the bodies were scavenged. The city smithies quickly built wheeled sledges so they could transport the remains.

The night before they were to embark, while Dam nestled with Hanhau in his barracks bed, Hanhau edged around the notion of Dam staying back. Hanhau held his face and gently traced the puffy half-moons beneath Dam's eyes. "You've barely rested since coming home. It wouldn't trouble our cause one bit if you let us go without you."

Dam knew that he was right. Since the battle with the snakes, he had been racing from one thing to the other, fueled by the collective excitement in the city. Exhaustion clawed at him. Dam laid his cheek on Hanhau's chest and clutched his thigh between his legs. Staying back made good sense, but he didn't want to be separated from Hanhau now that he knew what it felt like to be together.

Hanhau kissed the crown of his head and combed his fingers softly through his hair. "I'll be back before you know it."

Dam listened to the drumming of Hanhau's heart. "I'll follow your sound every moment that you're gone."

Hanhau chuckled. "You should be sleeping instead of checking up on me."

"You'll never know the difference."

Dam saw Hanhau safely off when the team embarked from the city gates, then he traveled to his house in the Honeycomb and lay down on his pallet.

His senses roamed into the distance to follow the rumble of the expedition's sledges. He searched for the familiar, calming sound of Hanhau's heartbeat, but his concentration was spent. His eyelids shuttered like lead weights, and sleep quickly engulfed him.

CHAPTER TWO

D am awoke to a room bathed in red, crystalline light. So it had
been nearly every day for a half year's passing, but for a strange
moment, he could not remember where he was or how he had come to
be there. Slumber had washed his mind clean. Dam even forgot that he
had been living in the underworld and wondered what had made the
light of day turn red and twinkle as though the sun had been caged in
stained glass.

The events of his recent past drifted back to him. He remembered
that the Old Ones had built a new tower for the Oomphalos. By
the faint light of that thrumming red, underworld sun, it was early
morning. Dam remembered Hanhau, which brought a grin to his face.
His stomach grumbled mightily. Dam thought about going down to the
dining hall and fixing himself a feast, but it was nice to just lie lazily
in his warm bed for a little while.

A figure stood in the doorway to his terrace. He was backlit by
the ruby glow of the Oomphalos like a messenger descended from the
heavens. Dam sat up and squinted, trying to make a better reckoning
of his visitor.

"It's about time you woke up."

Aerander strode up to the foot of Dam's bed. He was dressed and
groomed for a public outing in a tunic bearing his family crest and a
sash that had been cut and dyed for him. His fawn-colored hair was
damp from washing and tied back with a fillet.

Dam frowned. "It's early still. I can't have missed much."

"Can't have missed much? You missed an entire day and night."

Dam eyed his cousin crookedly. Could he have really slept that
long?

"You've every right to it," Aerander said, "but I brought food for you last night that's going to spoil." He walked over to the room's low calcite table, where there was a silver trencher with an ornate, domed lid. Now his cousin received fancy gifts from the metal workers as well as the silk workers in town. He was a champion of the underworld twice over. Some spoke of him as a demi-god.

Aerander lifted the trencher lid to glance inside. The smell of smoked fishes wafted to Dam and pulled at his stomach.

"It's cold, but it's still good," Aerander said. "Let's have a meal. You can get washed up afterward. We have business with Ysalane later."

That was mildly curious to Dam. Aerander never asked him to come along when he met with Ysalane, and Dam had been fine standing apart from those matters. He and Aerander had caught up since Dam had returned, but they hadn't talked about anything special related to Ysalane. Dam rustled out of his bed, pulled on a shift, and sat down at the table.

Hephad was already out and about. He had his morning rituals, which included feeding and exercising the kittens and bringing blessings to the old men in the below-houses. In addition to Silenos, three of those men had died during the time when the Oomphalos had been taken away. Others had turned wasted and bedridden. At night, Ysalane was focusing the stone's healing energy on them to repair their bodies. Naturally, Hephad believed that prayers to the mother of grace Pleione would help as well.

Dam and Aerander sat across from each other at the table and picked from the trencher with tines. The fish was good, and they ladled the rich broth at the bottom into bowls. They ate their meal in silence while the city awoke with the sounds of street sweepers and water lifts churning.

"I never thought I'd say it, but there are things I'll miss about living down here," Aerander said. "It's peaceful in its own way."

Dam gulped down a mouthful of his breakfast and nodded, and then he went back to the trencher for more.

"We can always come back and visit."

Dam glanced at Aerander's face, then looked at Calaeno's amulet hanging from his cousin's neck.

Aerander caught that glance. He winked. "It's time. Calaeno found fertile land where we can resettle, and there's a portal nearby.

It'll be a long trip for the old men, but the sledges will help. That's what I'm going to talk to Ysalane about. We'll need guides through the backcountry."

"Calaeno found land?"

Aerander nodded.

Dam brought out delicately, "Are you sure you can trust her?"

"What do you mean?"

"I mean, she's awfully fond of Zazamoukh."

Aerander scowled. "You can't fault her for that. They were lovers dozens of lifetimes ago. Calaeno's loyalty is to her country. Every day since we've been down here, she's been looking for a way for us to return."

"She's been looking to get to Zazamoukh."

Aerander gazed at Dam squarely. "Dam, she helped you when you were lost with no idea of what to do. If she hadn't led you to Zazamoukh, you wouldn't have gotten the Oomphalos. The New Ones would have made slaves of us again."

"She led me to Zazamoukh, and he almost took the amulet away for good."

"How was she supposed to foresee that? She's not omnipotent, you know. Zazamoukh has tricks that even she didn't know about. Tricks beyond her power. You're being too hard on her."

Dam gathered that Aerander had spoken to Calaeno about everything that had happened while he was on his own in the backcountry. He couldn't argue that she hadn't been helpful. Anyone would say that he owed her his life. They were words he could say himself, but somehow he didn't feel it in his heart.

"She's been wanting to talk to you," Aerander said.

That was the last thing Dam wanted to do. He pushed away from the table. A conversation with his cousin had been looming. Dam had pretended he didn't have to think about it because it had always seemed a long way off, but now Calaeno's big discovery had forced him into it.

"I'm not going back."

Silence thickened around him.

"You had to know that," Dam said.

"What are you talking about?"

"I like it here. It feels like I belong. I'm happy."

"You're happy," Aerander repeated. "What kind of reason is that to stay? You belong with family."

"I've made a family here."

"You know what I mean, Dam. If Hanhau cares about you so much, he ought to go with you instead of making you choose between him and your kin."

Dam felt like he was sprouting horns from his head. Why was it that his cousin never understood? "He didn't ask me to choose. It's my decision."

"A decision based on what? You barely know each other. What has it been—a season, two at the most?"

"We've had plenty of time to get to know each other. How does that matter anyway? Whether it's a day or many years, I want to be with him."

"So you'll stay down here. Giving up on your own kind. You know nothing about these people. Their ideas about family and loyalty could be entirely different from ours. Then what will you do? All alone."

Dam bit down on his bitter feelings. A strange moment of clarity came over him as he looked upon Aerander. He didn't see a bossy cousin, always criticizing him for not living up to his standards. He saw a desperate and fearful young man.

He reached out to clasp Aerander's arm. "You've got to stop worrying about me."

Aerander swung away from him. His voice turned brittle. "You won't let me worry about you. You took away my right to that. Ever since you left the palace. That was my fault, wasn't it? Letting my father split us up."

A cold draft passed through Dam, like a ghost drifting through his body. His cousin had never spoken of it that way. He had always said it had been Dam's choice, and he had never acknowledged that his father could have adopted Dam.

"You couldn't do anything about that. I suppose I blamed you. That wasn't fair of me."

"Why won't you let me make it up to you? That's all I ever wanted. For the two of us to be brothers again."

Dam edged around the table closer to his cousin. "There's nothing to make up. I turned out fine. We're grown now. None of that matters anymore."

"Brothers stick together even when they're grown."

"Aerander, you are my brother. The only brother I've ever had. You'll always be."

"A world apart." Aerander hid his face in his arm and wept. Tears filled Dam's sinuses. He encircled his cousin in his arms.

"How can you be so soft? You're the King of Atlantis. The greatest hero our country has ever known. Don't you know you're going to be just fine? You've made your father so proud. I never told you that, but I should have."

Aerander shuddered against him.

"You've got Lys and Dardy and so many people who love you. You don't need me by your side anymore. I'll always be there in your heart, like you're stuck in mine. We've just gone down different paths is all."

Aerander's choking, tearful breaths brushed against Dam's neck. It was the worst that he had ever seen Aerander come apart. "I do want you to be happy," Aerander said. "I just don't want you to go."

"I know."

They held each other for a while. Then Aerander stirred and wiped his eyes. He looked around, reawakening to the room. "I ought to go." A nervous smile sprung up on his face. "I haven't even told Lys Calaeno's news." Dam's arms fell away from him. Aerander stood up unsteadily. His voice came out stunted. "I wanted to tell him. But something made me want to tell you first."

"He doesn't have to know that."

Aerander shook his head. "I won't keep it from him. He'll be angry, but he deserves to know that I made a mistake."

"I guess you're right."

His cousin stepped past him in a muddle. Dam felt like he was shrinking from the world. Was he going to be the cause of a row between Aerander and his boyfriend?

Aerander came back to him before leaving, lifted the amulet from his head, and pressed it into Dam's hand. "The power is fading. Calaeno says it's because Zazamoukh won't survive much longer. Talk to her before she's gone."

CHAPTER THREE

The room felt empty when Aerander left. It was as though every vibration of life had died. Dam went back to his pallet and crushed himself into a tight ball.

Everything he said had needed to be said. Dam didn't regret any of it. But a well of emotions engulfed him. He had launched himself on a journey to make his own way. Dam had done that once before when he had left Aerander's family to join the priesthood, but then, Dam had always known that Aerander had been in the background of his life, there to help if Dam really needed him. Now they would be separated by continents of bedrock. It was like realizing for the first time that he truly was an orphan.

After a while, Dam noticed he had been clutching the amulet tightly in his fist. It had left deep, white streaks on his palm. Looking at that hand, he spotted the long groove of his life's trail and noticed a fifth cross-scratch he hadn't seen before. The fourth had been the destruction of the Oomphalos tower. The fifth now was his parting from Aerander. But that next scar didn't signify a betrayal or a disaster. It was Dam's decision.

Speaking to Calaeno still bothered him, but it had to be done. Dam sat up on his bed. He pulled the necklace over his head and shed the thoughts in his mind. He called out for Calaeno. It felt as though he was searching through a boundless void. Her voice reached out faintly, straining to connect with him. They joined in a psychic bond, but it was loose, like two gripped hands that could easily slip away from one another.

"Hello, Dam. It's so good to hear your voice again. Did Aerander tell you the news?"

"Yes."

"He told me how courageous you were, fighting the New Ones. I had no idea you found magic. That must be really special. It all sounds so exciting how you brought back the Oomphalos. But dangerous, I'm sure."

Dam joggled his head.

"And now Atlantis will thrive again. It's a lovely place, Dam. There's a river valley with fields like gold. The river current is very gentle, and it flows out to a beautiful sea—the Great Green, I call it, because it's deep and boundless and as green as ripened olives. And the land has hills that are rich in limestone. That will be perfect for building new homes. Has Aerander told the others?"

"He's just left to do it."

They were quiet for a moment.

"Dam, did you tell him your news?"

His nose twitched. "My *news?*"

"That you're staying in the underworld."

"How did you know?"

Calaeno chuckled. *"I could tell from the way Aerander described you. It's one of the reasons why I knew I would like you even before we met. I loved the underworld too. We really do have a lot in common, don't you think? Neither one of us feeling like we belong in the world above the ground."*

Dam thought on that. Calaeno had been raised to fit into a world that wanted her to be a prince rather than a princess. He had been taken in by a House Governor, but he wasn't meant to be part of the nobility. Dam had never met anyone who understood what that was like. So why had he been so distrustful of her?

"The Fates truly favored you, Dam," Calaeno said.

Dam's face shrunk up. It had never felt like that. Though Dam knew what he must do, it was more like the Fates had given him two ways ahead in his life and each one tore at his heart. *"How do you mean?"*

"They gave you two lives instead of one. That only happens to a lucky few. You were a child of nobles and a comrade of city folk. There's so much knowledge you must have from living in both worlds.

"The Fates gave me two lives as well, first as a boy and then as a girl. I couldn't be either in the earthly realm. But the blessing for both

of us was that the Fates gave us another choice, the heavens for me and the underworld for you."

"I wish I didn't have to decide. At least not so soon."

"That's my fault, isn't it?"

"Your fault?"

"If I wasn't around looking for a way for your countrymen to return home, you could stay in the underworld and live with the man you love as well as Aerander and all of your friends. I've been thinking about this a lot, Dam. I hope it doesn't make you angry. I think you were afraid of coming above and afraid of having to make a decision, and that's why you turned cold to me."

A blush scored Dam's face. He realized she was right. He had no other reason to have been so mean to her. *"I'm sorry,"* he said. *"It was stupid of me, wasn't it? I couldn't stop the others from leaving even if I wanted to. And I don't want to, deep down. Aerander and his friends belong above the ground."*

"It wasn't stupid, Dam. It was a hard and noble decision to make." Her voice brightened. *"I accept your apology. Aerander took it hard, I bet."*

"He did. He probably hates me."

"I don't think he could ever hate you. The two of you are so lucky to have each other. You're quite an unusual pair. Like the Old Ones' legend, the Twin Masters of the Underworld. Aerander, the Master of Light, and Dam, the Master of Sound. I hope someday the three of us will meet. You'll visit Dam, won't you?"

"I'd like that."

Her voice shrank into the background. Dam called out for her. He could feel the magical vibrations of the amulet dwindling.

Calaeno warbled back to him. *"I think this is good-bye, Dam."*

"Thank you Calaeno. I wish we had more time."

"Eudoros is fading..."

"Calaeno?"

No answer. The psychic bridge was broken. No power was left in the amulet. It was just a gruesome necklace with a trident amulet carved from bone.

CHAPTER FOUR

A few nights later, the expedition returned with the remains of Calyiches' party. Hephad presided over the funeral, and after the corpses were burned, they laid stones for each one of the deceased in the polyandrium.

The voyage to the surface proceeded right away. They had no time to waste given the condition of the old men in the below-houses. Ysalane commissioned a twenty-man escort and many cartloads of provisions for the journey. Based on the location of the portal described to Aerander by Calaeno, Hanhau and Backlum plotted out an expeditious route making use of underground rivers and a team of slug-sledges to scale to the highest regions of Agartha.

They needed barges, strung together from the trunks of the largest flax trees that grew in underground lagoons. They needed wheeled sledges that could make the climb to the country's upper shelf.

During the whirlwind of activity preparing for the trip, several boys stopped by to visit Dam, having heard he would be staying back. His close friends Heron and Callios visited, as did his old friends Lys and Dardy and his new friend Rad. Each one made a fuss for Dam to reconsider, but they respected his decision in the end. Even some boys who had hardly ever talked to Dam came by to wish him well. They had known him as Aerander's cousin, which made him a person of some notoriety in and of itself. Now Dam was a celebrity, a sorcerer of sound.

At the feast on the eve of their departure, there was a new shocking announcement. Hephad and Attalos told the others that they, too, would be staying in the underworld. For Hephad, the explanation was practical. His kittens had only known the world below the ground, and they were linked to the Oomphalos' magic. No one knew what would happen when they bridged the surface, and he couldn't abandon their care.

Dam saw beyond what little truth was in that story. He supposed most of the others did as well. Both Hephad and Attalos found places in Agartha. Hephad would tend the gravesite of their countrymen who had died, and he would be a priest of the Atlantean faith to any men who came back to visit the underworld city. For Attalos, the expedition to retrieve the Oomphalos had kindled a passion. He wanted to learn the ways of the warriors and explore the backcountry. Neither one was leaving without the other. They had vowed to forge a new life together. Hephad and Attalos would have the entire Honeycomb to themselves. Hephad already had plans to reconstruct a temple there. Dam and Hanhau would build a house across town among the Old Ones.

Dam requested to come along to see Aerander and his friends off to the portal. It was a lumbering journey with some eight dozen aged, infirm men to ferry through the backcountry. They traveled at a snail's pace with slug-sledges driving their wheeled carts and a slow routine of loading barges to ford the rivers and sending them back to ferry more passengers. They had to pitch camp frequently.

On flat terrain, with the Oomphalos hoisted like a standard at the lead, the caravan of evacuees looked like a torch-staked road stretching endlessly into the obscurity of the horizon. On portages to higher parts, it was a winding stream of light rising from the depths.

They reached an upper shelf where the air was cold and damp and not good for the elderly men's health. Dam helped the novices and the women to shelter them with blankets, administer the medicines given to them by Sacnite, and help the old men to drink and eat. Over days, some of the old men were lost to pleurisy. They wrapped their bodies in pallets and freighted them on sledges so they could be buried in their homeland.

A second fortnight of travel had passed when the warriors scouting the way ahead brought news that they had found the portal. That lifted everyone's weary spirits. A passage into an ancient cavern led to an excavated rotunda where a column of shadow signified the magical lift up to the surface.

After one night's camp, the caravan forged into the cavern in a single file of wheeled sledges and small teams of men to pull them through. To an unacquainted eye, the portal was no more than a dark shaft descending from a sightless distance. But Dam remembered traveling through the portals. He remembered the strange energy that had tangled up his stomach and the shocking, wintry chill like the clutch of death.

Aerander would go first with a team of boys to scout their landing. The remainder of the company would help the old men through. Dam found his cousin through the dense queue of people. It was time to say good-bye. He and Aerander regarded each other silently for a moment, and then they came together in a bear's embrace. Aerander sniffed back tears and patted him on the back. "Remember this place. I'll send a wreath of vine to let you know we're settled."

Dam nodded. The warriors were already etching the walls of the rotunda with their sacred symbols.

"You'll come visit, won't you?" Aerander said.

"Of course. I told Calaeno I would."

"Promise me."

"I promise."

Dam handed him back his amulet. "It's not magical anymore. But you'll need it to show your kingship."

Aerander smiled.

"We're always brothers," Dam said. "And more than that. Twin Masters. The Master of Light and the Master of Sound."

Aerander held Dam fast to his chest again, and he brushed a kiss against his cheek. He pulled the necklace over his head, and then he looked to Lys. Happily, Aerander had made any amends that he had needed to make after neglecting Lys. The two boys led the scouting party into the dark shaft of the portal.

Dam blinked once, and the group was gone, swallowed by magic crafted from an ancient time.

❖

On the trip back to the city, the escort party was untethered from the train of carts and barges to ferry the old men and the provisions. Their pace was doubled. They could rappel straight down gullies to lower shelves.

At the crests of mountains, the warriors unpacked winged contraptions from their freight. Harnessed at their shoulders, those wings of tarpaulin on scaffolds of light metal allowed them to glide great distances. It was a type of travel that required skill and practice, so Dam rode strapped beneath Hanhau. During their flight, the warriors summoned light into their bodies. They were a flock of man-sized fireflies coasting over continent and sea.

Parts of that journey were thrilling to Dam, but the freedom of their travel felt sorrowful to him as well. He was starting a new life with Hanhau, but now that Aerander was gone, a lobe of his heart seemed to have been cut away, as Calaeno had said when she had been separated from her sisters.

Thoughts about the future drifted into Dam's head and distracted him from that sagging feeling. Dam knew he did not possess the gift of the oracle. As his thoughts took form, what he saw in his mind's eye was more like waking dreams, though they felt clear and true.

After centuries, the old men would breathe the fresh air of their country and feel the strength of the sun against their skin. Their deaths, though certain, would be peaceful. At night, they would look up at the sky and see the multitude of their ancestors sparkling in the heavens and welcoming them to the afterworld.

For the boys, the return would be joyous. Dam imagined Aerander leading the charge of getting straight to work with lumber and limestone to build a new city. It wouldn't be grand, but in time it would be a home of which they could be proud. There would be marriages to the women. There would be cries of babies in time. That sound would lift their spirits high. They would forge a new country to continue the legacy of their fathers.

Calaeno would have the company of people after a millennium of exile. Maybe she would find a place among them as a priestess or a queen as was her right. Maybe she would prefer to live a simple life among her countrymen, and she would rediscover love with one of the men when her heart was ready. Perhaps, as she had said, she would still feel apart from the earthly world and decide to return to the heavens where she had gotten used to looking over everyone. In any case, she would know she was no longer alone.

Happiness welled up in Dam in such abundance that he felt that he might burst with tears. He thought about the life that lay ahead of him. He knew he had to retrieve Zazamoukh's body and put his soul to rest. That's what Calaeno would have wanted, and he owed her that. Strangely, it didn't feel dreadful to do it. As Hephad had said about Calyiches and his band of criminals, they could let the gods make a reckoning of the priest. Dam's time to judge him was done.

In the city, he would make a home with Hanhau. When the birthing season came, Hanhau would become a *nikwah* to the children as he always wanted. They had already talked about it, and Dam told him he would be happy to leave Hanhau to that vocation.

As for Dam, he knew where he would be most useful. His adventure in the backcountry had been astonishing, but the place where he felt he belonged was the infirmary. Dam would apprentice with the wise healer Sacnite to learn to set broken bones and to perform surgeries to save men's lives. Just as he had in the above-world, Dam would learn the cures that could be derived from the plants and minerals that the underworld provided. The magic of the Oomphalos kept people healthy and strong, but someone needed to mind the ancient knowledge of medicine in case the stone was ever lost again.

Dam's own magic was fading. His senses couldn't penetrate the darkness beyond a few yards to uncover the secret world of sound and vibration. Capturing those sounds was like trying to grasp fistfuls of sand in his hands.

He wasn't sad to lose that magic. Dam had claimed it because he needed it, and now it would be returned to the mori-mori well where it belonged. Perhaps someday, someone else would discover it when he needed it just as badly as Dam had.

It would make a good story for Hanhau to tell the children, a boy from the surface who became the Master of Sound. Hanhau would tell it with all its daring turns to make the children's eyes go wide and have them laughing in disbelief.

That story would always make Dam proud. He had done a very brave and honorable thing. Though if someone was to ask him to tell his story, he would say it was about a boy from the surface who discovered that he belonged below the ground.

About the Author

Andrew J. Peters is the author of the Werecat series and two books for young adults: *The Seventh Pleiade* and *Banished Sons of Poseidon*. He grew up in Buffalo, New York, studied psychology at Cornell University, and has spent most of his career as a social worker and an advocate for lesbian, gay, bisexual, and transgender youth. Andrew lives in New York City with his partner Genaro and their cat Chloë. For more about him and his books, visit: andrewjpeterswrites.com.

Soliloquy Titles From Bold Strokes Books

Banished Sons Of Poseidon by Andrew J. Peters. Escaped to an underworld of magical wonders and warring, aboriginal peoples, an outlaw priest named Dam must undertake a desperate mission to bring the survivors of Atlantis home. (978-1-62639-441-4)

Breaking Up Point by Brian McNamara. Brendan and Mark may have managed to keep their relationship a secret, but what will happen when they find themselves miles apart as Brendan embarks on his college journey? (978-1-62639-430-8)

The Orion Mask by Greg Herren. After his father's death, Heath comes to Louisiana to meet his mother's family and learn the truth about her death—but some secrets can prove deadly. (978-1-62639-355-4)

The First Twenty by Jennifer Lavoie. Peyton is out for revenge after her father is murdered by Scavengers, but after meeting Nixie, she's torn between helping the girl she loves and the community that raised her. (978-1-62639-414-8)

Taking the Stand by Juliann Rich. There's a time for justice, then there's a time for taking the stand. And Jonathan Cooper knows exactly what time it is. (978-1-62639-408-7)

Dark Rites by Jeremy Jordan King. When friends start experimenting with dark magic to gain power, Margarite must embrace her natural gifts to save them. (978-1-62639-245-8)

Driving Lessons by Annameekee Hesik. Dive into Abbey Brooks's sophomore year as she attempts to figure out the amazing, but sometimes complicated, life of a you-know-who girl at Gila High School. (978-1-62639-228-1)

Asher's Shot by Elizabeth Wheeler. Asher Price's candid photographs capture the truth, but when his success requires exposing an enemy, Asher discovers his only shot at happiness involves revealing secrets of his own. (978-1-62639-229-8)

The Melody of Light by M.L. Rice. After surviving abuse and loss, will Riley Gordon be able to navigate her first year of college and accept true love and family? (78-1-62639-219-9)

Maxine Wore Black by Nora Olsen. Jayla will do anything for Maxine, the girl of her dreams, but after becoming ensnared in Maxine's dark secrets, she'll have to choose between love and her own life. (978-1-62639-208-3)

Bottled Up Secret by Brian McNamara. When Brendan Madden befriends his gorgeous, athletic classmate, Mark, it doesn't take long for Brendan to fall head over heels for him—but will Mark reciprocate the feelings? (978-1-62639-209-0)

Searching for Grace by Juliann Rich. First it's a rumor. Then it's a fact. And then it's on. (978-1-62639-196-3)

Dark Tide by Greg Herren. A summer working as a lifeguard at a hotel on the Gulf Coast seems like a dream job...until Ricky Hackworth realizes the town is shielding some very dark—and deadly—secrets. (978-1-62639-197-0)

Everything Changes by Samantha Hale. Raven Walker's world is turned upside down the moment Morgan O'Shea walks into her life. (978-1-62639-303-5)

Fifty Yards and Holding by David Matthew-Barnes. The discovery of a secret relationship between Riley Brewer, the star of the high school baseball team, and Victor Alvarez, the leader of a violent street gang, escalates into a preventable tragedy. (978-1-62639-081-2)

Caught in the Crossfire by Juliann Rich. Two boys at Bible camp; one forbidden love. (978-1-62639-070-6)

Tristant and Elijah by Jennifer Lavoie. After Elijah finds a scandalous letter belonging to Tristant's great-uncle, the boys set out to discover the secret Uncle Glenn kept hidden his entire life and end up discovering who they are in the process. (978-1-62639-075-1)

Frenemy of the People by Nora Olsen. Clarissa and Lexie have despised each other for as long as they can remember, but when they both find themselves helping an unlikely contender for homecoming queen, they are catapulted into an unexpected romance. (978-1-62639-063-8)

The Balance by Neal Wooten. Love and survival come together in the distant future as Piri and Niko face off against the worst factions of mankind's evolution. (978-1-62639-055-3)

The Unwanted by Jeffrey Ricker. Jamie Thomas is plunged into danger when he discovers his mother is an Amazon who needs his help to save the tribe from a vengeful god. (978-1-62639-048-5)

Because of Her by KE Payne. When Tabby Morton is forced to move to London, she's convinced her life will never be the same again. But the beautiful and intriguing Eden Palmer is about to show her that this time, change is most definitely for the better. (978-1-62639-049-2)

Asher's Fault by Elizabeth Wheeler. Fourteen-year-old Asher Price sees the world in black and white, much like the photos he takes, but when his little brother drowns at the same moment Asher experiences his first same-sex kiss, he can no longer hide behind the lens of his camera and eventually discovers he isn't the only one with a secret. (978-1-60282-982-4)

The Seventh Pleiade by Andrew J. Peters. When Atlantis is besieged by violent storms, tremors, and a barbarian army, it will be up to a young gay prince to find a way for the kingdom's survival. (978-1-60282-960-2)

Meeting Chance by Jennifer Lavoie. When man's best friend turns on Aaron Cassidy, the teen keeps his distance until fate puts Chance in his hands. (978-1-60282-952-7)

Lake Thirteen by Greg Herren. A visit to an old cemetery seems like fun to a group of five teenagers, who soon learn that sometimes it's best to leave old ghosts alone. (978-1-60282-894-0)

The Road to Her by KE Payne. Sparks fly when actress Holly Croft, star of UK soap *Portobello Road*, meets her new on-screen love interest, the enigmatic and sexy Elise Manford. (978-1-60282-887-2)

Swans and Clons by Nora Olsen. In a future world where there are no males, sixteen-year-old Rubric and her girlfriend Salmon Jo must fight to survive when everything they believed in turns out to be a lie. (978-1-60282-874-2)

Kings of Ruin by Sam Cameron. High school student Danny Kelly and loner Kevin Clark must team up to defeat a top-secret alien intelligence that likes to wreak havoc with fiery car, truck, and train accidents. (978-1-60282-864-3)

Wonderland by David-Matthew Barnes. After her mother's sudden death, Destiny Moore is sent to live with her two gay uncles on Avalon Cove, a mysterious island on which she uncovers a secret place called Wonderland, where love and magic prove to be real. (978-1-60282-788-2)